JUDGMENT DAY
RETRIBUTION

JE GURLEY

Acknowledgments

I would like to thank the residents of Tucson and Phoenix for allowing me to maim, mutilate and kill for the sake of literary thrills. I would especially like to apologize to the city of Phoenix for destroying it. PETA should know that no animals were harmed during the writing of this novel and any resemblance to real coyotes was purely coincidental. I also thank Severed Press for their confidence in me.

Dedication

As always, I wish to dedicate this book to my lovely, loving wife, Kim, for her help in editing and proofreading my novels, and for putting up with me. I also wish to thank my cats, Shoes and Elsie, for walking across my keyboard and inventing new words, some of which I used.

1

Uncompahgre Plateau, Colorado

No one could have foreseen the results of one sloppily positioned alarm, a motion sensor attached to a metal pole driven into the ground directly beneath a lightning-struck ponderosa pine. Exhaustion, boredom, a wandering mind – whatever the reason for its haphazard placement, a dead tree branch that had been weakened by heavy winter winds, broke during the night and fell across the wires connecting the motion sensor to the solar battery used to power the array of sensor devices scattered around the camp. Had it happened two hours earlier while they sat around the fire discussing the next day's plans, someone might have heard it fall, but the branch broke while everyone was asleep, fatigued by their long journey.

The first sign of zombies in their midst was the scream torn from the savaged throat of Meara Corman, who, by sheer bad luck, happened to be sleeping farthest from the fire at the edge of the clearing. Jebediah Stone stirred quickly from a fitful sleep and reached for his rifle, an M14 automatic usually lying beside his sleeping bag. Too late, he remembered that he had left it in the back of the ATV in his haste to set up camp, a mistake that could cost him his life. Instead, he grabbed the machete he had used to chop firewood and stared at the scene of horror unfolding around him in the dim light of the dying fire.

Several zombies, merely dark shadows in the wan light, launched from the forest toward the sound of the scream. Jeb quickly assessed the situation and yelled to awaken anyone not already roused by Meara's frantic cries. He propelled himself from a sitting position to a full run and rushed to her side, ignoring the cold sharp stones biting into his bare feet. He brought the machete down on the back of the zombie's exposed neck with both hands. The sharp blade embedded deep in the dense flesh, severing its spine. The creature fell sprawling across Meara's still body. He placed his foot on the creature's back and yanked hard to remove the lodged blade. The savage blow would have easily decapitated a normal person, but the zombies were mutating into a new species – thicker skin, denser muscles, stronger bones, and smarter. He rolled the dead zombie off Meara and examined her, but quickly saw that it was too late for her. Her head lolled to one side, her once sparkling green eyes open and staring at him, her throat savagely ripped out.

The six others in the group, awakened by her screams and Jeb's shout, joined him in defending their small camp. Pandemonium reigned as shots rang out around him. It had been a year since the beginning of the zombie plague, and most of his companions knew how to shoot. They were experienced zombie killers. People who weren't good marksmen usually did not survive long, but awakening from a deep sleep during a zombie attack made for a certain amount of panic.

Someone – he hoped it was a zombie – fell into the fire and extinguished it, leaving them fighting by the gray light of a cloud-shrouded moon. He raced toward the crouched figure of a second zombie, a naked female heavy with child, pressing Mikal Antonov against a tree. The elderly Antonov was on his knees, holding his rifle in both hands and pushing against the zombie's chest to ward off her gnashing teeth. His strength was failing quickly. His eyes were wide with fright, but he did not call for assistance. He knew everyone else was fighting for their lives as well. Jeb planted the machete tip first in the zombie's back as hard as he could with both hands, but only managed to anger her. She knocked him to the ground with a vicious backhanded swipe that had his head reeling. She released Antonov and loomed over Jeb, growling. The eerie animal sound from deep within her throat reminded Jeb of a dog guarding its bone. Suddenly, her head exploded and she toppled to the ground beside him. He looked up and saw Karen, his wife, holding his rifle. The M14's 7.62 caliber slug tore through bone and muscle, leaving very little of the zombie's head intact, the reason he had chosen the weapon. He didn't have time to ponder what had roused Karen from her silent lethargy to help him. She averted her gaze from him as he rose from the ground, took his rifle from her, and joined in the fray. As he passed the ATV, he switched on its headlights, throwing the campsite into brilliant illumination.

They were lucky that only a small zombie hunting party, an extended family of six members, had stumbled upon them. Had there been more, they would have been in real trouble. The headlights distracted the zombies just long enough for the defenders to get organized. They quickly dispatched the four remaining creatures with no further loss of life. He knew the noise, the smell of blood, and the burned flesh that now hung over the camp would draw more predators, both zombie and animal. The seven people stood looking at one another, and then down at Meara's mutilated corpse.

"Was anyone bitten?" he demanded breathlessly as his lungs fought for air.

The blood or saliva of a zombie could infect even those immune from the airborne virus. Everyone shook his or her head to indicate no. They had been lucky.

"Pack it up," he called to them trying to break their stupor, "we're leaving."

"We have to we bury Meara." Sylvia Nabors, a middle-aged woman who had been a schoolteacher in the previous world, stared at Jeb. In her hand, she clutched the bloody hatchet with which she had beheaded one of the zombies. The hatchet looked incongruous in her pale, thin hand. Her graying, disheveled hair hung to her shoulders.

"There's no time," Jeb replied as he sat down to put on his socks and boots. He then rolled up his bedroll and shoved it into his haversack. Karen worked in the calm silence that had fallen over her since the escape from Biosphere2. She no longer wanted to die, or wished him dead, but she had not yet decided to join the land of the living. He helped her with her sleeping bag. She meekly accepted his assistance.

"Thank you for saving my life," he whispered to her.

She paused, nodded, and then turned away, her face as stolid and emotionless as ever. He resisted the urge to spin her around, make her talk to him, but this was not the place or the time for another confrontation with her.

Nabors remained standing over Meara's body, defiant, arms crossed over her chest. Blood from the zombie she had killed splattered her face.

"We could at least take the time to say a few words over her," she said. "She was our friend."

Jeb stopped packing and stared at her. He was sympathetic to her desire to mourn her friend's body, but he had seen too many deaths, witnessed too much tragedy the past year to feel pain. The living required too much attention to spare it for the dead.

"If you stay, you'll die. It's as simple as that. Say your words and pack up."

He continued gathering their meager supplies, including the motion detectors and the solar battery, and carefully positioned them in the back of one of the ATVs with his haversack. He breathed a sigh of relief, when out of the corner of his eye, he saw Nabors doing the same. The two Honda Polaris RZR4 All Terrain Vehicles they had picked up at a motorcycle dealership north of Taos sat four people each, but allowed very little room for supplies. Thus, they traveled light out of necessity. They packed with an efficiency born of practice in a world where constant movement was the norm. The vehicles were quickly loaded and ready to go. Remaining too long in one place invited disaster, either from zombies or from the military and its Hunter mercenaries searching for *munies*. The entire group was munies, people naturally immune to the airborne virus. Their blood was precious to the Hunters, who captured them for the Blue Juice their blood could produce, a temporary vaccine against the zombie virus. Blue Juice had become the new currency, replacing the almighty, worthless dollar. Without it, thousands of others would succumb to the mutated Avian flu virus and risk turning zombie.

"We'll go higher up," he told them, "maybe the snow will keep the zombies to a minimum."

They were traveling northwest along the Uncompahgre Plateau in southwestern Colorado through broken stands of ponderosa pine, blue spruce, and aspen. Ten-thousand-feet-tall Horsefly Peak, a silent sentinel to the east, wore its snowcap like a Spanish shawl cascading down its shoulders. Soon, winter snow would cover it completely. To the west, steep shale and sandstone bluffs dropped off sharply toward the Colorado River Basin. To the south, Telluride with its large population of zombies remained a bitter memory where they had lost two of their number and one of their vehicles. Avoiding the main roads served two purposes – evading people who used the roads and the zombies that followed the people. He had ignored that law of survival and it had cost them dearly.

Karen sat beside Jeb in the front seat, staring blankly ahead of her, hands folded in her lap, not because of any love for her husband, but because none of the others could tolerate her. Her head jerked with each bump and dip. He had thought she had experienced a catharsis during the fight at Biosphere2 three months earlier. For a time, she had quit fighting with him, paid more attention to her surroundings, and even initiated conversations with him, but lately she had slowly slipped back into her own silent world, albeit without the overriding desire to die. As a psychiatrist, he saw slight progress in her condition. However, her refusal to forgive him for abandoning her bitterly disappointed him. It mattered little to her that she had ignored his advice and had taken their ailing son to the hospital where the authorities had seized them and transferred them to the Marana FEMA camp. He could imagine the horror she had felt as she had watched those same authorities rip their ill, six-year-old son from her arms and dispose of him before he could turn into a zombie. Later, after the authorities had whisked her away to San Diego, he had risked his life to free her, but it seemed to count for little in her warped scales of justice.

They climbed north along little-used game trails into freshly fallen snow. The temperature dropped to ten degrees above freezing and the wind picked up. Night morphed into dawn with hardly a line of demarcation between the two. Thick, gray clouds rolled in from the northeast and were blotting out the sun. A storm was coming and they needed to find shelter. They had left their tents and most of their gear behind in their hurried rush to leave

Telluride. They had also left behind two of their number, Arthur Davis, and Willard Tempest, the man who had first convinced Jeb to bring the small party north into Colorado. He still had Tempest's maps, but without his intimate knowledge of the country, they were driving blindly through the wilderness.

Since leaving the glass domes of Biosphere2 in Oracle, Arizona, the group had flown in a Russian Mi17 helicopter piloted by Antonov to northern New Mexico. They took refuge in an empty school outside of Taos for several weeks to recover from their ordeal, and for the wounds of those injured in the fight at Biosphere2 to heal. At that time, they numbered fourteen. One had died of his wounds a few days later. Two had decided to leave the group when Jeb had suggested that the group continue north into Colorado. When they ran out of fuel, they abandoned the helicopter and walked. Two more had died during a zombie attack while foraging for supplies, another from an infected wound.

Jeb tried not to dwell on their losses for fear it would overwhelm him. His reins of leadership weighed heavily upon him. He had hoped to discard leadership altogether at Biosphere2, but its demise had thrust him back into a position of power. Mace Ridell, Renda Beth Kilmer, and Vince Holcomb had taken Erin Kostner's group of researchers to set up a new laboratory to find a vaccine. He wished Mace were with him now. He could use his single-minded determination.

Snow began to fall, lightly at first, but as the morning progressed, the flakes became heavy and wet, presaging the blizzard to follow. Driving became a challenge as visibility dropped. The second ATV driven by Craig Tyndale, dropped farther and farther behind. He drove slowly, fearing they might separate in the blinding snow. Finally, he spotted a dark opening in a cliff and nosed the ATV off the trail to investigate. It proved to be a narrow slit cave barely twenty feet deep and ten feet wide, but it was shelter against the weather.

They covered the ATVs with tarps to guard against the snow, weighted each down with large rocks, and then crowded into the cave. As Jeb watched the snow falling, he wondered if they would have to abandon the four-wheeled vehicles and find snowmobiles somewhere, perhaps the next town they encountered, thrusting them into even more danger. The small fire provided little heat, but its psychological value outweighed its functionality. Hot tea and a beef stew from scavenged cans warmed their stomachs and their hands, as they held their mugs close to their bodies. No one spoke other than banalities about the food or the weather. No one wanted to mention Meara Corman's death for fear of reviving the ghosts of their other losses. Jeb could feel their accusatory eyes on him as he sat at the cave's entrance with his back to them, staring into the white blankness outside. The long mournful howl startled him until he realized that it was a wolf and not a zombie. He relaxed slightly. If animals were around, then zombies weren't.

Jeb shivered as blast of frigid air found the cave entrance. He despised the cold. He missed Arizona winters, where a seventy-degree Christmas was normal. He enjoyed looking up at the Catalina Mountains with a blanket of fresh-fallen snow on Mount Lemmon from the cozy, warm comfort of his Foothills living room. Trekking through a frozen wilderness was not his idea of a good time. The zombies did not seem to mind the cold. Their thick, olive-hued skin rendered them immune from extremes of heat and cold. They preferred warmer climates only because of the greater availability of food, but as game at lower altitudes became scarcer, they would begin to venture higher into the mountains. No place was safe from zombies for long.

"Why so gloomy?" Antonov asked as he walked up to Jeb. "Come closer to the fire."

Jeb smiled at the old Russian, a friend since the escape from San Diego. Antonov moved with a slight limp in his right leg, the cold affecting his arthritis. "No, I'll keep watch for a while."

"Do you think they're out there?"

"We killed a hunting party. The snow will cover our tracks and our scent, but, yeah, they're always out there."

Antonov nodded his head slowly. "True. They are an ever-present danger." He made a fist and his voice became more strident. "I want to kill them all. They are an abomination."

Jeb snorted derisively. "Are they? Maybe we had our chance and blew it. Maybe God is having his revenge."

Antonov looked at him with a scowl. "Do you really think that? If that is so, then we have no chance."

"Hell, I don't know what I think anymore," he admitted. He clasped his knees against his chest with his arms to help warm his body. "All I know is that there are seven of us when there were fourteen – forty-five at Biosphere2. If there's a battle, we're losing."

Antonov shook his head. "Don't let the others hear this. You are our leader. You cannot have doubts."

Jeb reached out, grabbed Antonov's knee with his hand, and shook it gently. "You're right, old friend. I'm much too morose. I must shake off this lugubrious mood."

"The sun will come out tomorrow as it always does, and the day will be brighter. Your wife needs you." With this, Antonov limped back into the cave and settled down beside the fire.

Jeb stared into the mounting storm and wondered if Antonov was right about the sun. He knew he was wrong about Karen.

The storm blew throughout the night and the next day, piling snow three feet deep at the entrance of the small cave. Everyone grew restless. They had no destination, but all were eager to resume the journey. The storm ended just before sunset. The moon rose full that night in a clear bright sky filled with stars and the promise of better weather to come. After digging the ATVs out of the snow, they set out across a flat, windswept ridge free of snow and made good progress for several hours. Dropping into a shallow valley, they plowed through knee-deep snow, often dismounting to dig the ATVs out of snowdrifts. While crossing one frozen stream, Jeb's lead ATV broke through the thin ice. Luckily, the water was only two feet deep, and the other ATV easily winched it free. After that, he chose his route more carefully.

Steep slopes forced them to descend into a wide forested valley of junipers, spruce, and hollies, where they weaved through the trees at little better than a walking pace. By dawn, they were all exhausted and eager for a chance to stretch their cramped muscles. In a small clearing by a brook, they rested and ate a cold breakfast of cheese and bread. Jeb spotted an elk within easy rifle distance, but refrained from shooting it to avoid the noise. Their supplies were running low and they needed fresh meat, but the risk of discovery was too great. Just as Antonov had predicted, the day was beautifully sunny. Jeb hoped it was a sign of things to come, but the pessimist in him knew it was too much to hope for.

Back in the vehicles after their hurried meal, Jeb spotted a well-used game trail that made travel easier. He saw signs of a large herd of elk passing through – trampled earth, broken branches, and hoof prints in patches of snow. Free of mankind's hunting policies and of its restraining fences, the wild game population soared, increased by animals fleeing bands of foraging zombies. The presence of the large herd moving in a hurry made him uneasy. Animals could sense danger as they could detect the approach of a storm. From what were they fleeing? Jeb's apprehension mounted when they rounded a small rise and saw a hunter's log cabin nestled in the shelter of a small grove of ponderosa pines. As much as some undefined urgency pressed him to move on, he knew everyone needed a rest. Even he was feeling the weariness of weeks of restless sleep and hard travel. If he suggested they bypass the cabin, he would have a rebellion on his hands.

He called a halt and dismounted to check it out. The snow would have covered any tracks, but the cabin looked deserted. A rocking chair from the small front porch lay on its side on the ground, almost covered with snow. A wooden shutter on a front window had fallen off and leaned against the wall. Several large rocks had tumbled from the top of the river stone chimney. A small shed sat twenty yards from the cabin, its leeward side protecting a cord of stacked firewood. Despite the cabin's deserted appearance, he decided to announce his approach.

"Is anyone there?" he called and waited, shifting nervously from foot to foot. No one answered.

He approached cautiously, watching the shutterless window for any sign of movement within. He held his M14 in one hand, trying not to look dangerous, but keeping it handy in case of an emergency. A chain barred the front door, but there was always the possibility of a rear door. He stomped his boots on the front porch as a second warning. Satisfied no one was home, he jimmied the padlock on the chain that was securing the door with a piece of two-by-four that had been lying on the porch, possibly used as a door prop. The chain broke easily and seemed more for keeping the door shut than for keeping an intruder out. He stood to one side and peeked in. Light from the window revealed a sparsely furnished living room. He could see bunk beds through an open door to a second room. He stepped inside, hugging the wall for protection.

The two-room cabin was empty with no signs of its former occupants. A worn out couch, a broken down armchair, and four wooden chairs around a table comprised the room's only furniture. A quick search of a closet in the bedroom produced blankets, extra coats, and ammunition. Of greater interest to him was the full larder, enough food for several weeks. There was no electricity or television, but a rough plank shelf well stocked with books sat atop wooden pegs in the wall by the fireplace. Jeb noted several paperback thrillers, two cookbooks, and a dozen classics by Mark Twain, Edgar Allen Poe, H.G. Wells, and Sir Arthur Conan Doyle. He picked up *War of the Worlds* by Wells, and brushed its cover lovingly with the tips of his fingers, then shuddered at the similarities between Wells' fictional world and the real world. He had not read a book since before the plague began a year earlier. Soon, existing books would rot away. He reverently replaced the book in its spot and walked back outside to inform the others.

They chanced building a small fire in the fireplace. It was risky, but they had been cold for so long and they needed relief. The wood in the woodpile beside the shed was damp with snow, but a smaller stack inside beside the fireplace was dry. Jeb ripped pages from one of the cookbooks and shred it as tender, adding shards of wood shaved with his machete from the firewood for kindling. When the fire was roaring, he checked outside. The wood was well seasoned and only a small tendril of smoke rose from the damaged chimney, quickly dispersed by the wind.

Thick slices of Spam fried in a cast iron skillet, along with canned potatoes, made their first truly hot meal in days. They all ate until they were full, and then passed around cans of peaches and pears for dessert. It had been so long since Jeb had tasted anything sweet, he had forgotten how delicious canned fruit could be.

Another find that excited him were two pair of *Sherpa* snowshoes. The *Sherpas* didn't resemble the typical white ash framed snowshoe. They were hi-tech, made of strong aluminum tubing and used a durable synthetic material for the decking. Their shorter, twenty-one-inch length facilitated a more normal stride for the wearer. Whoever owned the cabin had not been stingy on their toys.

Jeb decided that as long as the group was determined to rest up for a few days, he might as well hunt one of the elk he had spotted earlier, using the compound bow they had brought to use when stealth was required. He would never qualify as an expert archer, but at close range, he was confident that he could bring down something as large as an elk. He approached Craig Tyndale to accompany him. Tyndale was the second best archer and an avid hunter, more at home in the woods than in the city. He had financed his frequent hunting trips by working as a bouncer and a semi-pro wrestler in Vegas.

"Are you up for a little elk hunt?" Jeb asked.

Tyndale smiled. "Always."

Jeb decided to waste no time. If the weather turned bad, they might need the extra meat. Having never worn snowshoes, he was pleased at how easy the snowshoes were to use. He had expected an awkward stride like the one he had seen on television, but after a few minutes, he hardly noticed he had them on. Tyndale moved quietly through the trees and underbrush for his size. Jeb, four inches taller than Tyndale at a stocky six feet, was not as at home in the woods as the avid hunter, but mimicked Tyndale's movements as best he could.

They travelled along the banks of a small stream until they found animal tracks, and then followed them for several miles. Jeb spotted movement in the distance at the edge of a small clearing, a grass-filled glade. It was not the elk he had hoped for, but a small herd of whitetail deer. He would take what he could get. Meat was meat. They carefully moved downwind and pushed through the underbrush until they were less than twenty yards from several of the deer. As Jeb lined up his shot with the bow, Tyndale grasped his shoulder. Jeb glanced at him angrily for spoiling his shot, but then noticed the perplexed expression on Tyndale's face. He followed Tyndale's gaze until he saw what had caught his attention – zombies.

The deer caught scent of the zombies and panicked just as Jeb saw them. The lead buck snorted an alarm and the herd raced the woods, right into a larger group of zombies waiting in ambush. It was a slaughter. The zombies leaped upon the deer's backs and killed them either with a quick bite to the jugular, or by snapping their necks with powerful arms. It was all over in seconds, twelve deer slaughtered by as many zombies. Still upwind, the zombies had been so intent on their prey that they had not noted the presence of him and Tyndale. Facing zombies with only a bow would be suicide. He motioned for Tyndale to move back quietly the way they had come.

As Jeb crouched and began to leave, another figure emerged from the woods. At first, he paid it no attention. Then he noticed something atypical about this zombie. It was tall and thin and moved differently than most zombies. It wore a heavy coat and hat and carried a long wooden staff. When the creature removed its cap and faced Jeb, he almost cried out in astonishment. The creature was no zombie, but a human walking unmolested among zombies. He wanted to remain and see what was different about the man that zombies welcomed and didn't treat as food, but one of the creatures began stalking along the edge of the clearing. He took one last lingering look at the man, who had the lean cheekbones and ruddy complexion of a Native American, and left.

2

"I tell you, he wasn't a zombie." Jeb had repeated his observations of the zombies in the glade half a dozen times, but no one believed him. He was tired and his anger was beginning to shorten his temper.

"Then just what was he," Sylvia Nabors asked, arms folded across her chest, "some kind of zombie shepherd?" Her gray hair was now pinned atop her head in a bun, making her look even more like the schoolteacher she had once been.

He had told them all about the staff the person carried, but they didn't believe that either. "He was a man," he insisted.

"A man walking with zombies. That's ridiculous," she replied.

Nabors's condescending attitude was getting to Jeb. She had been distant with him ever since he had refused to allow her to hold a memorial service for Meara, who was killed on the trail in a zombie attack. "What the hell do you know about anything," Jeb shouted at her, "you've been wearing blinders since we found you."

Her lips quivered and she blinked her eyes several times before replying. "What do you mean," she demanded coldly.

"You still haven't accepted what's happened to the world. You've seen zombies, and you've seen all the destruction, but you keep telling yourself that it's not real. You think that one day you'll turn a corner and there'll be a town just like there used to be, with cozy little houses with white picket fences, a church, and a preacher telling you that you've been a good Christian and passed God's test. It's not going to happen. The world's dead. We're in survival mode."

She remained silent, but her eyes blazed with anger. She turned to Craig Tyndale. "Did you see this … person?"

He glanced at Jeb uncertainly; then shook his head. "No, I was leaving, but why would he lie?"

"Yes, why would he?" she repeated.

Mikal Antonov took on the role of diplomat, a function he was assuming more often as the months passed. "Let's all calm down and discuss this," he suggested. "Whatever any of you think, the fact remains that zombies are nearby. What are we going to do?"

Jeb smiled at Antonov. "You don't believe me either. So be it." He turned to the others. "Look, I told you before that this isn't a democracy. I'm leaving tonight. If any of you want to remain here and take your chances, so be it, but one of the ATVs goes with me."

Reece Halliwell offered his objection. "We're tired," he whined. "We need rest. We can't just pick up and leave at a moment's notice." He looked at the others for support, getting some encouragement from Nabors and Tyndale. Emboldened, he added, "We need a chance to warm our bones and decide where we're going next."

Halliwell had been with them since Biosphere2. At twenty-nine, he was the youngest of their number and a chronic complainer. He voiced his resentment of Jeb's authoritarian approach at leadership at every opportunity, but adroitly avoided making any decisions himself. Jeb had tolerated Halliwell because he was a good shot with a rifle and a good worker, but his tolerance was wearing thin. Jeb stared at Halliwell until he swallowed deeply under the scrutiny, his prominent Adam's apple bouncing in his throat.

"You can stay if you want," Jeb repeated. "Any of the others can stay with you, but I'm leaving. If more than four of you decide to go with me, both ATVs go as well."

Halliwell flared his nostrils and gritted his teeth. His hands clenched and unclenched as if he was trying to decide to attack, but he knew Jeb could beat him. He turned away and strode angrily to the fireplace. Jeb eyed each of the others in turn.

"You wanted someone to take charge. I am. If you don't like it, you're free to choose another. We tried democracy at Biosphere2 and look what it cost us. We're on the run for our lives. If we stay, zombies will smell our fire or cross our trail eventually. We can't fire our rifles to hunt game or they'll hear it. That leaves snares or the bow, neither of which are reliable enough to guarantee a steady supply of fresh meat. If a heavy snow falls, we're stuck here until spring with zombies nearby. Without supplies, we will never survive."

He began packing his gear and saw that Karen had already started. She had not taken part in the discussion. In fact, she remained as aloof and as distant as she had been since her rescue from the blood bank in San Diego. Her hatred of him had changed into tolerance of his presence, but no more. She seemed as dead inside as the zombies. She was barely recognizable as the twenty-nine-year-old former Miss Arizona. Her emerald green eyes were sallow and sunken. She looked like a forty-nine-year-old crack whore, but without the whore's zest for crack. The only two things that drove her were her hatred of him and of zombies. He sometimes wondered if she was a changeling, a practical joke played on him by her captors in San Diego.

He did not turn but heard the others packing as well. He had almost hoped some would remain behind. He was tired of leading people. Halliwell was right about one thing – he had no idea where they were going. Even if they found an ideal spot to hide out from the zombies and the military, what would they do then? They were too few to start a colony and too many to wander aimlessly about the countryside. He was just winging it, hoping everything eventually worked out for the best.

A gut-wrenching howl outside the door turned his blood cold. They were too late. Zombies had found them. He whirled, grabbed his rifle, and raced to the window. Two dozen zombies faced the cabin in a semi-circle. More milled about in the woods beyond. A tall Alpha male wearing the remains of a filthy t-shirt and nothing more, stalked to the forefront of the massed zombies. He stood and stared at the cabin. One part of Jeb's mind was wondering why they didn't simply attack, while the other part frantically considered options for escape. There was none.

"We'll have to make a stand here," he yelled to the others.

As they prepared for the expected attack, the Alpha zombie grunted and the zombies in front split apart, forming a corridor down the center of their line. Jeb stared in amazement as an old man in a dirty white robe strode unmolested through their midst. Beside him, was the same man he had seen in the glade. The old man limped along, bent over using a large staff with a little assistance from the other man. As they drew nearer, Jeb saw that he was a very tall man, lanky and bearded like Abraham Lincoln. His eyes were dark and cold, and yet revealed a hint of inner joy as if he were at peace with the world. In his profession as a psychiatrist, Jeb had seldom witnessed such peace, since most people he treated bore the scars of their damage. The pair continued until they were within thirty paces of the cabin, and then stopped. When the old man spoke, his voice was strong and deep in spite of his apparent weakness and carried easily to those watching from the cabin.

"I am Brother Malachi." He waved his arm taking in the zombies around him. "These are the Children of God. Do not fear us. These Children have accepted us. They no longer hunt humans for meat."

Jeb saw no other option but to speak with the old man. He glanced at the others, leaned his rifle against the wall, and opened the door. He kept his pistol in its holster just in case. The musky, fetid smell of zombie greeted him as he stepped outside.

"What are you doing here?" he asked from the edge of the porch.

The man calling himself Brother Malachi, took a step forward and leaned on his staff. Jeb saw that the man was not as old as he had thought. He was closer to fifty years old rather than the seventy he had first appeared. "We fled our sanctuary in Phoenix when Major Corzine gassed the city. Ahiga," he glanced at his silent companion, "was accepted first by the Children and sought us out."

More Arizona ex-pats, he thought. "The Major's dead. We killed him at Biosphere2."

Brother Malachi nodded his head. "Good. He was an evil man. Ahiga was a Hunter with the Gray Man, but he changed when the Children accepted him."

Jeb flinched at mention of the Gray Man. Vince had described his narrow escape from the Gray Man and Major Corzine. He nodded at the Hunter and scowled. "My first impulse is to kill him."

Brother Malachi smiled. "Believe me, no one had a bigger hatred of Hunters than I did, but all people change. Besides, if you kill Ahiga, you will all die within minutes, perhaps me as well. The Children protect him." He glanced at the sky. "Snow is coming soon. You will be trapped here for weeks. If you come with us, the Children will not harm you. My people will see to your needs."

"Your people?"

"We are New Apostles."

Jeb's stomach tightened. "I've heard of you," he snarled. "One of my friends was your prisoner for a while. I understand you wanted to feed him to the zombies."

Brother Malachi's lips quivered in agitation. "Thinking God had abandoned us; we wanted to become one with them to redeem ourselves in His eyes. Now, we realize our task is to elevate the new Children of God. They are changing. Many are no longer the animals they were."

"One of our friends was killed by zombies two nights ago."

"None from this group, I assure you. There are other smaller groups nearby, but even they are changing."

"They're still zombies," Jeb reminded him.

"An unfortunate label. They are not the walking dead. They are something unique, a new link in the evolutionary chain. It is our belief that they will supplant man."

"Not if I can help it," Jeb snapped. The thought of zombies becoming the new dominant species sickened him.

"Nevertheless, they will. Man is too few and too scattered to matter. In spite of the apocalypse that has befallen us, we still kill each other. We have dedicated ourselves to enlightening the Children, setting them on the pathway of humanity. It is God's will."

Jeb barked out a quick laugh. "Huh! Some will argue that."

"Be that as it may, your decision is simple – will you join us, or will you remain here and starve? The Children will not harm you if you remain, but the game is moving north."

"We were preparing to leave."

"By tomorrow or the day after, the snow will come. There is no adequate shelter within a week's travel. You would die along the way."

Jeb knew he was right, but replied, "We'll risk it."

Brother Malachi shook his head. "I understand your fear. You must release your fear and let God into your heart."

"I haven't seen much of God lately," Jeb verbally shot at him.

Brother Malachi smiled at Jeb's retort. "He is why we are still alive. You must decide as you will, but I implore you to come with us. In the spring, you and your people may do as you wish, but you will never survive the winter alone."

"I have to talk to my people."

Brother Malachi waved his hand. "Please do."

As Jeb turned his back to walk back inside, he imagined the dozens of pairs of zombie eyes staring at him hungrily. Inside, the others looked at him expectantly. He glared at Nabors.

"Believe me now?"

She glanced at the floor.

"What do we do?" Halliwell asked trembling in fear.

Jeb shrugged. "What choice do we have? We can go with them, or we can try to hold out if they attack. Even if he's wrong about the snow coming, we wouldn't last long in the open with zombies around."

"Will they attack?" Halliwell pressed.

Jeb shook his head. For some reason he felt no threat from the old man, but it was difficult to believe he could control zombies. "I don't know. I'm surprised they haven't already."

"Maybe he's speaking the truth," Antonov suggested.

"Maybe," Jeb answered, "but is it worth risking our lives to find out?"

"We risk our lives every day. I must admit to a certain amount of curiosity, but as you Americans are fond of saying, 'curiosity killed the cat'."

"Those creatures murdered Meara," Nabors reminded them. She did not hide the bitterness in her voice. "We should kill them."

"Maybe, or maybe it was another group like he said. I don't know. These zoms seem different somehow. I do know that after we fire the first shot, we're dead. We have three choices: We can stay here, risk the storm, and hope they don't attack; we can head out, risk the storm, and hope they don't attack; or we can go with them and hope they don't attack."

"None of which are very appealing," Antonov replied with a humorless chuckle.

"A couple of us could go and see what this is all about while the rest of you remain here," he suggested. It was not a chance he wanted to take, anything could happen, but it only seemed right to allow everyone to choose for themselves, a brief resurgence of democracy.

"No," Antonov answered. "We should all go or all stay. Separating could be dangerous."

Jeb looked at everyone to gauge their reactions. A few faces turned away. He had been making the decisions since leaving Biosphere2. Some hadn't been the right ones, like choosing to rest up in Telluride, but no one else seemed willing to make the hard choices.

"Okay, we go with them. Keep your weapons handy, but for God's sake don't pull the trigger."

Karen glared at him but said nothing. Her hatred of zombies exceeded his own and her decision to go surprised him. He wasn't sure what he would have done if she had refused. It took them ten minutes to pack their supplies. He walked out first, stopping a few paces beyond the porch.

"You must leave the vehicles," Brother Malachi said. "The noise and the smell of burning fuel confuse the Children."

"We might need them," Jeb protested. "Besides, you look like you could use a ride."

Brother Malachi smiled. "The journey north has been a long one, but I will survive. The vehicles cannot maneuver through the forest. Cover them if you wish to protect them from the snow, but leave them behind. I must insist."

They secured tarps over the ATVs to protect them against the snow that Brother Malachi had predicted. By the time they had finished, Jeb noticed the temperature had dropped several degrees, and the wind had picked up. Bands of gray clouds scuttled across the sky from the northwest. *Maybe the old man isn't so crazy*, he thought.

They followed their silent Indian guide along a game trail in the woods. The zombies had gone on ahead, but Jeb suspected a few followed discretely behind them from a distance. His people were nervous. Even Karen stayed close to him, pressing her hand against his back for reassurance. At one time, he would have considered that a good sign that she was beginning to accept him again, but after so many false hopes, so many setbacks, he paid scant attention to it. She, like the others, was frightened. He hoped no one got too nervous and took a wild shot at a zombie. He quickened his pace and caught up with Brother Malachi.

"Does the Indian speak?" he asked.

Brother Malachi chuckled. "His name is Ahiga. Yes, he speaks, but very seldom."

"What's his story?"

"In the fight at our sanctuary at Twin Buttes Resort, he was severely wounded. He wandered the desert awaiting death, but death did not come. The Children found him and accepted him. He now believes that the Great Spirit saved him for a purpose. He is devoted to my people and to the Children." He glanced at Jeb. "Your friend at the Sanctuary? He is alive?"

"I wish I knew," he sighed. "He saved our asses at Biosphere2. He's the one who killed the Major. He went with the others when we split up. I haven't heard from them in months."

"It is a harsh and unforgiving land. We lost five on our journey here, two from accident and two from disease. One became one of the Children, a New Angel, but became so wild and dangerous that the Alpha male killed her. They are beginning to use tools, you know."

The offhand remark stunned Jeb. "Tools? What kind of tools?"

"Oh, just simple tools – stones for crushing bones for marrow, sticks for knocking fruit from trees, sharpened stones for cutting meat, but they are learning."

"Fruit? I thought they just ate meat."

"No, these Children are hunter gatherers. We grow vegetables, which we trade for meat. They might even have a rudimentary language. Not much, just a few simple grunts and calls, but they all understand them. I am no expert, but I am convinced that they are evolving. There are thousands of them in southern Utah and the mountains of Colorado. Most live in caves."

"If what you say is true, then mankind is doomed."

"Or being given a second opportunity. What we have considered as man's folly might have been God's plan. If the Children evolve, why can we not evolve with them, like Cro Magnon and Neanderthal?"

"Neanderthal died out," Jeb reminded him, "Cro Magnon probably killed him."

Brother Malachi shrugged. "We will have to do better."

3

Agua Caliente, Arizona

Elliot Samuels stood on the crest of a low, sandy ridge, looking back down at the Agua Caliente solar farm with its neat rows of solar panels spread out before him like a hall of glistening mirrors, or rather they would have been glistening if the day weren't cloudy and dreary. A northern cold front was moving through. Even for Arizona, the fifty-degree temperatures were chilly for late November. The cold weather exacerbated the dull ache in his right shoulder, caused by a poorly mended broken collarbone, a bullet-scar memento of the battle at Biosphere2 three months earlier. There had been no clear winner of the fight. They had killed the ruthless Major Corzine and eliminated his attack force, but only at a horrific cost. Over half of the defenders were lost and the integrity of the glass domes of Biosphere2 were compromised. The survivors had split up – the *munies* followed Jeb Stone. Elliot and those needing the Blue Juice vaccine were accompanying Mace Ridell and Erin Kostner's former CDC group that produced the temporary vaccine. Elliot rubbed the dull throb of the bullet wound in his shoulder, wondering how Jeb was faring. They had not heard from him since their parting.

Movement in the distance caught his attention, an ATV coming from the direction of the interstate. His body stiffened. Was this the moment they had all been dreading, when they would need to pack up and slink away or stand and fight? He relaxed when he saw that it was Vince Holcomb and Amanda returning from a run into the outskirts of Yuma for supplies. So far, their little group had managed to remain hidden in their new quarters, but discovery loomed over them like Gideon's sword. They had all the power they needed for the labs from the solar farm, 240 megawatts worth – power enough for the lab equipment, electric ovens and microwaves for cooking, hot water for showers, and electric heaters – but they still had to salvage supplies from intact stores or homes. Each trip exposed them to marauding zombies, frightened survivors who often shot first, or bands of mercenary Hunters seeking munies. He glanced up at the sky. Somewhere up there, spy satellites still circled the Earth. No doubt, the military had managed to add them to their arsenal of weaponry to locate survivors. The cloud cover would help, but every trip entailed risks. Eventually, their luck would run out.

Vince spotted Elliot and waved. Elliot returned his greeting. He genuinely liked the former Air Force technical sergeant. Though somewhat taciturn, a term often used by Erin about him, Vince was friendly, honest to the point of rudeness, and a deadly killer when necessary. His relationship with Amanda, whom he had rescued during his escape from the Gray Man and his Hunters, had soothed his bluntness somewhat, but he still spoke his mind, often to the ire of others. Elliot found it refreshing. As a former FEMA director and liaison with the CDC, being political had been his stock-in-trade, a useful tool to soothe frayed relations, but the time for politics was over, dead with the rest of civilization. Truth and honesty were needed now.

Vince roared up the slope, rolled the ATV to a stop beside Elliot, and removed his helmet. "Keeping watch?" he asked.

"Keeping out of Erin's hair," Elliot replied. "There's a bit of tension in the lab, and as the only non-scientist there, I felt out of place."

Vince jerked his thumb toward the back of the ATV piled high with boxes. "Maybe this will help."

Elliot strolled to the ATV and looked at Vince's haul. Among the cases of goods, bottled water, and a pile of extra blankets, he spotted a box of chocolates, several cases of beer, and much to Elliot's delight, a case of canned cranberries.

"Good job," he said, "maybe this will liven up the crowd."

Vince climbed out of the ATV and stretched by reaching his arms behind his back and clasping them. A sharp snap followed as bones realigned. Amanda remained seated. "I hope the hell it does. It's like a damn morgue around here. Mace sits beside that damned Ham radio like he's expecting a word from God."

"Word from Jeb, more likely. It's been three months."

"Jeb can take care of himself," Vince said, and then shook his arms to loosen his muscles.

"That's true," Elliot agreed, "but he insists on taking on everyone else's problems as well."

Vince shook his head and grinned. "Reminds me of someone else." He glanced at the sun low in the western sky. It blazed brighter as it broke free of the cloud cover but was already caressing the horizon. "Hop in and we'll give you a lift back down before dark."

"No. I'll stay here for a while and enjoy the fresh air."

"And the quiet," Vince added. He glanced down at Elliot's holster with his 9 mm automatic and nodded. "Good, you're armed." He reached into the back of the ATV and pulled out a blanket. "Here. You look cold."

Elliot accepted the blanket, a cheap, colorful Mexican blanket found at most truck stops or roadside souvenir stands for five dollars, and wrapped it around his shoulders. "See you later."

He watched the ATV head back down the ridge toward the concrete block building, the sheds, and the four salvaged FEMA trailers that comprised Agua Caliente. A light shone briefly as several people exited one of the trailers to help unload the supplies. Someone inside quickly closed the door to hide the light. Voices rose in greeting. A high-pitched laugh that could only have come from Dana Welch, a former Tucson morning show radio host, erupted from the crowd. Even in the relative safety of the trailers, Elliot noticed Amanda stood off to the side with her rifle on guard while the others unloaded the ATV. The supplies unloaded, Vince drove the ATV to the shed where they parked their vehicles out of the sight of prying eyes. Amanda stopped and looked back up the ridge at him before going inside.

The slim Afro-American woman was still a mystery to him. She was quietly observant and seldom ventured an opinion, except through Vince, but he felt that beneath her reserved façade, she was a woman of great emotional strength and stability. She never spoke of her captivity at the hands of the Gray Man, and no one dared ask about it. By mutual agreement, the past was as gone as the world they had lived in. Only the present and the future mattered. Vince had confided that she had killed the Gray Man during their escape in a manner best left unspoken. She was a good match for Vince and that was all that mattered.

A sudden gust of wind sent a small dust devil spinning at Elliot's feet, then racing down the slope toward the solar array. Dust was a prevalent problem with the solar panels, reducing their efficiency and scratching the glass. Its accumulation had to be kept to a minimum, but sparkling clean solar panels would be a dead giveaway that someone was maintaining them. The entire camp walked the fine line of maintaining a façade of desertion and accommodating fifteen people. Black drapes covered windows and doors to prevent light from leaking out. Large outside gatherings were strictly forbidden. Cold weather was the worst, forcing everyone inside for warmth, but southern Arizona was blessed with mild winters interspersed with many days of warm weather. The heart of the winter was still months away. Things would become more difficult then.

He clasped the blanket tighter and stared north until he saw it, a brief flash of light on the horizon. It lasted only a few seconds, but this was the third time he had seen it in as many days. It was why he had come to the ridge, just to be certain. It could be something innocuous like the setting sun flashing on some metal object or glass, but there were no houses in that direction, only the Agua Caliente Mountains. Strangers presented a problem. It had been someone passing through Biosphere2 that had revealed its location to Hunter spies, leading to many deaths and their eventual expulsion from their glass-enclosed Eden. The flash warranted investigation, but not tonight.

He trudged down the steep slope in the dark, mindful of his footing. He had already suffered one broken bone. He didn't need a broken leg to add to his list of scars. The cinderblock building serving as the laboratory, stood apart from the other trailers for safety reasons. When dealing with a potentially lethal virus like the mutated Avian flu zombie virus, certain precautions were not only warranted, but also expected. He knocked first to allow the people inside to slide the dark drape over the door opening. When it opened, he stepped inside quickly and closed the door behind him. Erin Kostner and Ang Lee were arguing in the far corner.

"It has been three months and we're no closer to a solution," he complained. "The direction of our research is fundamentally flawed. The degradation is not a genetic problem, but a chemical one."

Erin did not back down from Lee's accusations. "We've replaced all of our reagents and sterilized all of our equipment, all with the same results. Our original blood supply was contaminated in some manner that our limited equipment can't detect. We have all received treatments from the resulting batch of Blue Juice, further contaminating our blood supply." She glanced across the room at Elliot. "We can't drain our immune donors. It's a slow process."

He rubbed his arm where he had donated blood twice in the last two weeks. He was glad she had reminded everyone that those needing Blue Juice greatly surpassed the number of munies. He couldn't give blood every day.

Lee was adamant. "It's too slow. We need more blood."

Erin scowled at Lee and placed her hands on her hips. From personal experience, he knew Lee had gone too far. She was not quick tempered, but lately, she had become prone to explosive bouts of anger. He waited for the fireworks. Instead, she spoke quietly.

"I suppose you would like to return to the military base at San Diego and join them in killing hundreds for their blood, or maybe they've established one in Phoenix by now."

Lee's face reddened. "No, I, er, I …," he spluttered.

"I didn't think so. Nor would I. We work with what we have and pray for some good luck to come our way." She turned and smiled at Elliot, catching him off guard. "We're due for some."

Without waiting for Lee's response, she turned on her heel, strode back to her desk, and resumed entering notes on her laptop, one of the few items they had been able to save when they had fled Biosphere2. The rapid-fire *peck-peck-peck* as her nimble fingers struck the keys with more force than necessary, filled the suddenly quiet room. Elliot walked over to her, bending down so that his striking six-foot-two-inch-frame wouldn't seem so intimidating. When he rested his hands on the desk, she stopped typing long enough to reach out and clasp one of them for a few seconds, and then resumed typing.

"Vince is back with some more items for our Thanksgiving meal," he said.

"Thanksgiving. I'm not so sure that's a holiday we should revive, that and Christmas, not when we have three-hundred-sixty-five-days of Halloween."

He understood her reluctance to note the one-year anniversary of the beginning of the zombie plague. "We aren't celebrating the plague, but a year of survival. We all need something to break the monotony. It won't hurt to shut down the lab for one day and just relax."

She looked up at him over the rims of her glasses. "Won't it?" She waved her hand around the room. "Not you, maybe, but any one of them could die tomorrow, and they know it."

He stood straight. "We all know it, Erin. Maybe Ang has a point. It's been three long months. Take a day off and be human again." He smiled. "Vince brought cranberries." They had managed to shoot a few wild chickens and even bake bread for stuffing, but without cranberry sauce, Thanksgiving wouldn't be complete.

Erin removed her glasses and laid them on her desk. After rubbing the bridge of her nose, she looked up at him and smiled. It was a quick smile, barely creasing the corners of her mouth, but he accepted it as a sign he had gotten through to her.

"Maybe you're right. We're getting on one another's nerves."

"Some roasted chicken with stuffing, cranberry sauce, mashed potatoes and gravy, corn, and a cold beer, ought to make a new woman out of you."

She frowned. "Why? Is something wrong with the old me?"

"Not at all," he replied quickly, "but I don't see the old Erin much anymore except at meals and in the lab."

She winced at his implication. "I know I've been rather remote lately, but it has nothing to do with you, or with us," she added after a short hesitation.

He twirled the ends of his moustache with his fingers. "I hope not. I trimmed my moustache just for you. You complained it irritated you."

"I didn't complain, I ..." she began; then stopped and chuckled, "okay, I guess I did complain. It's lovely. Thank you."

"It's good to hear you laugh."

"It's good to remember that I still can." She sighed. "Oh, Elliot! Ang's right. We're just going through the motions. I don't know what to do."

He walked around behind her chair and began to massage her shoulders. She leaned back and closed her eyes, allowing some of the tension to drain from her body. Everyone else in the lab pretended sudden interest in something else, to allow the couple a moment of solitude. After a few minutes, he felt her body relax beneath his hands. Suddenly, she pushed away from her desk and stood. Elliot scrambled backwards out of her way.

"Everyone! Stop what you're doing and shut down the equipment. Tomorrow is Thanksgiving and we're taking a break, starting now."

Lee stared at her. "But we ..."

"We all need to take a break, take a few steps away from our work, and see if inspiration strikes us."

"Wahoo," Susan McNeil yelled. She threw off the hairnet she was wearing and shook out her long blonde hair. At twenty-seven, she was younger than the others were and suffered the most from their self-imposed isolation. Most who saw her, considered her beautiful, and those who knew her, labeled her vivacious, but no one ever doubted her ability or dedication to her work. "I feel like some music and dancing." She looked at Elliot and winked. "How about you, Elliot?"

He felt his face turning red. She had once had a thing for him, but his interest had lain in Erin. She still enjoyed flirting with him. Erin didn't seem to mind, so he ignored it.

"I have two left feet," he replied.

Susan sighed and shook her head. "You men. You would think at least one of you would know how to dance."

Seth Brisbane, one of the technicians thrust into the position of researcher by the expediency of surviving the plague, raised his hand timidly. "I can dance," he said. The others turned to stare at him. Brisbane, a few years older than Susan, was quiet, unkempt, and awkward around women, but he attacked his job with a single-minded perseverance that overcame his lack of formal training. His admission surprised them all.

Susan smiled. "Well then, Seth. You and I can take a turn around the dance floor while the others watch."

He withered under her smile and gaze. "N-n-now?" he stammered.

She placed a hand on her flat belly and laughed. "No, silly. Tomorrow at our party."

He smiled back. "S-s-sure."

"Be sure to return all cultures to the incubator in the Level 4 lab," Erin reminded them.

"I'll do it," Brisbane announced.

"Okay, Seth," Erin replied, "go ahead."

While the others shut down the equipment, Brisbane gathered the tubes of cultures the others had been examining into a slotted carrier. They had almost finished by the time he donned a bright blue biohazard suit salvaged from a FEMA medical center and cycled through the decontamination lock. He held his arms wide to allow the disinfectant and UV lights to scour his suit of any contaminants. The Level 4 lab, really just a ten-by-ten sealed cubicle in a corner of the building, maintained a lower air pressure than outside air in case of minor leaks. The door hissed as he swung it open. A single, double-paned acrylic window allowed outside observers to watch workers inside the room. Brisbane carefully attached the coiled air supply line to his suit, crossed the room, and opened the sealed incubator.

Elliot glanced at Brisbane while the others shed their lab smocks and prepared to leave. At first, he paid no attention to Brisbane's grabbing the air hose with his right hand. The looped coils sometimes became tangled and needed adjusting. When he set the carrier on the edge of a desk and yanked the hose with both hands, a loose aluminum strut supporting the hose mechanism pulled away from the ceiling and struck him in the shoulder. As he staggered backwards, his flailing hand knocked over the carrier, spilling its contents on the floor. One of the vials broke. Almost immediately, a biohazard alarm sounded, startling everyone.

"Seth!" Erin yelled and raced for the airlock. She was sobbing by the time Elliot joined her.

Brisbane rose from the floor, startled, and surveyed the overturned carrier. He then examined the broken strut. "I'm sorry, Erin. I'll clean this up." His voice was shaky, but calmer than Elliot would have expected it to be under the circumstances. When he turned his back, he heard Erin's gasp.

"Seth," she said with dread filling her voice, "look at your suit."

The strut had ripped a hole in the tough material of his biohazard suit just beneath his right arm, and as he had fallen, the airline had separated. He was breathing contaminated air in a compromised suit. Rather than panic, Brisbane turned to look at Erin through the glass.

"The Blue Juice might save you, Seth," she said. "Decontaminate in the lock, and we'll administer another dose."

He smiled and shook his head. "The vial that broke was one of the concentrated samples. Just my luck. If I open the inner door, I'll contaminate the airlock. I don't think the mist and UV lights are enough. I'll expose all of you."

Someone had thankfully silenced the alarm. The room was now deathly silent except for Brisbane's labored breathing coming from the intercom speaker.

"You know what you have to do," he added.

"No, Seth," Erin pleaded, "I can't." She turned away and began to sob into Elliot's shoulder.

Susan's eyes were moist as well as she said, "You owe me a dance, Seth."

He smiled; then turned away. Elliot saw Brisbane's shoulders shaking and knew he was crying as well. "You're more practical that the rest of us, Elliot," he said with his back turned. "Will you do it?"

Erin grabbed his arm to stop him, but she knew Brisbane was right. She could do nothing for him. He was a dead man. The Blue Juice vaccine would not protect him from the concentration of lethal viruses contaminating the lab air. It was just a matter of time before he died and the virus changed him into a zombie.

The Level 4 containment lab had a failsafe system. The large red button sat discretely in a metal box behind a glass cover on the wall. Its presence was known by all, but largely ignored for the implications of using it and what it would mean. By pressing the button, a flash fire fueled by natural gas would raise the inside temperature of the room to two-thousand degrees Celsius in a matter of seconds, immediately incinerating any viruses in the air or contaminating any surfaces. Unfortunately, it would do the same to Brisbane. Elliot hesitated, and then smashed the glass covering the red button. He hesitated again, his hand hovering over the button. He felt Erin's hand cover his.

"Together," she whispered.

He pressed the button and covered his eyes from the brilliant flash, as fire swept through the room. Liquids hissed as they boiled away, and metal screamed as it twisted and warped from the intense heat. Brisbane collapsed to the floor, barely visible through the flames as the heat scorched the inside of the thick acrylic window. Thankfully, the intercom went dead before they heard his horrible screams. Elliot held the button down until the natural gas tank emptied. Overhead, a powerful fan throbbed as it sucked the burning exhaust gases away from the building and expelled them harmlessly into the air from an outlet a hundred yards away. The sprinkler system sprayed the room until the flames died away.

The scorched and blackened window obscured their view of the aftermath of the fire, but the room was safe, its deadly contents vaporized. The intense heat would have left very little of Brisbane to remove. The damage was extensive. It would be hours before they could see what they could salvage, if anything. They would have to rebuild the Level 4 lab from scratch, a time-consuming effort.

"The rest of you go ahead," he told the others. "I'll take care of things here."

No one protested or offered to help, too stunned by the sudden sequence of events to comprehend fully what had just happened. All they knew was that they had lost a colleague. It would dawn on them later that many weeks of hard labor lay before them before they could continue their work. Perhaps Erin had been right after all. Taking time to give thanks for their bounty seemed incongruous now.

4

Salt Lake City, Utah

It hardly mattered to Bahati Adib that she was probably the only Coptic Christian in a land of Mormons. The daily tedium of simple survival erased most religious, social, and racial barriers. Few people had the time or energy for intolerance. The Mormons practiced their faith as they always had and bothered no one, allowing Christians, Buddhists, and atheists alike to do as they saw fit. Bahati had been an exchange student studying at Brigham Young University when the plague struck, with no way of returning to her native Alexandria, Egypt. Her name, Bahati, meant 'Fortune' in Arabic. She was not so certain of her fortune. She had no idea if any of her family had survived. Now, stranded in a foreign land among people she barely knew, she was trying to make a new home for herself.

To fit in, she had discarded her traditional Egyptian long-sleeved, long-hemmed *thobe* and sandals for Western wear – jeans, shirt, and boots. Even as a Christian, she did not wish to draw attention to her Arab origins. Some people held Muslims responsible for the plague, though Arab countries had been among the first to suffer and, with few hospitals or medical personnel available, had suffered harder.

She had joined in the massive effort to dig the Big Ditch, saving Salt Lake City from the zombie horde migrating northwards. The zombies had eventually scattered into the mountains to the east, but the city remained a virtual island, isolated from the rest of the country by mountains, desert, and the narrow band of water of the Big Ditch. The few airplanes that flew in brought mostly medicine and military supplies. No one left. There were few places to go.

The military was slowly reclaiming the hearts of San Diego and Phoenix, and had established a base on Vashon Island across from Seattle. Most of both coasts were zombie occupied, as was the Industrial Northern Corridor from Chicago to Boston. Using ships from San Diego and Vashon Island, railroads from Phoenix, and air travel from both Phoenix and Salt Lake City, a thin line of communications was kept flowing between these far-flung outposts of civilization. America's sparsely populated productive heartland had few large cities, most of which were deserted except for zombies. To rebuild the country, they needed farmlands and industry. For this, they needed people, but survivors were afraid of the military for their *pogrom* of capturing immune civilians to feed the blood bank mills that produced Blue Juice, the only vaccine available. Since its effects were only temporary, a lot of blood was required.

Only in Salt Lake City under the authority of Colonel Martin Schumer, was it safe for a munie to walk the streets. The Mormons donated their blood freely and without coercion. Their isolation enforced the colonel's authority. The Ditch that had saved them had been his idea. As an engineer, he had implemented its construction with the same dedication that he devoted to protecting the people in his charge.

Bahati finished the sandwich in her hand, washing it down with a bottle of fruit juice. Around her, the other women were returning to their jobs in the food processing plant. She worked on the vegetable line, operating the machine that today dumped a pre-measured portion of cooked corn into aluminum cans racing down the conveyor line. Beyond her, another machine sealed the cans and sent them onto a labeler. Her world had become one of corn, peas, beans, and squash, but people must eat. Soon, the storeroom of aluminum cans would be depleted. Recycling wasn't enough. Unless they reopened the mines and smelters, their diet would be limited to seasonal fresh produce and dried foods.

Her day passed mindlessly, hours of boredom interrupted briefly by a flashing red light accompanied by a lull in the noise level. She rose from her stool, cleared whatever had stopped the line, usually a bent can, pushed a button to restart the line, and resumed her seat. In this manner, the afternoon passed. She was aware of the time only when the whistle blew to announce the end of her shift. She donned her heavy coat, and with the other women, marched from the factory to the single women's dormitory a few blocks away.

She passed a brochure in the common area of the dorm announcing a movie that night – *You've Got Mail* – but she didn't want a reminder that such things as E-mail were obsolete. Her roommate, Elise Newman, another non-Mormon met her at the door of their room. Elise was short and somewhat unattractive, something she made no effort to alter by wearing her bright red hair short with deep bangs that almost hid her hazel eyes, which she framed with large, dark horn-rimmed glasses. She was thin, but well proportioned, and hid what Bahati thought was her best feature, her body, beneath bulky, formless dresses. By contrast, Bahati was tall and slim with long black hair and emerald green eyes. The blood of Cleopatra ran in her veins. She was aware of the looks of admiration she received from men, but ignored them. She had no time or inclination to fraternize.

"Are you going to the movie tonight after dinner?" Elise asked.

Bahati sighed. "No. I do not feel like a movie."

She tossed her coat on her bed, unpinned her hair, which she had kept covered with a cap, and let it fall around her shoulders. She glanced in the mirror and wiped a smudge from the side of her nose with her finger.

"You can't sit around moping all the time," Elise challenged.

"I'm not moping," she shot at her friend. "I'm tired."

"You're moping. I know you're worried about your family, but …"

"And you're not?"

Elise paused. Her face paled slightly and a quiver played on her lower lip. "My parents are dead. I saw them die. My brother … I don't know what happened to him. He was in Chicago."

Bahati plopped down on her bed and frowned. She could see that she had upset her roommate. "I'm sorry, Elise. I did not mean to be so rude. You go on to dinner and the movie. Once I've rested and cleaned up, I might join you."

"Do. It's Thanksgiving, Bahati – turkey and dressing. You need to relax."

"We do not celebrate Thanksgiving in my country, and I do not see that we have anything to celebrate."

"Living. We celebrate just living." Elise smiled at her one last time and disappeared out the door.

Bahati realized that Elise was right about one thing – she was moping. For days, doubts of her uncertain future had plagued her mind. Would she ever return to Alexandria? Did she have any family still living if she did? Could she adjust to life in a land with people so different from her? She had come to America to study economics and to improve her English skills to help with her family's date export business, but she had never dreamed of living here. Now, unless something changed, she was stuck in America, in Salt Lake City.

She couldn't recount the number the times someone had replied, "You must be used to the desert," when she mentioned her origin. Did they think all of Egypt was desert? Her city, Alexandria, lay on the southern Mediterranean coast near one of the Nile's two main outlets, a land of lakes, rivers, and the sea. Soft sea breezes swept inland and the scent of red lotus blossoms sweetened the air. It had been home to Cleopatra, most famous of the Ptolemy Pharaohs, and the city of Marc Antony's death. It was site of the renowned Library of Alexandria. Her family's house faced the sea along the *El Geish* Road in the *El Ibrahimaia Bahary* neighborhood. She grew up swimming in the Mediterranean's blue waters. The Nile Delta was an agricultural region. What did she know of deserts and sand dunes?

She needed something to take her mind off her problems, but she was certain a movie was not it, certainly not a romantic comedy. She had no stomach for food, even Elise's much touted turkey feast. Perhaps a walk through downtown would lift her spirits. She sighed. It would require wearing her heavy coat again. She did not think she would get used to Utah winters.

Her dormitory was located near the canning plant southwest of downtown in the Sugar House neighborhood, a once liberal bastion of small shops. Now, like many areas of the city, it was mostly deserted. The colleges had closed, though a few small schools still functioned for children. Two of the city's TRAX rail lines still operated, though with fewer stations. She hopped on a train headed downtown, one of only a handful of passengers. Two young men stared at her and whispered to one another. She glared at them until they stopped. When she had first come to America, such crude displays made her nervous, thinking they were whispering about her foreignness. Elise had informed her that men found her strikingly beautiful. She had dismissed her friend as being overly complimentary, but she felt a secret thrill at men's stares. She had lost her virginity in Alexandria to an older cousin at fourteen. She liked men, but at this time, had no desire for even a casual relationship.

She left the train at Temple Square and walked east along South Temple Street. A few snowflakes floated down from the low-lying clouds, but no one had predicted any accumulation. There was little traffic. Fuel was too precious to waste on automobiles. Volunteer work parties had removed most of the abandoned cars and corpses from this section of the city and boarded broken windows, but many areas of the city remained untouched. Groups of people strolled on the temple grounds in spite of the inclement weather. Her destination was a small former sports bar and grill a few blocks from the Temple that had lately reopened.

The name *Z-Bar* had been the owner's attempt to inject humor into the absurdity of the Zombie Apocalypse. The fact that his name was Miklos Zacharenias did not dissuade most patrons of the opinion that the name was an inappropriate reminder of the devastation surrounding them. However, it did not prevent them from drinking there. Bahati thought the name appropriate since most of the customers displayed the lifelessness of zombies, if not their penchant for devouring human flesh. The *Z-Bar* had a dance floor and a jukebox, but it was seldom playing, and she had never seen anyone dancing. Many of the patrons, far too many in her opinion, were individuals like herself, who simply sat alone and drank. She did not consider herself an alcoholic. She enjoyed the occasional dry martini, but she had never been drunk. In a community where even caffeine was frowned upon, a drunk would never have been tolerated.

As she entered, Miklos, a rotund former Athenian with a large black moustache and ever-present smile, nodded to her and began to prepare her martini. He knew what she liked to drink. She chose her usual table beside the jukebox, facing the street where she could watch passersby. The sun was setting, casting long shadows down the street and sidewalk. The glass windows of the buildings, those that still had windows, reflected a burnished golden aura. If not for the gaping, blackened windows and streaks of soot from fire-gutted buildings, it would have been a serene scene. Instead, it served only to remind her of where she was.

At first, she paid no attention to the black man standing frozen on the sidewalk, but something in his odd mannerism caused her to look more closely. He glanced at the bar, and then down the street, as if trying to come to a decision. Finally, he turned to the bar and walked in. He stood looking around for a moment before choosing a table, the one directly across from her. He cast a quick, nervous smile in her direction as he sat down. Miklos rushed over with a bar towel draped over his arm. She thought this odd, since he never waited on tables. The customer usually ordered and picked up their drinks from the bar.

"What can I get you, sir?" he asked, smiling profusely.

The man seemed undecided, then cocked his head, nodded and answered, "A beer."

"I have several good beers," Miklos informed him.

"Any beer," the man replied.

As Miklos rushed off to fetch the beer, the man glanced at Bahati and saw her staring at him. He smiled and explained, "I'm not much of a beer drinker, but I thought I should order something."

She returned his smile and nodded politely. Miklos returned with a bottle of beer and a cold mug and her martini on a tray. He placed her martini in front of her and then carried the beer and mug to the other patron. She took a sip. It was very dry with just a splash of vermouth, the way she liked it. There were no fresh olives, but a twist of lemon peel added a touch of tartness. She had learned to enjoy martinis while visiting southern France during her last year of high school with her friends. Sipping the concoction reminded her of those times. She wondered if any of them still lived.

The man ignored the frosted mug and picked up the bottle. He took a short experimental sip, smiled, and then took a longer swig. "Not bad," he said.

Miklos beamed. "Thank you, Colonel. I am most pleased." He muttered to himself as he walked away.

Bahati recognized the man now – Colonel Martin Schumer, commandant of the military and de facto head of the government of Salt Lake City. She had seen him once when she had worked on the Ditch, but she didn't recognize him now without his uniform. He seemed somehow smaller, more vulnerable. He seemed uncomfortable in the bar but determined to finish his beer, as if wasting it would be a major sin. She felt sorry for him.

"I worked on the Ditch," she said to him. "You saved us, Colonel."

He looked startled; then replied, "No, people like you saved us. I just drew a line on a map and let others make it happen."

His modesty surprised her. She had expected a high-ranking officer to have as large an ego. "I saw you digging with a shovel alongside the rest of us."

His smile seemed genuine. "I've always felt more comfortable doing than ordering it done."

"Have you tried Miklos's martinis?"

"I can't drink hard liquor."

She smiled. "Oh? A soldier that doesn't drink?"

"Never got a chance growing up in the Alabama Bible Belt. My father was strict. I didn't even drink beer until I joined the army."

"Why aren't you in uniform now?" she asked.

His eyes grew darker and the corners of his mouth sagged slightly. She immediately regretted her question. His reasons were his own and she had no right to pry, but a few seconds later, he smiled.

"Sometimes I like to get away and pretend I'm a normal man." He pointed down the block. She craned her neck and saw two uniformed soldiers standing on the corner, his escort keeping a discrete distance. "It's an illusion, of course, but it helps."

An idea flittered across her mind. It seemed silly, perhaps even wrong, but the colonel seemed like a nice man thrust into a position with which he was uncomfortable. "There's a back door, you know. Would you like to take a stroll, Colonel?"

He stared at her for a long moment, and then broke into a wide grin. "The name's Martin and yes I would."

"My name is Bahati. I'm not from around here," she said as a joke.

"Neither am I," he replied.

His easy humor put her at ease. She set aside her unfinished martini and stood. She heard the heavy metal back door creak as Miklos, who had had been listening to them, opened it for them. They left their unfinished drinks and slipped out the back door into the alley. The cold wind funneling down the alley was biting. She pulled up the collar on her coat.

"Sergeant Williams and Corporal Rollins are going to be angry with me for this," Schumer said, but Bahati noticed that he was smiling like a schoolboy cutting class.

"Just a quick stroll to assert your independence," she suggested.

"What are you asserting?" he asked.

She considered his question for a moment before replying, "My individuality."

Schumer frowned. "Do you not feel like an individual?"

"Not at the factory. Sometimes not even here in the streets. We all seem to be morphing into one people, drawn together by our despair, huddled together in our fear, and living quietly as if our next mistake could be our last."

They reached the end of the alley and turned south down an empty Main Street. A building warded off the worst of the cold wind, but without streetlamps, the area was dark and uninviting. She didn't worry about crime, almost unheard of in the city, but she was wary of the shadows, a holdover from the days of sudden zombie attacks.

"We're living at the edge of our limits," he said. "After a time, it plays on people's fears. I remember the celebrations when we completed the Ditch. People felt as if they had accomplished something grand. Parties erupted all over the city. We even had fireworks. Now, we simply survive."

"But things are getting better, right?" she asked.

His hesitation in answering dismayed her. She needed to hear a resounding 'Yes' from the man in charge of their lives, but he seemed to be choosing his words carefully.

"In general, yes. We've cleared parts of San Diego, Phoenix, and have a base in Washington state, but it's a slow go. Much of the country's infrastructure is in shambles. The real problem isn't recovering. There are … factions in the military that see a different path for the future of America. Here in Salt Lake City, we have it better than most areas of the country. We have some independence, some of that individuality you're talking about. I fear my influence may not be enough to keep us out of the conflict I see coming."

She grew suddenly cold. "War?"

"No, I don't think it will come to that, but there could be violence."

She considered his meaning. In spite of the time she had spent among them, Americans still baffled her. Even for a people whose entire history had been conflict, it seemed counterproductive to fight among themselves when so few remained.

Schumer continued. "In Europe, NATO keeps the munies sequestered from the general population in camps. The munies willingly donate blood, similar to here in Salt Lake City, but they have few rights. A few of our leaders want to go a step further. In San Diego, they sedate munies and harvest their blood. I've received numerous 'recommendations' that I do the same. I've refused in the strongest terms possible. I've expected orders to stand down at any time, but my popularity for saving the city has given me a reprieve. Attention was focused elsewhere. Now, I don't know."

Bahati had heard rumors of concentration camp-like facilities for munies, but like most, had dismissed them as spurious. After all, how could humans treat other humans like animals? The colonel's confirmation of the rumors shattered her world. It could happen here. It could happen to her. She was furious. She stopped walking and spun to face him.

"You won't let them, will you?"

Her sudden anger took him by surprise. "I'm just a colonel in the military. I follow orders. I won't do it, but I can't stop them from removing me from my position of authority."

"Position of authority? Is that all this is to you? Why did we work so hard to save ourselves if we are simply to become cattle? You're a colonel. You're in command. Your men worship you. Hell, the entire city adores you. Fight them."

"I have less than five hundred troops and most of them are involved in the logistics of feeding a city. Maybe two hundred have combat training. How can I fight anyone with them?"

"We'll all fight. I'll fight. I was there during the Arab Spring in Cairo. Ordinary people fought – students, shopkeepers, taxi drivers, and farmers. Give us weapons and teach us how to use them." Her voice rose in volume as she realized the enormity of what she was suggesting. Her anger gave her the courage to continue. "We'll fight for our lives. We'll fight for our freedom. If we have weapons and training, we might at least die like humans."

Spent, her courage discharged like a spark of electricity by her words, she suddenly became dizzy. Her body refused to cooperate. She felt Schumer's hands as he reached out to catch her as she collapsed. She tried to smile at his whispered words, but the effort was too great.

"You're right, Bahati," he said, "we have to make a stand for what is right."

5

San Diego, California

Admiral Anthony Van Ekland stood on Pier 17 at the San Diego Naval Base admiring the destroyer they had just completed refurbishing. In her year of idleness, she had accumulated a heavy coat of rust, pigeons and seagulls had covered her decks and railings with inches of poop, and rats had chewed miles of electrical wiring. Now, after months of hard labor, she had a trained crew and was ready to sail. The DD-567, guided missile destroyer *USS Watts*, sporting a fresh coat of gray paint, rolled gently in the bay as if eager for the journey. Soon, she would carry her new crew south to check on the status of the Panama Canal. Accompanying her, would be a team of canal and lock specialists gleaned from every port and canal in the U.S. if the locks were still operational or easily repairable, passage to the East Coast would be possible.

As far as Van Ekland was concerned, the Eastern Seaboard cities were death traps, difficult to provide for and impossible to defend. With so few people surviving, it made more sense to move the people to the Southwest or the West Coast where sufficient power was available and the weather was milder. San Diego had power, water, and transportation. What better place to center the new United States? He smiled at the prospect of being near the center of power. Power was like water; it tended to spread out. All he need do was to be ready with his cup.

He would not repeat the mistake of the base's former commander. General Perry had refused to follow orders due to a matter of conscience. Van Ekland had no such problem. He would not let the munie problem be his downfall as it had Perry's. He had orders to transfer the munies at the base to Phoenix, where permanent facilities were near completion. He would personally oversee the transfer of munies. He would be glad to get rid of them. He was a sailor, not the commandant of a prison camp. Upon his arrival, he had inspected the rows of comatose men, women, and children, their precious blood dripping into collection tanks, and had thanked God that he had been spared such a fate. He knew the necessity for their blood, the source of Blue Juice, but as a munie himself, he felt sympathy for their plight. However, he was pragmatic enough to know that he didn't want to join them in their miserable oblivion.

The tracks were nearly operational between San Diego and Phoenix. Within the next few weeks, medical trailers would be loaded onto sixteen flatcars, each containing twenty-eight munies, for a total of four-hundred-and-forty-eight bodies. Once they left San Diego, they would no longer be his responsibility.

"A Christmas present for General Hershimer," he said aloud thinking of the trainload of munies. "I wonder if I should add a bow and ribbon to the damn train."

Phoenix would become the new center for medical research and vaccine production, leaving him to concentrate on military matters. NATO was clamoring for a centralized military to meet any threats posed by the scattered former Soviet Republics, China, and Eastern Asia. Europe was a shambles, her population reduced by four-fifths. The fertile farmlands of southern France produced sufficient food to feed them, but Europe was poor in resources and looked to the U.S. with envious eyes. The U.S. President had so far resisted handing over command to NATO, but Van Ekland knew him as a spineless bastard and suspected a deal was in the works. If so, the U.S. would never rise higher than Europe allowed, becoming a source of valuable raw products and manufactured goods. The balance of power rested in the hands of the military. It was his intention to keep it there.

A figure waved to him from the ship. He squinted against the glare of the sun and recognized the ship's commander, Captain Leland Sheppard. At twenty-six, he was a bit young for command of his own ship, but he had proven himself up to the task as second-in-command of a missile frigate during runs up and down the coast. Van Ekland had few capable officers to choose from. Ships at sea fared poorly during the zombie plague. He hoped the young commander managed to reach Panama. He would hate to lose the *Watts*.

Van Ekland forced a smile to his face and waved back. "At least we still have GPS," he said under his breath.

Tucson, Arizona

Captain Nathaniel Lacey tried not to nod off to the monotonous, rhythmic clanging as the jigger passed over welds in the rails. The small, two-man motorized car, driven by Hugh O'Malley, a cigar-chewing gang pusher from Hoboken, New York, had left the rail yard in Phoenix four hours earlier for the convoluted journey from Phoenix to Coolidge to Picacho to the work gang north of Tucson. O'Malley, a stickler for details, had insisted on stopping to check every new section of rail along the way. Lacey didn't mind too much. He wasn't sure he entirely trusted the hastily formed railroad crews. They lacked discipline. He did trust O'Malley. O'Malley's thirty years on the railroad more than compensated for his own total lack of railroad experience. He knew men and O'Malley knew railroads. Together, he hoped they could quickly get the track cleared through Tucson so he could move on to other things. They had cleared the tracks from San Diego to Phoenix two months earlier, a backbreaking job in stifling heat and dust. No trains had yet made the journey, but they soon would.

"We're here," O'Malley announced.

The metal wheels of the jigger squealed in protest as he applied the brakes, jerking Lacey forward into his seatbelt. In front of them sat the Hi-Rail crane truck and the flatbed car used to transport the bulldozer necessary to clear away the debris from the year-old wreck. Ten men, mostly former railroad workers from around the country, sat idle or leaned against shovels staring at the newcomers.

He frowned when he saw their weapons stacked carelessly on the bed of the flatcar.

"I thought you said they were a good crew," Lacey said. "They look like a bunch of fuck ups to me."

O'Malley sneered at the man he thought of as dead weight. "The snipes heard us coming fifteen minutes ago. They're waiting for you."

Lacey grinned. When he had first heard the word snipes, he had immediately thought of snipe hunting, the practical joke of Southern good ole boys, not railroad work gangs. O'Malley climbed out of the jigger and walked up to the crew pusher, a tall black man with shoulders wider than any man Lacey had ever seen. He wore his green hard hat cocked at an angle.

"Soweta," O'Malley called out loudly, "how they hangin'?"

Soweta grabbed his crotch with one hand and broke out in a toothy grin. "Low to show, boss." The man's musical *basso profundo* voice carried easily to Lacey. It was just a shade higher in pitch than a low rumble.

"The captain here," O'Malley jerked his thumb over his shoulder in Lacey's direction, "is an impatient man. How much longer?"

Soweta scowled at Lacey and pointed to the crumpled, burned out hulks of boxcars and flatcars littering the area. Piles of charred cargo indistinguishable from the wreckage dotted the cleared spaces. "There was more than a mile of this shit on the tracks. Some fool parked a dozer down the line and derailed the entire train. The train took out a tank farm for a power station. Big mess. Burning oil melted and fused metal. We laid some new ballast and ties and replaced a few sections of rail. Luckily, the engines landed far enough from the track that we didn't have to move them. The dozer's no good for that sort of work. We're good to go."

O'Malley spat out the stub of his cigar and glared at Lacey. "Fuck ups, huh?" he challenged.

Lacey climbed out of the jigger, trying to hide his limp from camped legs. The nearer he got to Soweta, the larger the big black man loomed. He towered over O'Malley, not a short man at five-feet-seven-inches, by a good foot. His hands were large enough to pound spikes. The ten-pound sledgehammer he carried looked like a finishing hammer in his meaty hands. Looking up at the big gang pusher, Lacey felt like a child at his father's knees.

"Dingane here is from South Africa, a Zulu, but don't worry, he won't eat you."

Both O'Malley and Soweta laughed hysterically. He ignored them.

"How far has the track been cleared?"

Soweta stopped laughing and stared at Lacey for a moment before replying. He raised an arm and pointed down the line. As he did, Lacey noticed the pearl-handled automatic stuck down the back of Soweta's pants. *Maybe he's not such a fuck up after all.* "We've been all the way to the outskirts of Tucson, maybe fifteen miles. Many zombies. Any farther and we'll need you army boys." He grinned. "My men handle shovels and picks better than rifles."

"So I noticed. My men are on their way by truck." Lacey checked his watch. "It's four now. They'll be here before sunset."

"I hope so," Soweta growled. "We hear all kinds of noises in the dark. Not good. Many zombies moving northwest following the Catalina Mountains. More there." He glanced around nervously. Lacey followed his gaze to a line of ghostly airplanes parked in the distance, Pinal Air Park. "This is a bad place."

Lacey wondered what the big South African would think if he knew that six nuclear-tipped missiles lay housed less than a mile away in the abandoned underground Red Rock nuclear first strike base, each capable of delivering over five kilotons of destruction. Part of his mission was to secure the nukes and transport them back to Phoenix. First, they had to clear the area of zombies.

"Don't worry. My boys will protect you, so you can sleep tight. You just see that the trains can run. If we're going to reclaim the cities, we need the rails. Fuel's too scarce for airplanes. The oil fields and the refineries come next."

"We'll do our job, boss. You do yours."

With that, Soweta turned his back, whistled loudly, and trudged off toward the crane. The others followed behind him. Seated inside the cab, he moved the boom over to a line of wheel assemblies and dropped the cable. Two workers clamped the cable to one of the assemblies and stepped back as Soweta lifted the rusty wheelset, and then gently lowered it to the flatcar. Lacey wondered why he was bothering salvaging a hunk of rusty steel.

"We can refurbish the wheelsets," O'Malley said observing Lacey's concern. "Most of the bogies, or trucks, that the wheelsets attach to beneath the cars were too damaged by the wreck to salvage. We've got plenty of rolling stock but no way to re-forge damaged wheels. Once we get the marshalling yard in Tucson back in operation, we won't depend on Phoenix for everything."

Lacey nodded. O'Malley's job was handling his crew and repairing the rails. His was commanding his troops. "I've got no problem with that." He jutted his chin toward the work crew. "They look like they know what they're doing."

O'Malley grinned. A fresh cigar protruded from his mouth. Lacey wondered where he got them. He seemed to have an endless supply. O'Malley removed his battered Union Pacific cap and wiped his brow. "Soweta's been doing this since he was fourteen and swinging a hammer in South Africa. He came over here at twenty-one to learn about American railroads and stayed. Zombies trapped him and six others in a repair yard in Cincinnati. He's the only one who made it out alive. He can do as much damage with a twelve-pound spike hammer as you could with a machine gun. Don't underestimate this crew, Captain. Railroad men are born brawlers." He pointed to a pile of burned corpses Lacey had dismissed as more rubbish. "They just don't like to fight and work at the same time."

"I'll keep that in mind. Can we go farther?"

O'Malley shrugged. "Sure. We'll have to go back about half a mile to a spur to get around the work car."

"Good. I want to be back before my men get here. We'll set up a base camp here; then we're going there." He pointed to the airpark across the I-10 expressway.

O'Malley squinted to see where Lacey was pointing. "What's over there? Looks like some old planes. You want to take a spin in the sky?"

"I'm more interested in what's below ground."

O'Malley shuddered. "You army boys scare the crap out of me. Well, hop in if you want a lift."

The railroad man reversed the jigger to a point just past a turnout, hopped out, and threw the switch. The switch points moved smoothly into place. He then guided the jigger past the turnout.

"I'll leave the switch open for our return trip. I'll be glad when we get power to all the electrical switches. If we have to throw the switches by hand, it'll take days to get a train from Phoenix to New Mexico."

"They're working on it," Lacey replied.

O'Malley rolled his eyes. "They've been working on it for two months."

They passed the repair crew and continued south until they encountered another train blocking the tracks. Lacey spotted a few zombies in the distance but none paid attention to the small jigger or its occupants. He pulled out a map, checked it, and then surveyed his surroundings. He spotted downtown Tucson in the distance.

"Looks like we're near Orange Grove Road. There's a Costco nearby. It might be worth investigating."

"Not now," O'Malley ventured.

"No, not now," Lacey agreed. "I'll bring some men with me."

"You know," O'Malley said, stabbing his cigar toward the train, "if I can get the engine started, I might be able to switch this locomotive to another set of rails on down the line, free up some track."

"If you can get it running, we need it in Phoenix."

"Whatever you say, Captain. What now?"

The sound of zombie calls in the distance sent a shiver through him. Movement near the expressway caught his attention. He spotted more movement closer to them on the opposite side of the expressway. The zombies were closing in on them using a typical hunting pack technique. He would have liked to stay and watch it unfold, but they were outnumbered and too vulnerable to attack. He had his rifle sitting beside him in the jigger, but he didn't relish the idea of defending the small open car against a horde of zombies.

"Now we go back."

O'Malley threw the jigger in reverse and headed north. He didn't bother looking over his shoulder to see where they were going, but Lacey did. He didn't share the railroader's confidence that the vehicle would stay on the rails. A few zombies came and stood at the edge of the tracks watching them leave, but did not pursue them.

He was eager to tackle the challenge of Tucson. Once they had secured the city with deadly *Sarin* gas, the entire southwest would be accessible by rail west to California and east to New Mexico and Texas. Too bad he had to depend on a cigar-chewing Irishman and a black Hulk to get the job done. He chuckled at the thought.

"Something funny, Captain?" O'Malley asked.

Lacey shook his head. O'Malley cast a suspicious look in his direction but said nothing. Lacey closed his eyes and listened to the rhythm of the rails.

6

Agua Caliente, Arizona

Brisbane's funeral was short and sad, marked mostly by its lack of ceremony. No one spoke a eulogy. They sang no hymns. They could not gather outside in large groups for fear of discovery by satellites or planes, so they paid their respects in groups of three, all except Erin Kostner. Brisbane's death had deflated her like an empty bladder. She felt used up, spent. She sat on the cold ground beneath the cover of one of the sheds and stared at the small, unmarked grave. Only ashes remained to bury. The grave's very diminutive size dismayed her, so child-like. It seemed impossible that all that Brisbane had been, his laughter, his youthful awkwardness, his dedication to work could fit in such a small vessel.

She recalled her colleague Lyle Medford's gruesome death in Atlanta. At the time, he had simply been a colleague, not a friend. She did not have many friends or the time for them. She had been a loner, dedicated to her job. She had watched the zombie-bitten Medford die slowly as the virus changed him into a snarling, vicious creature. Elliot had shot him in the head when he turned. At the time, she had hated Elliot for it, but now she was grateful for his act of kindness. Since then, she had witnessed too much for it to affect her as Brisbane's death did. Maybe it was because it seemed so senseless, so futile, like their efforts to find a permanent vaccine. Perhaps it was because she now thought of Brisbane and the others as friends. The world had grown too small and too empty to remain alone in it.

The Level 4 lab was in shambles, their samples gone. They could do no work. They had enough Blue Juice to last a month at most, and its effectiveness was still in question. Faced with the enormity of rebuilding the lab, Erin questioned the wisdom of continuing for the first time in her life. It was as if she had been pounding a door with her fists seeking entry and suddenly discovered that she longer wanted what was on the other side. The military had all the resources and the munie blood supply. She had been fooling herself to think that they could find the answer when others had not. Maybe it was time to give up, live what life she had left. She rose from her seat and sought out Elliot.

She found him in the vehicle shed speaking with Vince and Mace. She approached him silently and slipped her hand into his. He glanced at her, squeezed her hand gently, and smiled.

"We were discussing a little trip," he told her.

"Where?"

"Elliot thinks we're being spied on," Vince said.

Elliot shook his head. "Not spied on, maybe, but I think someone's out there."

"It won't hurt to look," Mace suggested. "I'll leave before dark."

"Alone?" Erin questioned.

"Elliot has volunteered to go."

Erin looked up at Elliot. "Why you? Why not Vince?"

"I suggested the trip. It's only right that I go. Besides, Vince just got back. He needs time to recuperate."

Vince said nothing but shuffled his feet.

"Can I go?" she asked hesitantly. She didn't really want to leave the safety of the camp, but she also didn't want to be separated from Elliot, not when her morale was so low. He always managed to lift her spirits.

Elliot's grimace at her request was all she needed to see to know that he would not agree. "What about the lab?" he reminded her gently. "Vince can help locate the material and supplies, but he'll need you or one of the others to tell him what to look for."

"What good is it?" she sighed. "We've gotten nowhere. Seth's dead. Lyle's dead. We're all going to die before we find a vaccine."

Elliot squeezed her hand. "You can't think like that. If the military finds a vaccine, they'll keep it for themselves. You have to do it."

She lowered her head and sighed again. "I don't know if I can. It's so useless. I feel as if I'm just making work so I don't feel bad about getting nowhere."

"If anyone can do it, you can. I have faith in you."

She looked up at him. His honest, loving smile pained her. "Faith? I'm not sure if faith is enough."

"Forget faith," Mace interjected. "The only reason we're together is the hope that you'll find a full vaccine. If you give up, we might as well go our separate ways and take our chances. Do you want that?"

"No, but ..."

"Take some time off," Mace suggested. "Get some sleep. Hell, get drunk. Make a list of what you need and where we might find it. In the meantime, Elliot and I will check out his flashing light."

She turned to Elliot. "You'll miss Thanksgiving dinner."

Elliot inhaled deeply. The hearty aroma of roasting chicken and fresh-baked bread fought against the lingering scent of burned metal, plastic and death. In spite of the setback, the festivities would continue. As much as the holiday seemed inappropriate to her, she knew that Elliot had been looking forward to it. Even if she didn't feel like celebrating, he and the others deserved any comfort they could find.

"Save me some stuffing," he said. "We'll be back by morning."

"Why not wait until morning?" she asked.

"If someone unfriendly is out there, I'd much rather approach them in the dark than in broad daylight. They're probably friendly, but ... just in case."

She removed her glasses, stood on her tiptoes, and kissed him on his lips. He responded quickly. She broke away and said, "Come back safely." She replaced her glasses and glared at Mace. "You'd better bring him back."

Mace grinned. "We'll watch out for each other."

While Elliot and Mace gathered supplies for their trip, she stood outside the lab building remembering Seth Brisbane. His youthful exuberance had kept her pushing forward with their work even through her doubts. She would miss his unabashed enthusiasm and conviction that they would find the answer to the vaccine problem. The dynamics of the small research group would once again be twisted and morphed into something different. She supposed that they had been extremely lucky to make it this far without further loss. Through Atlanta, Colorado, San Diego, and Biosphere2, they had faced challenges and had come through them intact. Their luck had changed.

She did not like change, but change now seemed a constant companion.

"Come on, Vince," she said, "I'll make out that list of equipment."

Mace's mind was somewhat distracted as he powered the Kawasaki Mule 4010 ATV over the rough terrain north of Agua Caliente. His common-law wife, Renda, was now over seven months pregnant and concerned for the safety and welfare their unborn child. Since both he and Renda were immune to the virus, they hoped their child would be, but neither Erin nor any of the other medical people could assure them that immunity was genetic. The rigors of childbirth were problem enough without the added trauma of a child born without immunity to the virus present in the air they breathed. While no one in their group had yet turned zombie, they all knew about the possible failure of the Blue Juice. Mace judged such a failure would be more than Renda could bear.

"Watch it!" Elliot's voice blared in Mace's ear as the ATV tilted to the left as the right tires climbed over a rocky outcropping. Mace jerked the wheel to the left and the vehicle shuddered as it righted itself. He also slowed to a more cautious speed. He had been barreling along absentmindedly at close to the vehicle's top speed of twenty-five miles per hour. He tried to pick the clearest path with the ATV's headlights, but the uneven terrain and the constant bouncing made seeing very far ahead almost impossible. The four-passenger ATV weighed over fifteen-hundred pounds. If it tipped over, the two of them would never be able to right it. They had plenty of rocks to serve as fulcrums but no trees to use as a lever.

"Sorry," he mumbled into his headset mic to Elliot. Without the walkie-talkie's headsets, they would never have been able to communicate over the roar of the engine.

"Just pay attention to where you're going," Elliot responded.

Mace tried to push his thoughts to the back of his mind and concentrate on driving but they remained with Renda.

"I'm worried about Renda," he finally said. "Something's bothering her."

"I thought you said her last checkup was just fine."

He swerved to avoid a patch of prickly pear cactus that suddenly appeared in the headlights; then swerved again to avoid a saguaro that lay beyond it. "I don't think it's her health. I think it's the possibility that the baby won't be immune."

"Erin thinks it will be."

"But she won't guarantee it."

"Look, Mace, it's almost two months until her due date and there's not one thing we can do about it. Erin seems confident, even if she won't offer any guarantees. There are no guarantees about anything anymore. Don't let it eat at you. We've got more pressing problems."

"Don't you think I know that," Mace snapped. "The lab's gone. No more Blue Juice for a while. Try to convince Renda that other things matter more than her child, our child. She's worried."

"I didn't mean to sound so heartless. We're all concerned that her child be perfect. I just meant watch the road."

The ATV left the ground as they cleared a ridge and bounced hard as it landed, jarring Mace's teeth. "What road?"

Elliot had estimated the reflection had been at least fifteen miles away. To be seen at that distance, it would have to be located atop a ridge. They had timed their leaving for just before sunset to arrive after dark, hoping the darkness would provide some cover. After traveling nearly twelve miles in the dark, he wasn't so sure it had been a good idea.

"I think I see a light ahead," Elliot said.

Mace slowed to a crawl and searched the skyline but saw nothing. "Where?"

"It vanished as we went over that last ridge. It's to our right."

Mace gunned the ATV up the next slope and killed the engine at the top. "I see it. About two o'clock."

"It looks like a campfire."

"Let's approach on foot."

As he climbed from the driver's seat, he picked up his AK47 and pack. Elliot grabbed a hunting rifle and his pistol. They decided not to use flashlights. The moon played peek-a-boo from behind the wind-tattered clouds, but sufficient light filtered through for them to pick a path. The temperature had dropped quickly after the sun had gone down. Mace's breath clouded in front of him as he exhaled. There would be frost by morning. He was glad he had worn his gloves. They walked carefully, avoiding twigs and debris littering the ground that would snap under foot. As they climbed the final ridge that separated them from the campfire, they listened for noise from the camp but heard only silence.

Kneeling behind a thirty-foot saguaro cactus, they surveyed the camp. A blue and white helicopter lay on its side, its rotors and tail section sheared off by the crash. One person sat beside the small fire, occasionally feeding it twigs and bundles of dried grass. A second person lay close to the fire wrapped in blankets. Neither appeared armed.

"Do we see who they are?" Mace whispered.

"They're not military," Elliot replied. "It looks like some kind of commercial helicopter."

Mace nodded and stood. He made certain his AK47 was visible. "You by the fire," he yelled. "If you're armed, don't reach for a weapon or I'll shoot."

The person sitting jumped up, said something inaudible, and waved his hands.

"We're coming down," Mace said.

They approached slowly in case they had missed a third person. The person wrapped in blankets did not move. The other one, they could now see that it was a woman, danced around the fire laughing.

"Thank God," she cried as they walked into the scant camp. Her eyes filled with tears. "Bob's badly hurt. His leg is broken and he has a high fever."

While Elliot knelt to examine the injured man, Mace tried to get a story from the woman. He almost had to restrain her physically to prevent her from helping Elliot.

"Who are you?" he asked.

"My name's Trish Moon. He's Bob Krell, the pilot. We were on our way to Yuma when the engine started smoking. That was," she stopped to think, "that was four days ago."

"Where are you from?"

"Tucson. Bob was from Yuma originally. He wanted to see if his family had made it."

Mace was skeptical. "After a year?"

"I know. I know. We tried to dissuade him, but he wouldn't listen, so I went with him."

Mace did not miss her use of 'we' but let it slide. Her reluctance to reveal too much information to strangers was natural.

Elliot completed his examination of the injured man. "His right leg's broken in two places and he's feverish. His color is bad and his breathing is shallow. Did you splint the leg?" he asked Trish.

Trish smiled. "I was an EMT, but we had no medical kit. I used a piece of metal from the helicopter. Do you have anything for pain and fever?"

"In the ATV," Elliot said. "I'll go get it and drive it here."

As Elliot disappeared into the night, Trish asked Mace, "What are you two doing out here. We must be miles from anything."

"Elliot saw a reflection from the windshield of the chopper. We came to investigate." He looked around and saw no supplies. "Do you have food or water?"

"Just a thermos and some granola bars, but they've been gone since yesterday. Bob won't eat or drink anything. I was waiting until daylight to try to walk for help." She pointed to the west.

"You'd have had a long walk in that direction." Mace dropped his pack and took out a canteen. "Here," he said handing it to her.

She downed several large gulps of water, and then remembering her injured friend, offered him a sip, but he was unconscious. She poured some water over his brow and patted his feverish cheeks with a damp hand. She accepted a handful of dried fruit from Mace and chewed it quickly, washing it down with a mouthful of water.

"How many people in your group in Tucson?"

She winced when she realized that Mace had not missed her mistake. She stared at him as if judging how much she should reveal. Finally, she said, "There are twenty-three of us." She chuckled. "We call ourselves the Tucson Survivors Society as a kind of joke, I guess. You know, spitting in the Devil's eye. I guess we're all immune; at least no one's gotten ill yet. Some gangs gave us some trouble early on, but we killed a few of them, and they leave us alone now. We've got water, power and food, but no way to know what's happening around us. We're safe from zombies, but they infest the area like cockroaches. It's tough to get out except by helicopter." She glanced at the wreckage. "I guess that's out of the question now."

"You wouldn't have found anyone alive in Yuma. Tens of thousands of zombies passed through months ago, killing everything in their path."

"Poor Bob."

As if realizing someone had spoken his name, Bob roused just long enough to moan, cough several times, and then passed out again.

She looked at Mace. "Where are you from?"

"Agua Caliente, the solar power farm near here. We'll get your friend back there for medical treatment. We have some doctors with us."

She sighed, "Thank God. I was afraid I was going to lose him."

The sound of the ATV grew louder as Elliot approached. He skidded to a halt in a cloud of dust. "We've got problems," he said as he jumped out of the ATV. "Let's get him loaded and get out of here."

"Zombies?" Trish asked, scanning the ridge for movement.

"Coyotes – dozens of them. I spotted them in the next ravine over."

Working quickly, they strapped Bob into one of the passenger seats, carefully avoiding further injury to his broken leg. He was still unconscious and his breathing was ragged. Mace settled his helmet on the injured man's head to protect it.

"Grab your gear and let's go," Mace told Trish.

She reached behind a boulder and produced a Remington double-barreled shotgun. "I'm packed."

Mace smiled at her. "I can see you are."

The blood-curdling sound of a large pack of coyotes howling echoed through the darkness.

"Too late," Mace said. "We need some light." With that, he raced to the helicopter and punched a hole in the fuel tank with his knife. "Stand back," he warned as fuel gushed out the hole and pooled up beneath the helicopter. He withdrew several feet, struck a road flare on a rock, and tossed it underhanded at the helicopter. The fuel erupted into a fireball as soon as the flare landed, engulfing the helicopter in flames and illuminating the entire ridge and ravine below. Nearly fifty coyotes milled about, frightened by the flames but so driven by their hunger that they refused to slink away into the night. Mace knew they could never fight their way through a pack that large while driving.

Trish didn't wait for the others. She fired both barrels of the shotgun into the massed coyotes, scattering them and killing two. As she reloaded, Elliot began picking them off with carefully aimed shots from his 9 mm pistol. Mace joined in with short, sweeping bursts from his AK47. The 7.62x39mm cartridges travelled at over 2300 ft/sec. When they hit, they tore large chunks of flesh from the coyotes. In their hunger, the coyotes turned on their injured comrades, overpowering them and ripping out their throats. However, enough of them remained to pose a serious threat to the humans, who watched the pack savaging its own members with growing horror. Reloaded, Trish took careful aim at the nearest coyote and fired. It yelped and leaped into the air as the buckshot ripped into its flank. A well-placed shot from Elliot's 9 mm ended its contortions. Mace fired another burst into their midst, clicked on empty, and shoved in a fresh clip. The burning fuel ran down the side of the ridge, splitting the pack in half. Mace decided to use the opportunity to its best advantage.

"Come on," he yelled and ran for the ATV, firing into the nearest pack of coyotes.

He dropped his rifle beside him in the seat and slammed the ATV in gear as Trish and Elliot climbed in. He drove as close to flames as he could to limit the coyotes' attack to one side. The heat singed the hair on his arm and the side of his head. Trish let loose with both barrels at one coyote that raced for the ATV, almost beheading it. Elliot continued to fire his pistol. Coyotes dropped around them. Mace drove down two coyotes foolish enough to stand yelping in the path of the ATV. The vehicle thudded over their crumpled bodies, and then the ATV was up the next ravine and pulling ahead of the pack, who had to race around the burning fuel to pursue them. Behind them, the helicopter finally exploded, showering the ridge with burning fuel. Several coyotes caught in the shower raced away in flames.

Trish dropped the shotgun beside her seat and cradled her companion's head as the ATV bounced and shuddered across the rough terrain. He was still unconscious but moaning. Finally, when he felt they had outdistanced the pack, Mace slowed the vehicle and picked a smoother path. Neither he nor she were wearing a helmet or headset mic, so he could not ask her how the injured man was doing, but he realized that time was of the essence. He had not had the heart to tell Trish, but he had caught the unmistakable smell of gangrene as he had helped Bob into the ATV. Amputation would probably be necessary, if he survived the journey

The remainder of the return trip was uneventful. They arrived back at Agua Caliente just after ten p.m. Erin met them as they drove up, frantic with worry.

"We saw the explosion," she burst out.

"We had to dissuade a few coyotes," Elliot told her. "We have an injured man here. Can you do something for him?"

Kevin Houseman and Charles Bemis, two of her technicians, helped Elliot move the injured man to one of the trailers.

"I want to go with him," Trish said.

"Better if you come with us," Mace said. "He's in good hands. You could use a good meal."

Her eyes continued to follow the group carrying her companion until they disappeared into the trailer, then looked at Mace and smiled weakly. "Yeah, I guess I could."

Renda met Mace at the door of the trailer they had set up as a combination kitchen/dining room. She crossed the room quickly, hugged him tightly, and then cast a suspicious glance at the woman accompanying him. In the dark, he had not noticed that Trish was, in spite of the dirt and grime covering her face and clothes, a very attractive woman, but Renda had. Trish's short, dark hair framed a thin face with large, blue eyes and a short, pert nose. He suspected Renda was jealous. He quickly made introductions.

"Trish, this is my wife, Renda. Renda, this is Trish. Her friend is injured. Erin and the others are seeing to him."

Renda's expression softened. "Sorry to hear about your friend. Is he badly injured?"

"A broken leg and a fever, but he should be fine."

Mace's expression revealed to Renda that things were more serious than Trish believed. "Mattie and I were just finishing up the dishes," she said. Mattie, a short, rotund woman smiled at them and returned to scrubbing a pot. The hearty aroma of Thanksgiving dinner lingered in the air, quickly reminding Mace of his own gnawing hunger.

"How about some leftovers?" he suggested.

Renda opened the oven and removed a platter laden with pieces of roasted chicken, mashed potatoes and stuffing, and rummaged through the refrigerator for cranberry sauce and something to drink. Mattie stopped scrubbing long enough to place a container of gravy and a bowl of peas in the microwave oven. As the food warmed, Renda set three plates and three wine glasses on the table and opened a bottle of white wine.

"Nothing for you?" Mace asked.

"Nothing for me," she replied, patting her belly as she laboriously seated herself. "I've eaten. I'll just nibble from your plate."

Mace grinned. Since her sixth month of pregnancy, her 'nibbles' had become grazing, but except for her obvious bulge, she still retained her physically-honed body. She continued her exacting regimen of exercise and workouts with her *Guan dao*, a pole-mounted weapon with a three-feet-long curved blade, the only personal item she had brought with her during the hasty evacuation of Biosphere2.

Trish was obviously famished, tearing into her plate of food with reckless abandon. Mace tried to match her enthusiasm, but surrendered graciously as she started on seconds. Renda, true to her word, picked over Mace's plate with a practiced eye, choosing a piece of untouched chicken and spooning a few peas into her mouth, but passing on the calorie-filled mashed potatoes and stuffing. Mace sat back in his seat to finish his glass of wine.

"We have apple pie," Renda said around a mouthful of chicken. "Canned apples, but it's still good pie."

Mace groaned. "No thanks, Hon, I'm full."

Trish pushed back from the table looking embarrassed by her ravenous appetite. "I ... I guess I was hungry."

She picked up her glass to take a sip of wine. Just as she did, the muffled sound of a pistol shot startled her, and she dropped the glass to the floor. Mace watched it fall almost in slow motion. Trish's scream of "No!" silenced the sound of its shattering.

As she tried to rise from her chair, Mace restrained her with a hand to her shoulder. She fought back, frantically pounding his chest with her fists and kicking the table with her feet, shouting obscenities at him. He tried to calm her with reassuring words he did not feel and was not surprised that she did not believe him. Her smoldering eyes silently accused him of betraying her and her companion. When Elliot walked in a couple of minutes later, she ceased her thrashing and stared at him in silence.

"I'm sorry," Elliot said, "he was infected and turning."

"No," she cried, "he's immune."

Elliot shook his head. "His injuries were too severe. He had gangrene. It was too much for his system to handle. The virus took over."

Mace released her and she slumped back in her chair. She shook her head. "No, it's not true," she protested.

"I think you knew," Elliot said. "All the signs of infection were there – his ragged breathing, his color."

She covered her eyes with her hands and burst out in tears. "I hoped ... I couldn't ..."

Renda laid her hand on Trish's shoulder and said softly, "Come with me. You need a shower and some sleep."

Trish rose from her seat and accompanied Renda without protest. When she stumbled, Renda wrapped her arm around her shoulder to help her. Mattie looked first at Mace, and then at Elliot before following the two women outside. After they had left, Mace turned to Elliot.

"You're certain?"

Elliot let his shoulders slump. "Erin was."

"If he was immune, that means a serious injury can weaken the body enough for the virus to take over."

"Erin said it might be mutating again."

Mace slammed his fist on the table hard enough to rattle the dishes. "Damn this thing! We can't catch a break."

The efficacy of Blue Juice was already in question. If an injury could trigger the virus, they could all be in jeopardy. Mace noticed Elliot's haggard look.

"You look done in. Sit down and have some chicken and a glass of wine."

Elliot shook his head. "I don't have much of an appetite right now. Maybe later."

Mace understood Elliot's reluctance. His recent meal now lay heavy in his stomach. Instead of an air of Thanksgiving celebration, he now sensed a pall of death hanging over the camp. First, they had endured Brisbane's gory death and now the disheartening news of the death of a stranger. Word would spread quickly of the man's zombie conversion, sending rumors of infection scurrying through the group. He knew that he should move quickly to dispel the rumors, but exhaustion, the meal, and the wine conspired against him.

"Later," he mumbled to Elliot, closed his eyes and leaned back in his chair.

The group at Agua Caliente attended their second funeral in as many days, the first for one of their own, and the second for a stranger. Once again, they paid their respects in small groups to avoid detection by satellite. Trish, jolted by the sudden death of her friend and still harboring resentment at his killing, held herself apart from the others. She had showered and changed into borrowed clothes, revealing just how striking she was. Looking at her, Mace hoped they didn't have another Janis Heath among them. Heath had been a beautiful troublemaker at Biosphere 2, finally meeting an ignominious fate at the hands of Hunters sent to spy on them.

"Everyone seems suspicious of her," Mace said to Elliot as the two paid their respects to the man they had tried to save. "They're giving her a wide berth."

"Word's out that Krell turned zombie before I shot him. They're scared. At least it jolted Erin out of her depression. She's eager to rebuild the lab now, but we have a bigger problem."

Mace nodded. "Trish's friends. With the military moving south from Phoenix along the railroad, they might be in danger."

After one of Vince's recent expeditions into Tucson, he had reported that the military was busy clearing the railroad tracks, and he had observed a train heading south toward Tucson heavily laden with spare rails, cross ties and repair equipment. After the military's indiscriminate use of the toxic nerve gas Sarin in Phoenix to eliminate zombies, Mace and the others expected a repeat in Tucson soon. Any human survivors would be at risk.

"Do we warn them?"

Mace was concerned with another aspect of the problem. "Do we dare bring them here? We're crowded as it is. More people make it harder to hide. Can we risk another Biosphere2 fiasco?"

"No, a larger group would only draw attention to us, but we should at least help Trish get back with a warning. They can find their own place to run to."

Mace was glad to hear Elliot agree with him. He and Renda had discussed Trish the previous night in bed. Renda had gotten over her initial jealousy and expressed concern for Trish's plight, but like him had no desire expand their group. Like Elliot, she thought that they should at least warn the other group of the danger they faced. However, she was not keen on the idea of risking anyone to return Trish to Tucson, especially her husband.

"We'll need the bus."

They had converted the school bus in which they had escaped from Biosphere2, into a zombie-proof vehicle, adding metal plates to the windows and a makeshift snowplow to the front. Slots beneath the metal plates allowed the passengers to fire weapons into attacking zombies in safety. A .30 caliber machinegun swivel-mounted in the enlarged rear emergency door made short work of pursuing zombies. A slide out ramp allowed for quickly loading salvaged supplies.

"And at least four people," Elliot added, "a driver and three shooters."

"Vince and Amanda?" Mace suggested. He trusted Vince more than most in their group, and both he and Amanda were excellent shots.

"And you and I."

"We'll give Trish a few days to recuperate. In the meantime, Vince and I can try to locate Erin's new equipment." *And I'll have plenty of time to convince Renda that I have to go.*

The last group of people paid their respects to the man who had now brought fear among them. His normal-sized grave dwarfed Brisbane's, which contained only a small box of ashes, all that remained after his immolation in the Biohazard Level 4 lab. The freshly turned soil served as a reminder to everyone that the world had not changed. Their Thanksgiving dinner had been but a very brief respite from reality and even that marred by Brisbane's death. They faced death every single day no matter how comfortable they tried to make their lives or how far they removed themselves from others. The virus was alive in the air they breathed, in their lungs, waiting on any opportunity to attack. The thought sent a chill through Mace as he unconsciously scratched his chest. He could well imagine how those not immune, those who were dependant on Blue Juice, felt. Was the virus doing its evil work on one of their number even now? Would one of them go to sleep normal and awaken as a zombie?

The one member of their group who seemed most affected by Brisbane's death was eighteen-year-old Cy Adler. The two, both quiet loners, had formed a friendship based on their mutual unease in large groups and their shared love of video games. With plenty of electricity available and no television broadcasts, keeping a television set strictly for X-Box presented no problem. Cy, who had first arrived at Biospehere2 calling himself Billy Idol and wearing only black Billy Idol t-shirts, had been one of the Hunters sent to spy on the Biosphere2 group, but in the end he had cast his lot with the survivors, even saving Mace's life, for which Mace was extremely grateful. Cy's close friendship with Renda, almost a mother-son relationship, had brought him part way out of his fantasy world of dead rock stars and video games, but he still mingled with the others in only a limited way. With Brisbane's death, Mace feared he might slip away entirely.

Mace spotted Cy leaning against one of the solar cells staring at the graves. With his ear festooned by a dozen piercings, a diamond nose stud gracing his right nostril, and rings encumbering the fingers of both hands, Cy still resembled a punk rocker, but his attitude had changed after the Biosphere2 battle. He was still a loner but no longer aloof. Mace decided to speak with him. Though wearing only a light, short-sleeved shirt, Cy seemed oblivious to the cold. Focused on the two graves, he paid no attention to Mace until Mace was within a few feet of him.

"Aren't you chilly?" Mace asked.

Cy shrugged his shoulders and turned away, eyes downcast. "He didn't suffer."

Cy jerked his eyes up and leveled them on Mace. "How do you know?" he challenged.

"Elliot told me. Seth knew what had to be done. He asked Elliot to do it."

Cy's chest heaved one time and a sigh burst from his lips. "It's not right. He didn't need to die."

"It was an accident, son. It was no one's fault. He didn't want to risk infecting anyone else. He died heroically."

"Do you really believe that?" His voice held no touch of sarcasm. Mace believed Cy was truly grasping at a reason for Brisbane's death.

"Yes, I do. He could have whined or begged for his life. Maybe Erin or one of the others would have felt sorry for him and tried to help him. Others could have died, maybe all of us. He knew that and did the right thing, the only thing he could."

Cy stared at him for a moment; then nodded his head. "He said he would like to face death like a man when the time came."

"Sometimes you have to ante up. He did. You should be proud of him."

"He was my friend. I don't have many."

"That's because you avoid the others. They would be your friends if you offered the same in return."

Cy turned away. His voice cracked slightly when he replied, "It isn't easy."

No one knew Cy's history. He had refused to talk about it. Mace did know that Nick Harris, the Hunter spy, had lied to and used Cy to do some things for which Cy was terribly ashamed. Since joining them, he had worked hard to earn their trust. He was one of the few people that Mace felt he could trust, if only he could forgive himself.

"Don't grieve too long," he told Cy. "Let's go eat some lunch."

Cy shook his head. "I don't think I can."

"Then come and sit with the others. It will make them feel better. Brisbane was their friend too."

He might not have really believed Mace, but he forced a slight smile to his lips. "Really?"

"Sure. Come on." Mace waited until Cy began walking and then followed him to the dining trailer.

The midday meal was a subdued affair. Trish's absence was duly noted, but no one commented. Somehow, the leftovers from the previous day's celebration held less flavor and provided less comfort to those gathered around the large table, chewing slowly, their thoughts more on recent events than the food on their plates. Occasionally, someone would look up in a quick furtive glance, and then resume contemplating their food as if fearing that their innermost thoughts and fears would be visible on their faces, or conversely, that they would see those fears mirrored in their companions' eyes.

When Trish walked in toward the end of the meal, all eyes turned toward her. She stopped at the door, coldly returned their stares, and sat defiantly at the end of the table where they could all see her. Like the others, she picked at her food, eating little. The rattle of dishes and the clinking of silverware on plates became quietly thunderous in the silence. Erin was the first to break the silence.

"Your friend was past all help. He died minutes after we began working on him."

Trish set down her fork and glared at Erin. Her hands curled into fists on each side of her plate. "His name is Bob Krell."

The bitterness of Erin's reply surprised Mace. "I don't care what his name *was*. We did all we could do for him. I'm sure you did all you could do."

"He was my friend. You shot him."

Erin's face turned hard. "We shot a dangerous zombie. We buried him beside my friend who died two days ago. If I don't have time to grieve for my friend, I'm certainly not going to take time to grieve for a zombie."

"You people are cold. Don't you have any spark of humanity left? Bob just wanted to find his family."

"Bullshit. Your friend wasn't on a rescue mission. He was trying to assuage his guilt. He waited a whole year to see if his family was safe, knowing they were long dead. He just wanted to bury the past so he could get on with his life. We all do. I've been shuttled around the country to five locations since the outbreak. I've watched people die all around me. My colleagues and I have spent every waking moment working on a vaccine, when we've not been fighting Hunters or the military or zombies. One foolish death more or less doesn't move me. I've become inured to death. My friends risked their lives to rescue you." She turned to stare at Elliot. "Now, they're going to risk them again to return you to your people. I'm not sure you're worth it."

She stood and left the room. As Elliot began to rise to follow her, Mace gently shook his head. He realized Erin was saying what everyone else was thinking. It was better that Trish grasped the reality of the situation. Silence returned to the table in Erin's absence. After a while, in twos and threes, they left the dining hall. The two people on kitchen duty began to silently clear the table. Trish sat with her eyes closed, her head lowered over her plate, slowly clenching and unclenching her fists.

Elliot remained. He cleared his throat and said, "Erin takes every death as a personal affront to her ability to save people. She did all she could for your friend. We'll get you back to your group."

Trish raised her head and stared at him. "Why?

"We need you to warn them that they aren't safe. The military is moving into Tucson. If they follow their pattern, they'll gas the city to kill the zombies. Your friends will just be collateral damage."

"Why should you care what happens to them?"

"They're survivors. There are few enough as it is."

"But we're not welcome here."

Mace joined in the conversation. "We tried that once before. Too many people died as a result. Our job is to find a vaccine. There's not enough room here for more people."

"So we're on our own."

"You've been on your own for a year and you've survived so far. That shows a certain degree of resourcefulness. We're sitting targets here. The military wants Erin's group. The rest of us are expendable. If I did what I should, you wouldn't go anywhere. You know where we are. That makes you a threat."

A quick look of fear crossed Trish's face. "So now you're going to kill me?"

Mace shook his head. "No. I might have, once, but the others are a little more forgiving than I am. We'll take you to your people and hope you don't talk."

She shook her head at him. "I don't understand."

"What he's trying to say in his long-winded, roundabout way," Elliot said, "is that we'll help you and your friends, but we won't take you in. We can't. It's not safe for you."

She visibly relaxed as the tension drained from her face and her body. "When?"

"Eat some food, rest up. You're in no condition to travel. In a few days. Maybe a week."

"Thank you," she mumbled.

They left her there to finish her meal and walked outside. Elliot went in search of Erin, while Mace sought out Renda. He found her outside one of the trailers practicing with her *guan dao*. He had tried the double-bladed weapon a few times, and though he liked the three-feet-long blade at its business end, found it unwieldy. He preferred a machete as a cutting blade. In her practiced hands, it became a part of her body, an extension of her fighting will. She planted her left foot, took a step forward on her right foot as she lunged the blade forward and up in a blow that would have split a zombie in half. Stepping back, she swung the blade in a vicious decapitating arc, ending with the *guan dao* across her right shoulder. She then spun her body as she lowered the *guan dao* in a blow designed to hack off the legs of any opponent, rendering him immobile. In spite of the coolness of the day, sweat poured from her body.

"How are my babies doing?" Mace asked from a safe distance. Renda looked fine, but she was breathing harder than she usually did after exercise. He wished she would take it easier on herself.

She turned and smiled. She planted the *guan dao* in the dirt at her feet and patted her rotund belly. "We're both tired and hungry."

"You missed lunch," he pointed out.

"I needed to work off some tension," she replied.

"About what?" He knew the answer, but he had learned over time to let her articulate it in her own words. As he expected, she came directly to the point.

"You're taking her back."

"I have to."

She stared at him. "No, someone has to, but why you?"

He smiled and shook his head. "Erin asked Elliot almost the same thing last night. We need to do this quickly and deliberately. We drop her off and hurry back. For that, I need people I trust. Elliot, Vince and Amanda make a good team. I'm just driving the bus."

"We made a good team once," she answered, glancing away.

He walked to her, reached out, and brushed her cheek with his hand. "We're the best team, but you're almost eight months along. If anything happened to you ..."

She leaned into him. He inhaled the scent of her perspiration as if it was a fragrant perfume. "I have a confession to make," she whispered.

"What?"

"I went to Erin a couple of days ago for an examination. She confessed that her Obstetrician's skills are limited but that she had been reading up on the subject."

"So?"

"She admitted that her estimation of my due date might be off."

Mace took a deep breath and asked, "By how much."

Renda turned her head and smiled. "Let's just say that instead of a January baby, we might get a Christmas present."

His legs felt wobbly. That explained her large belly, but it was a shock nevertheless. "M-maybe you should rest," he stammered.

She chuckled at his nervousness. "I'm fine, but you see why I want you here."

He clasped her hand in his. "I understand, but I have to go. Look, you're one of the solidest people I know. They need you here while we're gone. I need you here. If anything happens, I know you'll get them motivated."

Her eyes began to tear up. She swiped them away with the back of her hand. "Oh, dammit! These damn hormones are working overtime."

He wrapped her in his arms and buried his lips in her hair, kissing her head. They clung to each other for several long minutes, basking in each other's love. He smiled when he felt the baby kick once. For that brief second, he was the happiest man in the world. Too quickly, Renda broke free and frowned.

"I need a shower. I stink."

"You smell like love to me."

She stared at him a moment. "If you're not too busy, once I've showered, I could use some of your special brand of comfort."

She ground her hip against his groin. He glanced around to see if anyone was watching, but they were alone. "Dang it woman, you're just using me as a sex toy."

"You betcha. Batteries are hard to come by."

"Are you sure? With the baby ..."

"Be gentle with me," she whispered, and then laughed.

"Give me ten minutes."

She cocked her head to one side and said, "I'll be ready in nine. Don't be late."

He watched her saunter off, feeling a warm stirring in his loins. He failed to notice her slight limp. "Damn that woman knows how to push my buttons," he muttered to himself. "Christmas present. My God."

7

Phoenix, Arizona

General Chadwick Lawrence Hershimer sat at his desk signing papers as the arriving C-130 Hercules rumbled overhead. He thought it strange but somewhat comforting that even during an apocalypse, the paperwork never seemed to stop. Somewhere in the very building in which he sat, scores of army clerks worked feverishly to see that every 'T' was crossed and every 'I' dotted. He needed soldiers and he had a platoon of paper shufflers.

The C-130's wheels screeched as it touched down, it's four turboprop engines roaring and the brakes squealing as they fought to stop the massive sixty-five ton plane. It taxied down the runway until met by light baton-waving men who directed it to a parking spot. The former Phoenix Sky Harbor International Airport was now a hub of activity. Supplies came into Phoenix by rail from across the country for distribution by plane and rail to areas most in need. Phoenix was secure. There had been no zombie attacks in months. The zombies not immediately killed by the Sarin gas had all moved north. In fact, scouts reported that many zombies from other cities were moving toward the north and into heavily forested areas. He did not know why nor did he care as long as they were no longer his problem. Rebuilding a country was. President Samuel Hastings, a former Senator from New Hampshire, had declared the retaking of western cities a major priority. The East Coast with its collection of dead dinosaur metropolises could wait. Phoenix was the key to the entire operation.

The death of Major Corzine at Biosphere2 had not affected him overly much. Like most commanders, he feared and resented the wide scope of the Major's power. News of his death had almost brought a smile to his lips. However, the loss of men and materiel had been unacceptable. There had been no survivors to relate the whole story, but the defeat of trained men at the hands of civilians had sent waves throughout the entire military chain of command. He didn't like waves. They drew attention to him. Put him in the spotlight. Before the zombie plague, he had been just another bird colonel, riding a desk at a training facility outside Des Moines. Phoenix was his chance to shine, to rise above the rest. He intended to make the best use of the opportunity. Setbacks like Corzine's disaster made him look bad.

He had known General Perry, late commander of the Naval Station in San Diego, personally. Perry had attempted to buck the system and it had cost him his rank, maybe his life, since Perry's whereabouts were presently unknown. He had simply dropped off the face of the Earth. General Hershimer intended to see that things in Phoenix went by the book.

Dissent in the ranks rankled him. That upstart ditch-digging colonel in Salt Lake City, Schumer, wanted an end to the forced detention of munies; called it inhumane, as if letting thousands die was somehow more humane. Times had changed. The Judgment Day Protocol had kept the country's government relatively intact when most nations had withered. Someone had to pay the price of freedom. When the lab guys created a real vaccine, things would go back to normal. Then they could get on with the process of ridding the country of zombies.

A grimace of disgust crossed his face. "Damn over-breeding animals," he said to the empty room. A second C-130 rumbled overhead preparing to land, eliciting a wry smile from him. He eyed the four armored vehicles parked near the first C-130 waiting to load. The two C-130s and eighty men would go to Salt Lake City and take control.

"We'll show that damn ditch digger he can't buck the system."

8

Uncompahgre Plateau, Colorado

The small New Apostle village was a collection of tents, log cabins, and lean-to huts centered around a larger tent with a hand hewn six-foot wooden cross outside. Jeb counted roughly thirty people involved in the daily tasks of washing clothes, cooking meals, and building more cabins. Except for the occasional pair of glasses and the solar oven standing side-by-side with a haunch of elk roasting on a spit over an open fire, it would have passed for any medieval European village from the Middle Ages. Most men wore loose robes over blue jeans or work pants. The women wore longer robes, leaving no doubt that they were a religious order. None wore coats or jackets, but Jeb suspected that beneath the robes they wore multiple layers of clothing to ward off the cold. Ahiga disappeared into a tent, but Brother Malachi escorted the group to a small knoll some fifty yards from the village proper.

"This is a good spot for you, near the stream and away from my people. Until we establish mutual trust and a bond, it would be best for us to remain apart. No Children will harm you. We will share our food with you. Canvas for tents will be brought to you." He pointed to the tent with the cross. "That is our Temple. Services are at sunrise and sunset. You are not required to attend, but I hope you will show some curiosity about our purpose."

With this, he walked off. Ahiga emerged from the tent with a second tall man, younger than Brother Malachi, wearing a white robe. His face was stern as he surveyed the strangers. He spoke a few words with Ahiga, and then strode briskly to intercept Brother Malachi. The two exchanged heated words, but the older man waved his hand to dismiss him. By his glare as he stared at the group, Jeb knew the younger man was not happy with their presence. Jeb expected trouble from him.

His own group was quiet and subdued, overwhelmed by the enormity of their situation and the ten-mile hike. They stood around close together as if expecting trouble. Many still had their weapons at hand and looked nervous enough to use them. He watched with interest when half an hour later, four women brought bundles of canvas to them. They left without speaking and without making eye contact with the newcomers. His people continued to look torn between staying and running. He knew he had to get them focused.

"Okay, set up the tents. It looks like we're staying for a while."

"If we stay here for the winter, we'll need more than tents," Halliwell complained.

"Then we'll start cutting wood for a cabin," Jeb shot at him and turned to check on the others.

"I don't like this," Halliwell continued.

Jeb spun on his heel, marched up to Halliwell, and jabbed him in the chest with his index finger. "You're welcome to leave. I'm tired of your bitching and moaning. If you don't shut the hell up, I'll feed you to the zombies myself."

He left Halliwell standing speechless with his mouth open and his face pale as a ghost. Karen laughed aloud. He turned on her but she just glared back at him a moment, and then walked away. He didn't know if she found humor in his confrontation with Halliwell or in his threat, but he didn't need her stirring up more trouble. No one trusted her. A few feared her. Any sympathy they may have once felt for her plight had vanished long ago, drowned by their own struggles to survive. In their eyes, she was his problem.

In many ways, she had become more independent – doing her share of the work, cooking, even killing zombies – but in other ways she still clung to him. He wasn't sure if she still harbored some love for him, or if he was simply a reminder of all her troubles and being near him fed the anger that she needed to survive. He had given up trying to reach her, to break through the barriers that separated them. Each effort left him exhausted, bewildered and angry and drove her farther away. Hope that time would heal her wounds had faded. Now her presence only served to remind him of just how much he had lost. She was a shell of the woman she had been and he was becoming a shell of the man he had been.

After the tents were set up, they sat by the fire watching the New Apostles preparing for night. The group worked in close harmony, each doing his or her assigned task without complaint. A feeling of jealousy swept over Jeb as he watched. He could see that they were satisfied with where they were and what they were doing. They had no other goal than the immediate task set before them. He envied them their joy. At the ringing of a small bell, they dropped what they were doing and filed into the large tent. He was curious about Brother Malachi's message, but no one in his group suggested that they attend the evening service. He chose to remain with them.

A few curious zombies wandered around the edges of the camp but none entered it. Jeb tried to define the differences between this group of zombies and those that had attacked them a few days earlier. Physically, they were identical. Some wore articles of shabby clothing, while others remained naked, oblivious to the cold. Once or twice, he heard a series of calls and grunts repeated and wondered what message, if any, was being conveyed. He saw no sign of tool use, though a few carried broken branches that they could use as weapons, a decided advance over brute strength.

An air of unease permeated the camp. He couldn't blame his people. In spite of the show of non-belligerence, he didn't trust the zombies. He wasn't sure if he trusted Brother Malachi but was willing to give him the benefit of the doubt. As his people prepared their meal, they kept one eye on the church tent and the other on the woods surrounding them. Finally, curiosity won out over caution.

"I'm going to check them out," he said and rose from the stump upon which he had been sitting.

"I'll go with you," Antonov said.

"No. You stay here. Keep an eye out. I'll go alone."

Antonov shrugged. "If you want."

On the way to the tent that Brother Malachi had called the Temple, Jeb examined a few of the other tents and buildings. Most contained only blankets, clothing, and a few personal items, though a few had some pieces of simple hand-made furniture. He noticed no weapons. He remembered that Vince had said the New Apostles had been armed when he had encountered them. He wondered if they no longer felt the need to defend themselves. It made a weird kind of sense. The things they would most need defense against, zombies, now protected them. They lived in a topsy-turvy world.

He heard Brother Malachi's voice calling for silent prayer as he approached the Temple. Suddenly, the tent flap threw back and the Indian named Ahiga stepped out. He looked at Jeb for a moment, finally moving aside as the man who had gazed at them upon their arrival with distrust emerged. Jeb noticed that he was almost as tall as Brother Malachi was, with snow-white hair that cascaded to his shoulders and a long white mustache and goatee. His eyes held no warmth as he stared at Jeb.

"I am Brother Ezekiel," he said, "Brother Malachi's assistant. Did you come seeking solace?"

"I came seeking answers."

Brother Ezekiel smiled, but like his eyes, it too held no warmth. "Answers depend on the question."

"Your leader, Brother Malachi, has the look of a zealot to him. I understand what he's trying to do." Jeb squinted at Brother Ezekiel. "You look like a fighter. Why are you here?"

"I follow Malachi. I keep him safe. I keep him from making foolish mistakes."

"Like bringing us into your midst?" Jeb ventured.

"The New Apostles have dedicated themselves to assisting the Children to grow. You are killers."

"Zombies are killers. We killed to survive. I understand you sacrificed a few people to the Children of God. I would call that murder."

Brother Ezekiel frowned. "It was God's will."

"God changes his mind a lot." Jeb jabbed his finger at Ahiga standing silently beside the tent. "He was a Hunter responsible for a lot of misery." Jeb leaned closer and spoke quietly to Brother Ezekiel. "If you cause any trouble to any of my people, I'll put a bullet in your head and call it God's will. Now, do we understand each other?"

If Jeb's directness bothered the New Apostle, he didn't show it. Neither did Ahiga's expression betray what he was thinking. "Brother Malachi has offered you sanctuary. The Children have accepted you. You will be safe here as long as you follow our rules. They are few but you must adhere to them strictly. If you harm one of the Children, you will die."

Jeb backed off. "Fair enough."

"If you wish to build more permanent structures, we will help you. We will share our food with you. My personal beliefs will not color my allegiance to Brother Malachi or our goal. Do not let yours."

"My only belief is that man is better than the zombies. Forced to choose, I'll take man every time. We'll stay until the weather clears, then be off. Personally, I think you people are insane."

With that, he turned and stalked off. Behind him, he heard the worshippers exiting the Temple. Sounds of life returned to the small village – snatches of conversation, laughter, the sounds of preparing and eating dinner. In the distance, a howl reminded him that zombies, the Children of God, surrounded them. Could he leave or was he a prisoner? As the thick forest swallowed the last vestiges of sunlight, he decided not to test their boundaries at night.

During the first week of their stay, they slept in tents and kept their bags packed, ready for a quick exit, but as the days grew shorter and the weather worsened, Jeb decided to accept Brother Malachi's offer. Over the next two weeks, they built two small wooden huts, hardly larger than the tents, but a small stone fireplace with a chimney made of discarded #10 food cans provided warmth and a place to cook meals. Most settled into a routine – making chairs and beds to sleep above the cold ground, mending worn clothing, cooking, eating, and wandering the New Apostle camp. No one ventured into the woods. However, Karen became morose and turned inward, refusing to talk or interact with anyone, even Jeb. Her sullen behavior drove most of the others outside or into the other hut. On one particularly bad day, Jeb confronted her.

"Karen, you've got to stop this," he said. "You're making the others hate you. We're in close quarters here. You need to snap out of it and try to cooperate."

Her reaction stunned him. "Snap out of it?" she screamed. "We're living with stinking zombies and you want me to be happy? I can smell them from here, corrupt, filthy creatures. We should kill them all and these fools who worship them."

"Shut up," he snapped at her. "We have to stay here, at least until the weather changes."

She glared at him. "In another month, you'll be wearing a white robe and kissing zombie ass. Get away from me you murderer."

She pushed him to brush past him. He grabbed her by the arm, spun her around, and slapped her across the cheek. A smear of blood ran from her busted lip. "I should have left you there in that place," he told her. "People died to save you. You weren't worth it."

She stared at him and then pulled away rubbing her arm. "Never touch me again."

She pushed the door open and walked out. He followed her to the door and slammed it behind her, symbolically closing the door on their unsteady relationship. He realized that his wife was lost to him now, had been lost to him since the day she had rushed to the hospital with their son, Josh. He had been dead or dying of the Avian flu by then, but to her the world had conspired to remove her son from her care, starting with Jeb, who in her eyes had abandoned them to find food. Her trauma at the hands of the military had been too much for her fragile mind to handle. Given time and the proper surroundings, he might have made her whole again, but in a world gone mad, the mad fit in too well. It became impossible for them to see their defect. In Karen's mind, everyone else seemed insane.

A soft knock at the door drew his attention. He sighed and called, "Come in."

He was surprised to see Brother Malachi. He offered the New Apostle leader a seat on the bed. He graciously accepted the offer, grunting as he sat down.

"My arthritis is getting much worse. These cold days don't help," he chuckled. "A year ago I would have taken *Glucosamine* for my joints. Too bad there's no pharmacy handy."

Jeb was in no mood for idle chitchat. "You didn't come to discuss your aches and pains."

Brother Malachi spread his arms and nodded. "No, I came to see if you would accompany me to the Children of God village."

In the weeks since their arrival, Jeb had refused to visit the zombies or see how the New Apostles were interacting with them. His first instinct was still to kill them on sight, though he knew such an act would doom everyone in his group.

"Maybe it's time I go," he said.

His answer pleased and surprised Brother Malachi. "We should go now."

The zombie village was two miles from the New Apostle village on a point of land at the junction of two streams. They approached from a low ridge overlooking the village, a collection of daub and wattle huts strewn randomly across the point. Zombies sat around fires or waded in the ice-rimmed streams grabbing fish with their bare hands and flinging them onto the bank, where others used wooden clubs to kill them. Children clung to mothers or scurried around the village grunting and yelling.

"Did you do this?" he asked, incredulous at what he was seeing. It could have been a scene from a page of a history book, prehistoric man in his environment.

Brother Malachi leaned heavily on his staff, exhausted by the long walk. He smiled. "We showed them the basics of construction. They caught on very readily. Their results are somewhat crude, I admit, but they keep out the snow and rain. Fire was more difficult, but they have learned to keep it burning and use it to sear their meat."

"It's … incredible." Jeb was enthralled in spite of himself. He had thought of them as dangerous, mindless creatures, humans thrown down the evolutionary chain by a virus. Now, he was witnessing their rapid rise.

Jeb noticed two zombies watching them from the edge of the woods from which he and Brother Malachi had emerged. The two had not confronted the visitors, but kept a close eye on them.

Brother Malachi continued. "The children learn very quickly. Often, they are the teachers of the parents. I've listened to their sounds for hours. I think I now recognize a dozen or so of their meanings – eat, hunt, go away, danger, etc. I don't think they have a word for 'mine', as they share everything."

"Do they let you into the village?"

"Oh, yes, but we don't venture there too often for fear of disturbing their behavior. A few come to us, Alpha males usually. We show them things and they in turn teach the others."

"But you don't know why they tolerate you?"

Brother Malachi became pensive. "I think it is because God speaks to them. We stopped listening to God centuries ago. That is why mankind fell. They are a young species, closer to their creator. Our purpose is to guide them."

Jeb recalled the friends who had been killed by zombies. "Not all zombies are so friendly."

"No. Some are still closer to animals, but they, too, will evolve."

"Not if the military has anything to say about it. I'm not sure I disagree with them. Man didn't die out. He just slipped. In the future, it will be man against zombie for survival. What then?"

"Some, like these, sought remote places where contact with humans will be limited for many years. They will learn. Perhaps man can learn as well."

Jeb grunted derisively. "Considering what we've done to ourselves, I'm not as optimistic as you seem to be."

"Perhaps it is my belief in God."

"Or maybe you're just naïve," Jeb retorted.

"That is possible, though I prefer to think my life has purpose. Before Judgment Day, I was a plumber. Even on the best day, I dealt with people's crap. God offered me a vision of the future. I do not declare myself a prophet. I do not say it will come to pass, but I must do all I can to help bring it about. There will be room enough for both mankind and the Children of God for many years. Perhaps by then, we will have learned to coexist."

Brother Malachi's unyielding faith roused Jeb's latent cynicism, made more profound by his recent fight with Karen. "We don't do so well with our own species. Extending the hand of friendship to creatures that eat us might not be so easy."

"The task is daunting, I agree, but most worthy tasks are. Now, I think it is time we return."

As they were leaving, Jeb glanced back down at the village. It was easy to imagine the creatures as primitive humans. His attention was drawn to one zombie male making marks on the side of one of the huts with the charred end of a stick from the fire. The marks looked remarkably like a crude rendering of an elk. The significance of this act was not lost on him. Were the zombies developing a sense of wonder about the world around them, appealing to a God, perhaps the same God Brother Malachi swore by, to aid them in the hunt? He shook his head.

"Next they'll be painting cave walls."

Brother Malachi looked at him. "What?"

"Nothing," he replied, "just musing."

9

Tucson, Arizona

Fifteen wary men crossed silently on foot beneath Interstate I-10 traveling west on Orange Grove Road. Opposite them on the eastern side of the Interstate, the cloying stench of death rose from an abandoned sand pit that had become a funeral pyre for tens of thousands of bodies during the onset of the plague. Overwhelmed by the sheer number of dead, burying them became impractical. Later, dead zombies had been tossed into the flames, which had smoldered for weeks. Staring down into the pit with its grisly remains and the pool of dank, putrid water at its bottom, Captain Lacey had fought back the horrors that the scene invoked. His clothing still reeked of the foul odor.

So far, they had spotted no live zombies in the area, but still, they carefully followed a standard infiltration procedure with small groups moving forward while others covered them from secure positions. It seemed a method more suited for advancing under enemy fire, but the military had its traditions, and they were slow to change even in the face of a zombie threat. As they passed beneath the elevated Union Pacific tracks, their booted footsteps echoed like applause from an invisible audience. Captain Nathaniel Lacey was hoping they had no audience. He wanted a simple get in-get out mission with as little difficulty as possible. He carefully scanned the area for possible lurking zombies. In the past year since the plague began, they had become more organized and more dangerous. They were no longer mad packs of hungry animals. He detected method in their madness.

Debris from the summer monsoon rains littered the cracked asphalt and blocked the drains in the low-lying underpass, creating swamp-like conditions. Mounds of moldy newspapers, election posters, broken beer bottles, and plastic water bottles protruded like islets from murky pools of water. Brittlegrass, saltbush, buffel grass and young palo verde saplings thrust sunward from piles of dirt, like sea oats clinging to sand dunes. Chuckwallas and Sonoran Collared lizards rushed for the safety of holes dug in the packed earth. The tracks of Gila woodpeckers, wrens and mourning doves, lizards, and small mammals, like jackrabbits and packrats, marked the mud at the edge of the pools. The bare footprint of an even larger creature caught Lacey's eye – a zombie. He cautioned his men to make as little noise as possible as they waded through the puddles. Sun-bleached human skeletons showed white through rotten, tattered clothing as a grisly reminder that Tucson was a dead city. However, not all of its inhabitants were dead. If the fresh footprint was not proof enough, some of the bones around them were fresher than others and showed signs of recent gnawing

"Stay sharp, men," he advised as he kicked away a jawless human skull with the toe of his boot. It rolled away and ended face up staring at him through empty eye sockets. Around him, he heard the soft click as soldiers disengaged the safeties of their M16's. He did the same to his weapon.

Lacey was pleased with the progress that Hugh O'Malley's railroad snipes had made on the tracks. The line was clear as far as Vail, southeast of Tucson. Trains would soon be able to supply a permanent base in Tucson. The obvious choice for such a base was Davis-Monthan Air Base with its plethora of jets, but first he had to secure suitable temporary quarters for his troops and O'Malley's railroad men, preferably where the two groups had as little contact as possible. His men were soldiers, disciplined and on a mission; O'Malley's crew were drinkers, brawlers, and as undisciplined as men came. As long as they did their job, he didn't mind, but any conflict between the two groups could prove disastrous. A few disparaging words had been flung carelessly about already. It was only a matter of time until the conflict became more physical.

He had chosen a farmhouse near the tracks at Tangerine Road where it crossed Interstate 10. It seemed the ideal location – easily defended, secluded, surrounded by acres of open fields and a stucco wall. Several outbuildings on the property allowed each group their own separate quarters and mess. Dingane Soweta, the big black South African gang boss, was directing his gang to make the farm habitable while he and his troops secured supplies.

Costco, a large food warehouse off Orange Grove, seemed the obvious choice to find what they were seeking. It was unlikely that hectic buyers would have emptied the store before the plague, and pillaging by small groups of survivors wouldn't make a major dent in its inventory. They brought two trucks with them, but parked them a short distance away to avoid the sound of their engines attracting zombies. He could use his radio to call them in when they reached and secured the warehouse.

They followed the road until they could climb over the retaining wall, cutting back to the tracks and following them north, and then cut across strip mall parking lots as they marched the two clicks to Costco. They passed scores of human and zombie skeletons, the rusted hulks of torched trucks and cars, and dozens of burned out businesses. Fires started by gas leaks, lightning strikes, or careless looters had swept unchecked by decimated fire brigades through large sections of the city, leaving behind blackened piles of rubble surrounded by scorched adobe walls. Though he had never been in a battle, Lacey could well imagine himself walking through a battlefield. The only thing missing were the bomb craters. The large parking lot at Costco was surprisingly empty, a good sign that the store had closed, rather than been left open to looters.

"Higgins," Lacey called out to one of his privates, a veteran of Afghanistan, "take four men and set up a perimeter on the southeast corner of the building where you can watch the front entrance and the side of the building."

Higgins nodded silently, pointed to the three men nearest him, and made a sharp downward motion with his hand. They trotted after him to a position thirty yards from the building and scattered. The storefront was intact, the overhead roll-type door closed. Working quickly, two men inserted a six-foot pry bar under the door and jumped up and down on the end of it until they had raised the door high enough to insert a hydraulic jack. With the jack, they created a space large enough for one of them to slip beneath the door, while the second shined a flashlight and covered the first man with his rifle. Safely inside, he raised the door.

Lacey entered. "You two stay by the door," he said. The pair looked relieved at their assignment.

The yawning cavernous interior was dark and still bore lingering traces of the odor of rotten vegetables and fruit, spoiled milk and dairy products, and decomposing meat. Whether the meat smell was from shut down refrigerators or from corpses, he couldn't tell and wasn't eager to find out. Some shelves were nearly bare, while others remained untouched.

"Spread out by twos. Stay sharp," he cautioned. "Find canned foods, water, juice, first aid supplies, blankets, cooking utensils – whatever we might need for the next few weeks. Propane heaters would be nice if you don't want to freeze at night. Locate pallet jacks, load it on pallets, and bring it all to the front of the store." He checked his watch. "I want to be out of here in thirty minutes. Move out."

By pairs, they scattered into the darkness, the beams of their flashlights crisscrossing the store, one man holding the flashlight, the other covering with his weapon. Most of the food items were at the rear of the store and along one wall. He grabbed a shopping cart and headed to the pharmacy section, passing the long-dried remains of pretzels hanging from pegs inside a deli booth and bouquets of dried flowers, their petals littering the tile floor. Oddly enough, a faint scent of roses still drifted up as he crushed the petals beneath his boot. He swiped bottles of alcohol and hydrogen peroxide into the cart. He plucked boxes of cotton balls, bandage material, tape, cold and flu medications, anything that he thought might be useful, from the shelves and piled it in the cart. Razor blades, razors, shaving cream, soap, shampoo – all difficult to come by personal hygiene products went in with them. He heard a propane-powered forklift cranking up that one enterprising soldier had located. Its beeping backup alarm seemed incongruous in the dark, cavernous building. He checked his watch – fifteen minutes had passed. Passing a battery display, he grabbed all the 'C' and 'D' batteries and extra flashlights. His men had stacked five pallets of products by the front door before he heard the first shots from outside.

"Move it!" he yelled, leaving his full cart and racing for the entrance.

Two men from the four-man squad were already down, buried beneath a swarm of attacking zombies. The remaining two walked backwards toward the store, firing into the zombies pressing them. Nearly fifty zombies surged toward them. A dozen more lay dead on the asphalt.

"Set up a defensive perimeter," he ordered, pointing to a brick wall used to house shopping carts. He pulled his walkie-talkie from his belt. *"Victor Charlie to Victor Foxtrot. Victor Charlie to Victor Foxtrot.* Bring in the trucks. Be warned, zone is hot." He didn't wait for a reply. If they didn't come, he and his men were dead. He unslung his M16, crouched on the ground, and began picking targets with slow, carefully aimed bursts.

Private Higgins dove for cover behind the wall with two zombies on his tail. He came up huffing for breath and shot one zombie in the face at point blank. Its head exploded, splattering the wall with blood and brains. Lacey put two bullets in the second one's chest. The dense muscle and fused bone of the zombie's modified sternum could stop a bullet at twenty feet, but from a distance of ten feet, the 5.56 caliber slug tore out half its back. Pearson, the other survivor, turned to fire one last parting shot, but went down as two zombies grabbed him from each side. He screamed as one ripped his arm from his shoulder as easily as one would twist a leg from a cooked chicken. Both died in a hail of bullets from the defenders, but not before one of the zombies had ripped out Pearson's throat with its teeth, ending his screams.

Now, twenty dead zombies lay scattered across the parking lot, but the remainder did not relent in their attack. They came at the soldiers relentlessly. Two more of Lacey's men died as zombies clambered over the chest-high wall, flailing at them with inch-long claws and assaulting them with teeth as sharp as knives.

As Lacey's rifle clicked on empty, he pulled out his .45 automatic and placed three rounds in the back of a zombie's head as it bit into the neck of one of the downed defenders. Blood splashed across his face and mouth. He quickly wiped it off with the back of his hand but not before tasting the bitter blood. The sound of the two two-and-a-half ton diesel GMC cargo trucks rounding the corner turned a few zombie heads. The canvas top of one had been thrown back, revealing a .30 caliber machine gun. The heavy weapon swept through the massed zombies like a red-hot scythe, exploding skulls and dismembering limbs. Zombies fell to the ground, either dead or writhing in agitation if not pain. The noise more than fear of the weapon, forced the remaining zombies to retreat. To Lacey, an avid hunter from Iowa, they scattered like a covey of flushed quail.

He quickly assessed the damage. Five of his men lay dead. A sixth held his injured wrist almost severed from a zombie bite. He knew the horrible fate that awaited him. He stood stoically at attention and closed his eyes as his companion shot him in the head. Lacey shook his head. Six men dead and he would be getting no more replacements anytime soon. They had their supplies, but the cost had been too high.

"Load the trucks," he barked, taking out his anger on his men.

They rushed to load cases of food and equipment into the back of the two trucks while one man stood guard with the .30 caliber. Lacey returned for his shopping cart of toiletries. When the task was finished, he ordered the door of the store resealed for a future, hopefully less costly, salvage operation. As the two trucks loaded with supplies and men roared away from the Costco, zombies peered from behind abandoned autos and overgrown hedgerows of oleander. Lacey resisted the urge to place a bullet between the eyes of one particularly curious zombie, the Alpha male, for fear of unleashing another attack. The Alpha male stood defiantly beside the road glaring at the departing troops, its red eyes fixed upon him as if it recognized him as the leader. Lacey noted the creature's long hair, the dark olive skin, and the wide shoulders. It wore no clothing, its genitals dangling free, seeming inured to the chilly temperature.

Zombies were a mystery to him. He knew how to kill them. He knew how they attacked. He even understood the basics of their spectacular transformation from dying human to a flesh-devouring creature, but not the mechanics involved. He, like many, found it difficult to believe that such an abrupt mutation could come about solely through an act of nature via a lowly virus. Nature operated more slowly, a slight change here, a modification there, not a wholesale restructuring of the human body. Someone, some group, some country had wrought this apocalypse upon the human race. He hoped it had not been his own country.

He relaxed slightly when they reached the Interstate and the trucks picked up speed. He saw that his men were in a subdued mood after the loss of so many of their comrades. He had no cheerful words for them. He had seen too many men die. They all had. Death was something they had learned to expect and to live with its consequences. The trauma was too recent, the blood not yet dry on their fatigues. By morning, they would revert to their old selves, the memory of their fallen comrades fading as the sun brightened on a new day in which they had survived. It was not callousness or selfishness. It was life.

His mind drifted on the journey to more pleasant moments in his life – his farm near Des Moines, his ex-wife on whom he had cheated with her sister, his bird dog, Rascal. He wasn't sure which he missed most. They all seemed to meld together in a quasi-unreal daydream in which zombies threatened everything. He awoke with a jerk as the truck turned onto the access road near their base.

O'Malley was waiting for them, his ubiquitous half-chewed cigar resting in the corner of his mouth as if his lips had developed a permanent pocket for it. He immediately sensed the mood of the returning men.

"How many?" he asked as the soldiers began unloading the bodies of their fallen comrades from the rear of the truck.

"Six," Lacey answered taking off his cap and slapping his thigh with it. "Too damned many." He turned to Higgins. "Divide this stuff up – half for us, half for the snipes. Then, dig holes for the dead." He checked his watch. "Services at sixteen hundred." Returning his attention to O'Malley, he added, "Damn things were everywhere."

O'Malley nodded. He pulled the cigar from his mouth and waved in the general direction of Tucson. "Same with my crew. Soweta radioed in that his men had fought off a small party not far from you, near downtown. I told him to bring them in."

Lacey frowned. "Bring them in? It's barely fourteen hundred."

O'Malley spat on the ground, jammed the cigar back in his mouth, and shrugged. "Two o'clock. I know. They couldn't do much more until we receive supplies from Phoenix. We're out of rails. No reason to risk them just for survey work."

Lacey realized that O'Malley was right. He rummaged in the back of the truck and withdrew a box of cigars. He grimaced; then wiped a spot of blood that had come from one of his dead soldiers. "Merry Christmas. White Owl Blunts. Hope you like them. I never see you light them anyway." He tossed the box to O'Malley, who caught them and smiled. He ignored the hastily wiped smear of blood.

"Fifty count. Thanks. I didn't get you anything." He removed the much-chewed stub from his mouth and dropped it on the ground. Ripping the plastic wrapping from the box, he opened it and inhaled deeply. "Ah. Still fresh." He jammed a cigar in his mouth, moved it around experimentally, and smiled. "Very nice."

Lacey eyed the dropped cigar butt and discarded plastic, and frowned. He would have his men police the area later. A clean camp is a happy camp. It would give them something to do besides dwelling on today's fiasco. "Glad you like it. You can finish the damn railroad for my present. When's the train due?"

O'Malley shrugged. "Tomorrow. The day after. Who knows?"

The gang pusher's lackadaisical attitude annoyed Lacey's sense of military discipline, but he understood. In a normal universe, he wouldn't have to lose six men to resupply the rest. "I bet Dingane appreciates the break." Lacey had lately begun to appreciate the brusque Zulu. Soweta had explained that his first name, Dingane, meant 'One who searches.' He had further explained that his name had been one of his reasons for coming to America, to search for a land in which blacks were not considered inferior, unlike in his native South Africa. Until the plague struck, he had failed. Now, his skills made him indispensible.

O'Malley shook his head. "Not him. Soweta's not happy without a hammer in his hand pounding spikes. Railroad rust runs through his veins." O'Malley jerked his head toward the tracks. "Speak of the devil."

The bright yellow crane truck pushing a flatcar loaded with men rolled down the tracks, stopping on a siding. Men spilled off the flatbed and headed for the farm. Soweta's tall form stood out in their midst. Unlike Lacey's men unloading the trucks in silence, the track crew moved with the swagger and bluster of a winning football team, laughing and joking as they crossed the open field.

He turned to O'Malley. "I can't wait around. I have to wash up, and see that these goons don't screw things up."

Turning his back on the approaching work gang, he entered the metal barn recently converted to a military barracks. His eyes immediately were drawn to the empty cots of the six dead men. Tomorrow he would have them removed. They were a reminder of his failure and bad for morale, his and his men's. A shoulder high makeshift wall built from two-by-fours and corrugated metal divided his quarters from the main space. The ten-feet-by-ten-feet space held his cot, a low table, and a Coleman lantern. His extra uniforms hung from a nail driven into the wall. Its sparseness reminded him of how much he had lost, some from his own poor decisions, but most because of the plague. After his divorce, he had enlisted in the National Guard, mostly for the extra cash to supplement his dwindling income from his failing farm. The Apocalypse had made him a full-time soldier and, in his estimation, had made a new man of him.

Two of the men set up propane heaters at each end of the room and lit them. The day was not cold, but the metal building held onto the chill of the night. All they needed now was a shower with hot and cold running water and a working toilet. Alone and in pairs, his men returned to the barracks, exhausted by their labors and disheartened by their recent ordeal. Conversation was minimal, the general mood poor. He filled the washbasin with cold water and washed the blood from his face. The cold water invigorated him and removing the blood acted as a sort of mini-catharsis, re-instilling in him a sense of purpose. He had a job to do. More men might die doing it, but it was necessary. He was U.S. Army and believed in what he was doing. He was rebuilding his country and he wouldn't let a pack of mindless zombies, or a few deaths, stop him. He stripped off his blood-spattered shirt and replaced it with a clean one. First thing tomorrow morning, he would visit the underground *Red Rock* facility and secure the nuclear warheads for transport to Phoenix. The thought of being near such powerful weapons gave him an erection. He glanced around nervously to make sure no one had witnessed it.

10

Salt Lake City, Utah

Bahati and Colonel Schumer arranged to meet once or twice a week at the *Z-Bar*. Miklos Zacharenios, the bar's owner, began preparing her martini and poured his beer as soon as they sat down. She took this as a hint that Zacharenios approved of their relationship. Her roommate, Elise, was ecstatic that she had found someone to, as she put it, "To do the nasty." Their relationship had not reached the sexual stage, though Bahati did find the Afro-American colonel attractive. For his part, he made no advances, steered their conversations away from anything of a sexual nature, and behaved like the perfect gentleman.

The weather was growing colder with snow often covering King's Peak in the Wasatch Range, so they remained inside drinking and talking, often about his or her childhood. Hers had been an upper middle-class family – the best girl's school, servants, vacations, and a good college – while his parents had struggled simply to keep food on the table. He had risen to his present position through hard work and resolve, something she had yet to learn. Before the plague, she had vacillated between college majors. Now, she simply drifted with the tide, working at the cannery, no thoughts on what she wanted to do with her life. It was during one of these conversations that he made a surprising proposal to her.

"Do you remember our conversation a few weeks earlier when you suggested we resist those in the military trying to impose a new order on society?"

"Of course," she replied, curious as to why he had broached a subject she had thought long dead.

He smiled. "Well I've done it."

"Done what?"

"I contacted President Hastings and demanded a return to civil law. No more citizens being treated as test subjects or killed as collateral damage."

"What was his reply?"

He waved his hand in the air. "Oh, he agreed in theory, but insisted that the military was working in the best interests of the civilian population."

"What did you do?"

"I contacted the commanders of several other bases who think as I do, and we formed a cabal of sorts. We decided to refuse any order that harmed the civilian population under our care, whom we swore an oath to protect."

She was very proud that he had made a stand, but worried now that her rash suggestion might doom them all. "So what's next?"

"I received a shipment of weapons from General Perry in San Diego. Now I need to speak to everyone, civilian and military. If they're willing to risk death to protect their freedom, I'll lead them. Anyone who doesn't agree can leave. I'll use up precious fuel and fly them to another city." He leaned across the table and clasped her hand. "I want you to be my liaison to the people."

She drew back her hand in surprise. "Me? I'm not even American."

"You are now."

He reached into his jacket, removed a folded slip of paper, and handed it to her. She glanced at him puzzled, but took the paper and began reading.

"But ... but this says I'm a United States citizen. I don't understand."

"It's within my powers to grant citizenship in an emergency. The oath of allegiance is on the bottom. Read it and sign."

She hesitated. "But I'm Egyptian."

He frowned and sighed. "Bahati, we don't know if there is an Egypt any more. The Middle East heated up during the plague. A few nukes got tossed around. Your home may be gone. Alexandria may be gone. Even if it survived, you may never get the chance to return. Become a citizen. We need you here."

His plea made her dizzy. The thought that her family, her friends, even her country might be gone sickened her to her stomach. "I ... I don't know."

"If you sign this, I can make you my liaison to the civilian population. No one will question you."

She stared at the paper; reread its words and the oath. The writing blurred as her eyes swelled with tears. His proposal moved her, but signing the paper would be admitting that everything she loved would be gone. "I have to think about it."

"Please do. It's a big step, I know." He leaned back in his chair. "In a few days, I'm going to bring everyone together and announce my plan. Weapons training will start immediately afterwards."

"I want to fight," she said, surprised at the certainty of her words.

He shook his head. "I need you as my liaison. I'm not comfortable around most people. I am with you. With you, I can be honest. You make me honest. That's a rare quality; one I need. There are plenty of people that can shoot a rifle," he smiled, "or dig a ditch."

"I'll think about it," she promised.

"Good. Now, maybe I'll try one of those martinis you're so fond of."

Five days later, she was a U.S. Citizen, liaison for Colonel Schumer, and the envy of her roommate Elise.

"Do you need a secretary?" Elise asked upon learning the news. "I can type, a little."

The two were sitting outside in the cold for a little privacy. Bahati pulled her head down inside her collar when a strong gust of wind whipped down the street. "I don't even know what my job entails yet."

"Maybe he just wants you close by." Elise smiled wickedly. "I'll bet he's hot for you."

"He's a perfect gentleman," she replied, feeling the need to defend his honor more than hers.

Her roommate nudged her in the side with her elbow. "Those are the ones you have to watch out for."

"Really, you are so wrong about him. He feels comfortable around me. We talk. That's all."

Elise shook her head. "It's a waste of a good man, if you ask me. Still, he is handsome."

Bahati smiled and giggled. "He is that."

"Mark my words," Elise said, "any man that says he can be comfortable around you is either hot for you or gay."

"He's not gay," Bahati insisted.

"Then there you are. He wants you."

Bahati quickly discovered that her new job consisted of countless meetings with citizen groups and community leaders, some not fully supportive of Schumer's plan but sickened into action by his revelation that the rumors of blood banking people were true. Another task was coordinating volunteers. True to his word, the Colonel accepted over two thousand civilian volunteers and immediately began training them in the basics of weapons handling. More difficult was teaching them to work as a cohesive force. Most had worked on the Big Ditch surrounding the city. He reminded them of that unity, that sense of pride of accomplishment. Lastly, was the matter of military discipline. This proved almost impossible. Realizing the effort was not worth the time involved, he settled for a reasonable degree of cooperation, reminding them that their lives and the lives of their friends and families were on the line.

Only twice did the shooting instructor allow her to fire a rifle. The first time, the sudden unexpected recoil sent her flying backwards, landing her on her butt. She was more embarrassed than injured. The second time she managed to hold onto the weapon as she fired it, but missed the target by several yards. She quickly realized that her talents lay elsewhere. She discovered she had a flair for organization. Following Colonel Schumer's guidelines, she arranged the volunteers into units with as many of the most experienced people in each unit. She was surprised to learn that a very large number of women had volunteered, many of whom excelled in marksmanship, vehicle maintenance, and even heavy weapons This made her ineptness with the rifle even more unbearable, driving her to work doubly hard at her new job.

By month's end, Schumer was satisfied with his new militia.

"They're better than I expected," he confided to her in his office one evening as they sipped coffee. A cold, drizzling rain outside made the night seem even gloomier. Long gone were the lengthy conversations over drinks at the *Z-Bar*. She missed the intimacy of the bar, but at the same time was glad that work kept them from growing too close together. She found Schumer charming, but she wasn't eager to begin a relationship with him in spite of her growing attraction to him. She needn't have worried. During their several weeks of close contact, his manner and conduct had been exemplary, much to the disappointment of Elise. *Am I disappointed?* She wondered.

"They trust you," she said as she set her cup aside. The hot coffee helped combat the chill she felt when looking outside.

"I hope I'm right."

"People have to make a stand. They realize that what happens to others can easily happen to them. Fighting for survival in a post apocalyptic world sometimes means taking chances."

He took a sip of his coffee, eyeing her over the rim of the cup, and replied, "We might soon get a chance to test that theory."

She cocked her head to one side stared at him. He had been close-mouthed all afternoon, as if hiding something. She realized he had been so since receiving a radio dispatch just after lunch. "What do you mean?"

"General Perry in San Diego has been replaced. No one seems to know what happened to him. I received word from a sympathizer that two C-130 Hercules are in Phoenix. The troops there are on alert. I think they mean to replace me as well. I think this is the showdown."

Her breath caught for a moment. "How many men?"

"Each C-130 can carry up to ninety men. I suspect they are bringing armored transports as well, so maybe one hundred to one-hundred-twenty men."

She brightened at the prospect of so few troops. "We have more people."

He shook his head. "Up until now it's been a game. Faced with an enemy willing to kill, they might think differently. Only seventy of my men chose to leave, but who knows how many might change their minds rather than kill fellow soldiers."

"Shoot them down. Don't let them land. You have helicopters and jets." Her bloodthirsty comment startled her, but she was more frightened than she was willing to admit.

His reproachful tone chastised her. "I can't kill innocent men. First, I have to talk to them. They might surrender or even join us."

"You could die." Once the words left her mouth, she realized how she really felt about him. She could not even bear to contemplate his death.

"We've all faced death one way or another. I don't expect to get out of this life alive."

His cavalier attitude toward death angered her. Her voice became more strident. "What about the rest of us? If you die, what do we do?"

He looked at her as if her anger surprised him. "Why, carry on, of course. Is one death so important?"

She fell back in her chair, closed her eyes, and sobbed, "To me it is."

She hoped that he might come to her, offer her comfort. Instead, he remained where he was, silent. She heard him take another sip of coffee, set down his cup, and cross the room. When she opened her eyes, he was staring out the window.

"It's beginning to snow now. Perhaps you should leave before the streets become impassable."

He had changed the subject in an attempt to dismiss her concerns. She decided to press further. "Do you want me to go?"

He turned to her. Silhouetted by an outside streetlamp, his profile seemed hard, but she noticed a slight grin on his lips.

"Of course, I don't. I've come to enjoy your company, perhaps more than I should. You must know that if things go badly, anyone associated with me might be in for a rough time."

"I'm willing to risk it."

He lowered his head and sighed. "I'm not. Later, if things go well …"

"You mean when all's right with the world," she shot at him. Her words came out more harshly than she had intended. He was trying to protect her and she knew it, but she didn't want protecting. She wanted him to hold her in his arms. She wanted him to show her that he cared.

He shook his head and met her harshness with kindness. "Not that long, I hope. If we can hold this conversation a few days from now,   it   might   go   differently."

She slumped down in her seat. She had lost. He was adamant about playing the perfect gentleman in spite of his obvious feelings for her. "Very well." She retrieved her coat from the coat rack and slipped it on. "Are you going to stay here all night again?" She suspected that he had slept on the short sofa in his office more than once.

He smiled at her. "It might be a long night."

She made one more attempt to break through his self-imposed wall of propriety. "Let me stay here with you."

He shook his head. "I have to think. When you're around me, I find I think of you too much."

She was stunned. It was the first time he had openly confessed his feelings for her. It was a triumph of sorts. "Then I can't stand in the way of military matters. I'll leave."

"I can have someone drive you home," he offered.

"No, I'll take the train. The cold air might do me some good."

She glanced back at him as she closed the door. He was leaning with his hands on the windowsill, head bowed, eyes closed. His lips moved in silent prayer.

Once outside, she immediately regretted her decision to walk. A brisk cold wind from the north drove the snowflakes at her like frozen raindrops. By the time she had travelled the few blocks to the train station, she was shivering. The heater in the TRAX train barely kept the inside temperature above freezing, but even that small comfort was better than the alternative. Few passengers shared the car with her – a young couple clinging to each other and whispering, an old man and his dog, and a young soldier. Everyone else was inside their homes avoiding the inclement weather. On a whim, she walked the length of the car and sat down beside the soldier, no more than a boy, reading a paperback novel.

"Are you ready to fight?" she asked.

He stared at her for a moment before answering. "That's my job. I'm not so ready to die, though, but then Thoreau said, 'The price of anything is the amount of life you exchange for it.' Every day is a gift isn't it?"

His answer caught her off guard. She hadn't expected such a philosophical thought from a soldier or from one so young. "Yes, I suppose it is."

"If you mean am I ready to protect you and the other civilians, then the answer is yes." His face twisted into mask of rage but his voice remained quiet. "I've seen what munies look like hooked up to those machines. I won't let them do that to my friends, my buddies."

She nodded. "We're all ready to fight. That's why we'll win," she said with certainty.

He smiled. "I wish I had your confidence. We might beat them the first time, but they won't give up that easily. If you want to control the enemy, you can't leave an intact fort on your lines of communication."

"What do you mean?"

The soldier carefully placed a bookmark on the page he was reading, closed the book and laid it beside him with his hand resting on reverently, as if he knew such books would not be printed again for many years. As his gaze lingered on it, she suspected he would rather be reading than holding the conversation into which she had drawn him.

"They won't give up. They'll just keep sending more men, more planes, until we're beaten. In the end, we'll lose."

She stared at him in disbelief and shook her head. "No. They can't."

He offered her a sympathetic half smile. "They're not zombies. The Big Ditch won't stop them."

She leaned back in her seat, silent until the train reached her stop. The soldier resumed reading where he had left off. He acted as though he had shrugged off their conversation, but his words disturbed her. He was willing to fight though he knew they would lose in the end. It took a special kind of courage to fight in the face of such adversity. Such courage should not suffer a tragic end. Did Colonel Schumer share the young soldier's sense of hopelessness? Was he even now pacing the floors of his cold, empty office fretting about the coming battle? She wanted to reverse her journey, join him in his uncertainty, but he had sent her away. The train jerked to a stop. She hopped off, gathered her coat tighter about her against the pelting snow, and hurried home.

11

Tucson, Arizona

Two armed men stopped the bus at the gate. Mace kept the engine idling just in case, but when the men saw Trish, they rushed to roll open the gate. They ushered the bus into the warehouse through an overhead garage door where curious onlookers quickly surrounded it. Arms eagerly embraced Trish when she stepped off the bus. Her news of Bob Krell's death dampened the joy of seeing other survivors, but the small community greeted them warmly.

Trish's mood toward him had turned somewhat icy. Instead of the few days delay he had promised, she had remained at Agua Caliente for almost two weeks. Erin had been so distraught at the loss of the Level 4 lab and her inability to work that he, Vince, Elliot and several others made trips to Yuma and Casa Grande to find replacement medical equipment. Five hospitals and three medical supply warehouses later, they had located most of the items on her list. A sheet of thick acrylic large enough to serve as an observation window had been the most difficult to find, but after much deliberation, it was decided that a smaller piece would serve just as well. The dimensions of the observation window could be reduced to accommodate it. They had left Erin and her crew eager to resume their work.

The warehouse, a 50,000-square-feet cinder block building containing mounds of canned food, bottled water, clothing, and electrical appliances, was partitioned to provide dozens of smaller rooms with a common eating area. A basketball court took up a small area near one of the dozen metal delivery doors. It looked cozy and safe, but Mace wondered just how secure it was. Outside, coils of razor wire topped the fourteen-foot-high, reinforced fence surrounding the warehouse, but by itself, Mace doubted that even the formidable fence could have kept the zombies out. Trish had informed him that the Tucson Survivors Society, as they called themselves, manned the roof twenty-four hours a day with automatic weapons and a cache of Molotov cocktails. On the way in, he had noticed the two men at the edge of the roof, weapons ready. The scores of zombie skeletons outside the fence testified to their determination to defend themselves.

Emmanuel Garza, a short, stout, thirty-two year-old Mexican-American veteran of Afghanistan, led the group. Because of their common backgrounds, he and Mace hit it off from the beginning. After exchanging greetings, Mace got down to specifics. He was distressed to learn that of the twenty-two survivors – ten men, nine women, and three children under the age of twelve – only fourteen had any experience with a weapon.

"We're secure here," Garza boasted. "Luckily, we don't have to venture out for supplies. We have water from a tank on the roof, propane for generators, and a few solar panels. Zombies come at us from time to time, but we beat them back easily." He scratched his head. "Though it's odd there weren't any around when you arrived. Usually there's at least a handful around the fence. I would have thought the sound of your bus would have brought more."

Trish had also commented on the absence of zombies upon their arrival, but he had dismissed her observation as unimportant. In his eagerness to drop her off and return to Agua Caliente, he ignored her unease. Now, he had a gut feeling that he had made a big mistake. That feeling was reinforced when a call rang through the warehouse from the men on the roof.

"Zombies!"

Mace stared down at the crowd of zombies surrounding the fenced warehouse from the roof and felt a moment of dismay. He had walked blind-eyed into a trap. Garza approached him across the roof after speaking with one of the guards. Mace flipped his hand-rolled cigarette off the roof and watched it flutter to the ground.

"Frank says they're not milling about like they usually do," Garza said. "They seem to be waiting for something."

"They suckered me easily enough. They waited for us to come inside."

"They're not that smart," Garza noted.

"Oh? They're smart enough."

"That remodeled bus is pretty effective. You shouldn't have a problem."

"It keeps them at bay, but if that gate opens long enough for us to leave, they'll pour through in a flood."

He turned to Mace. "What do you suggest?"

"We could concentrate all our fire around the gate. That might keep them back long enough for us to get out, but we had to drive pretty damned slow through that maze of wrecked cars and trucks coming in. Without momentum, they could mass in front of the bus and stop it cold. Then we would be sitting ducks."

Garza sat on the edge of the short wall atop the edge of the building, his back to the zombies as if dismissing them and the threat they posed. "So, you were with Blackstone. Was it rough?"

Mace wondered why he had changed the subject. "Not as rough as slogging through the sand with a sixty-pound backpack and a gas mask."

"No, I mean, well ... I heard stories."

Mace sat down beside him, removed his pouch of cigarette papers and tobacco from his pocket, and slowly rolled another cigarette. Renda was after him to quit, but he enjoyed the act of rolling them. It helped calm his nerves more than smoking it. *Maybe I should roll them and toss them away. Nah, too wasteful.* He stuck the cigarette it in his mouth and lit it before answering. "A lot was the same ole same ole. You didn't know friend from foe most of the time. Some of the guys were a bit heavy handed, I suppose, but when the enemy hides in crowds and wears the same clothes as everyone else, you don't take chances. I did my job. If I killed innocent people, well, innocent people die in a war. I came back. I'm not sorry I did."

Garza nodded. "Yeah. I get it. I wasn't casting stones. I did things I'm not proud of, but like you say, we made it home."

As they sat there, Mace slowly became aware of the silence. The occasional growls and howls from the zombies as they fought for territory stopped. He stood and looked out over them.

"Son of a bitch."

Garza turned at Mace's statement. Beyond the crowd of waiting zombies, several dozen more approached carrying wooden utility poles across their shoulders. It was not the unexpected cooperation that stunned Mace; it was the fact that he guessed the use they were going to make of the long, wooden poles – scaling ladders.

"Get everyone up here quick!" he shouted.

Garza, also realizing what was happening, barked an order. One of the guards rushed to the opening in the roof and yelled down. Within minutes, everyone that could fire a weapon was on the roof, including Elliot, Vince, Amanda, and Trish. Mace watched the pole-bearing zombies approach. He fired two quick shots that dropped two of them. The utility pole fell to the ground and rolled away, but other zombies quickly picked it up and continued drawing nearer. They moved with such intent and purpose that it alarmed him.

"Start firing," Garza yelled. "Don't let them near the fence."

They swept the zombie herd with a deadly volley of bullets from a variety of automatic and semi-automatic weapons. Dozens fell but it was like shooting whitecaps on the beach. The tide kept rolling in. Two poles reached the fence. The zombies carrying it placed it atop the wire, and then scurried up the pole and over the fence. They died in a hail of gunfire before they managed ten paces, but others were quickly taking their place. Mace saw that it was just a matter of time before sufficient numbers made it inside to present a problem.

"Keep firing," he told Garza. "I'll take some Molotov cocktails and get closer to the fence; see if I can stir things up."

He spotted Vince and Amanda and motioned them to him. "Vince. I need your help," he said, and raced for the bin where the gasoline bombs were stored. He looked back and saw Vince shaking his head at Amanda, who wanted to accompany him. She didn't look happy at Vince's decision to leave her behind, but she took a position at the edge of the roof and resumed shooting zombies. She was an excellent shot and brought down one of the creatures with each shot.

By the time he and Vince reached the parking lot outside the warehouse, half a dozen poles were in place and zombies were climbing over faster than the defenders could stop them. He prayed those on the roof would keep the zombies at bay long enough for them to reach the fence. Lighting the gasoline-soaked wick stuffed into a liter wine bottle, he cocked back his arm and tossed it as far as he could. Vince followed suit. The two Molotov cocktails landed on the fence beneath several of the poles and shattered, sending flames shooting high into the air. Burning zombies fell from the poles, writhing on the ground to extinguish the flames. Their tough skin prevented major burn damage except to hair and faces, but it made them easy targets for those on the roof. They died quickly under a hail of bullets.

He and Vince tossed Molotov cocktails until they had covered the gate and the fence on each side of it in a roaring wall of fire. Luckily, the zombies had concentrated all their efforts in the one spot. Mace hated to think of what would have happened had they different picked points around the entire perimeter to breach the fence. Zombies continued to pour through the flames, but most held back, their instinctive fear of fire working in the defenders favor. The utility poles were in flames, the creosote-soaked wood popping and hissing from the heat. He concentrated on zombies within the fence. One rushed at him, its ragged clothing in flames, its hair singed and melted to its scalp. He sidestepped the creature, drew his machete, and planted it in the zombie's neck, withdrawing it as the creature fell at his feet. Vince had his pistol in his hand, firing at a small group rushing them. Two dropped from well-aimed gunfire from the roof. Vince shot two more in the head at close range. The remaining zombie stopped a few yards away, stared at the two of them, threw back its head, and howled in rage. Before he could question its bizarre behavior, the other zombies outside the fence took up its haunting call. The sound was deafening and unnerving, one of intense rage and fury. The zombie then chose Vince as its target and sprinted toward him. Vince raised his pistol; then began to back up as it clicked on empty. Before the zombie could close the gap between them, its head exploded. The creature fell and slid to a halt inches from Vince's feet.

Vince looked toward the roof and smiled at Amanda, who had brought it down with a single Winchester .308 round from Vince's Remington R-25. "God, I love that woman," he said.

Over twenty zombies had managed to breach the perimeter fence. They all lay dead on the asphalt. Several dozen more lay piled against the outside of the fence, some burning furiously. As the utility poles burned and collapsed in broken pieces, Mace stood watching the zombies. The remaining zombies stood howling outside the fence for several minutes before retreating to the safety of the surrounding buildings. They had acted as a coordinated group, planning an assault and almost carrying it out successfully. This was something new. The fence was no longer an effective barrier. The Tucson Survivor Society's refuge was no longer sacrosanct. They were already in a state of siege. They would have to relocate or face eventual defeat at the hands of a highly determined and fast-learning enemy.

Garza met them at the door, visibly shaken by the assault. "They didn't act like dumb brutes," he said. "They came at us as a unit."

Mace nodded. "Something's changed. They're getting smarter, more determined. You can't stay here. They'll eventually get inside."

"But all our supplies …," he waved his hands in the air, "this is our home now."

"You might be safe inside the building," Vince said, "but how long can you go without seeing the light of day. I was in the Air Force, a Tech. Sergeant. I was stationed in an underground base. All it took was one person turning into a zombie, and it became a slaughterhouse. There was nowhere to run. Believe me, you don't want that."

Garza stared at him. "What do we do?"

"Leave," Mace suggested. "Load up one of those tractor trailers with food and water, load your people in our bus, and leave. If the army comes in with gas, you'd die anyway."

"Where can we go?"

"There are people on Mt. Lemmon," Mace offered. "If you offer them a truckload of food, they might take you in."

Garza frowned. "We know about them. We sent two men up there a few months ago. They shot both of them on the road. One died and the other barely made it back. He died later. They don't want visitors."

Vince and Mace looked at one another. Neither suggested inviting them to Agua Caliente. Finally, Mace sighed. "It looks like we aren't going anywhere for a while. I guess I had better radio Renda the bad news."

Agua Caliente, Arizona

"You're certain?" Renda asked as she sat on the edge of the bed, refastening her bra. She wore only bra and panties because Erin had just completed a thorough examination at her request. Even though Erin was a doctor and had examined her several times before, she still felt embarrassed being naked in front of someone, other than Mace, that she was around every day. Thankfully, Erin had chased away the workmen repairing the Level 4 lab with the equipment Mace had brought back.

"I'm sorry, Renda. There's no doubt. The cancer has spread to your right leg. We could try a drug regimen, but ..."

Renda smiled at Erin's unease. "I know. I'm pregnant. That's why I stopped taking my *Paclitaxel* in the first place. I knew the risks, but ... you know." Though she had suspected that her cancer had returned, having her suspicions confirmed hit her hard.

"You wanted a child. I understand. The baby's fine, but I'm afraid the cancer will progress. If it was just a matter of amputating your leg...," she let the sentence hang before continuing, "it's too late for that. It has metastased to the bone, spread through your body. It would be like trying to stop forest fires as they erupt. I could try *Tamoxifen*."

Renda shook her head. "No, no more drugs. How long?"

Erin hesitated. "It's difficult to say. If I could treat it properly, five years. Now ..." She lowered her head and turned away.

Renda felt sympathy for Erin. As a CDC virologist, Erin had little need for or chance to practice proper bedside manners. Her role as physician was much more difficult than as a researcher.

Renda honestly thought that Erin was more upset by her news than she was. "I understand."

Erin lifted her head suddenly and looked at Renda. "Does Mace know?"

Renda finished buttoning her shirt. "No, and I don't want him to know until after the baby is born. He has enough to worry about."

"After the baby's born, we could start you on drugs. It might … delay the spread."

Renda shook her head. "I don't want to spend my time lying in bed sick. I want to spend the time I have left with my family."

Erin nodded. "I understand. I can provide a sedative safe for the baby if the pain becomes too intense."

"I have a slight twinge every now and then, but I can manage." She pulled up her pants and snapped them; then stepped into her shoes. "Remember, this is our secret."

"I'll honor it, but I really think you should tell Mace."

"Later."

Erin's sigh was the sound of pent up emotions escaping. "Okay. It's your decision."

Outside, the day promised to be sunny, warm and bright in stark contrast to the darkness swirling around in her head. She knew when the full impact of the return of her cancer hit her she would probably give in to a fit of crying and self-pity, but for now, she was too numb to cry. Just then, her baby kicked her hard, reminding her that she had at least one last task to perform. To bring life into a dead world was a daunting task. Erin had assured her, as best she could, that the child would be healthy and immune to the zombie virus. She wanted to believe that. She had to believe that. Otherwise, what did it matter that they struggled to carry on, to keep civilization going. She patted her belly and continued the short walk to the dining hall.

She didn't have much of an appetite, but she grabbed a cup of coffee and sat at the table listening to snatches of conversation. Dale Cuthbert and Ang Lee were arguing about the placement of equipment. Other than Cy Adler, Charles Bemis seemed to have taken Seth Brisbane's tragic death the hardest. He sat at the end of the table apart from the others staring at the untouched food on his plate. Several others were playing a word game that had suddenly become popular. She wished Mace were with her. She needed his arms around her.

When she had first met Mace in the FEMA camp in Marana outside Tucson, he had struck her as cold, uncaring and dangerous. She wasn't sure why he had included her in his escape plans. He said it was because she refused to give up. Maybe he was right, but even when his survivalist friends had died freeing the remaining prisoners from the camp, including Jeb Stone, he had showed very little emotion. His stint in the army and his years with Blackstone Security in Afghanistan had hardened him, made him the perfect man to survive in a cruel world, but left him scarred. Slowly, over the months, he had opened up to her, and she had come to love him.

She knew that but for her, he would abandon the others to their own fates. He had little faith in crowds and detested being the one in control or the one to whom they turned in times of trouble, but only through his perseverance had they managed to survive so far. There were times that she heartily agreed with him and would have gladly left with him, but not now with a baby coming. Especially now. Unable to finish her coffee for the deepening, sinking feeling settling in her stomach, she decided to wait for Mace's radio call. He had promised to contact her by radio at noon, just a quick message to let them know all was well. The military might intercept and trace a longer message.

The Ham radio was set up in one of the outlying sheds. She worried that Mace spent too much time there waiting for calls that never came, particularly one from Jeb. Now she was doing the same, certain Mace would call if possible. He had selected a frequency for his walkie-talkie that the Ham radio could receive. She whiled away the time in the choice of baby names, a pursuit that had occupied expectant mothers for millennia. For a boy, Mace was partial to Luke. The name conjured an image of strength but sounded too biblical. She preferred James, after her father. If the child was a girl, she liked Tia. Mace seemed convinced the child would be a boy and she had not been able to convince him otherwise. Strictly from a standpoint of repopulating the Earth, she wanted a girl.

Precisely at noon, the radio crackled to life. "Mace to base. Mace to base."

She grabbed the mic. "Base here. This is Renda. Hello, love."

The next words pierced her heart like a sharp knife. "Looks like daddy's going to be late."

12

Salt Lake City, Utah

Colonel Schumer watched the sky and prayed the snow would continue. It wouldn't stop the coming assault, but it might slow them down. He had been standing on the runway since he had received word from the radar tower that two large bogies and two smaller ones were inbound with an ETA of one hour. It was barely enough time to prepare for his unwelcome visitors. He knew he should be thankful that they had sent only the two C-130's and two escort jets, probably F-16's. It would have been impossible to defend against a ground assault. Bahati had suggested shooting them from the sky as they approached, but his answer had been no. It might have been the safest option, but he wanted to deliver the same choice to the soldiers aboard the transports that he had offered his own men. They should be free to choose. Killing them would only incur a stronger retaliation.

He stood at the edge of the runway huddled against the driving snow. The bitter cold reminded him of winters in Northern Alabama as a child, except then, he had no warm place to seek shelter. The thin plank walls of the two-room tenant farmer's shack in which he lived offered little protection from the wind, and the small coal heater produced little heat. He had survived that; he would endure this.

The roar of the two F-16's as they flew low over the base shook the ground, but the low-lying clouds and the darkness prevented him from seeing them. He had ordered all radar and anti-aircraft missile batteries to go cold to avoid drawing any incoming fire. He didn't want a war. A short time later, the two Hercules C-130 transports circled the landing field twice before touching down and taxiing to the far end of the runway. The loading ramps dropped and they immediately began disgorging armored personnel carriers and Humvees. Men scattered into the darkness. He took a deep breath to steady his nerves, removed the flare from his coat pocket and lit it, holding it aloft and waving it over his head. The vehicles approached slowly, searchlights panning the field and surrounding buildings for targets. They halted twenty yards away, but he knew the .50 caliber machine gun mounted on the lead Humvee could easily cut him in half at the first sign of trouble. The footsteps of many men racing down the tarmac broke the stillness of the night. Overhead, the F-16's made another pass.

A man dismounted from the lead Humvee and approached. "Colonel Schumer?" he asked.

"I'm Schumer," Schumer answered, surprised that his voice didn't squeak from fear.

"Colonel, my name is Captain James Buras. I have orders from General Hershimer for your arrest and return to Phoenix." He stared into the darkness surrounding them. "Our Infrared scans show you have about fifty men nearby. We have more. Will you order your men to stand down and come quietly or do we fight it out?"

"First, let me ask you something, Captain. Do you believe in what you're doing?"

"What do you mean?"

"I mean, do you think it's right to capture civilians, treat them like lab animals, and bleed them for their immune blood?"

The captain's tone became cold and hard. "I follow orders, Colonel."

"That's been the mantra for most of the torture and killing throughout history. Do you really believe following orders relieves you of personal responsibility?"

"It's necessary for protection against the plague. Some die so that many can live."

"You mean civilians die so that you might live. It used to be the other way around, Captain. That was the reason for a well-trained military – to protect its citizens. Look around you. Here in Salt Lake City, the civilian munies willingly donate their blood for Blue Juice. They do it because they care. We don't sedate them, line them up like cattle, and drain them dry. Is this really what you signed up for, took an oath to preserve? Our leaders are frightened, but they're more frightened of losing control. You can take a stand, Captain. You can decide right now that what you're doing is wrong. Throw down your weapons and join us. We can make a difference."

From the captain's hesitation, Schumer knew his words had had some effect on him, but years of following orders was a difficult discipline to break.

"I can't. You're under arrest. If you resist, I'll have to shoot you."

Schumer sighed. He had lost him. "Last chance, Captain."

The captain looked around nervously. He knew where Schumer's troops were, but Schumer's confidence made him uneasy. "Don't force me to shoot, Colonel."

"If you pull that trigger, you and your men will die within seconds."

"We have jets overhead."

Schumer dropped the flare to the ground in front of him. The captain watched it fall. Seconds later, twin streaks launched at the jets. They exploded in flames and disintegrated, targeted by missiles whose radars had remained inactive until his signal. Simultaneously, tarps flanking both sides of the landing field were thrown back, revealing four hundred armed men and women standing in waist-high ditches, armed with automatic weapons, LAWS rockets, and heavy caliber machine guns. They had lain in the freezing cold for almost an hour, waiting. It was a simple trap, but effective.

"I don't want to kill any more people, Captain. The jets were a necessity. Your deaths would be a tragedy." He raised his voice so that the soldiers behind the captain could hear him. "I offer you a choice. You can stay here with us and join us in our fight to take back America, or you can throw down your weapons and board one of the C-130's and return to Phoenix. You can see that here, our civilians are willing to fight and die for their freedom. That's what made America great. It's what will rebuild America again. Your leaders are lying to you. They want to rebuild the country in their image, an armed state controlling its citizens. The real enemies are the zombies and the plague. If we continue the way we're going, they'll win the war and we'll be the ones forced into hiding. Will you stay and live free?"

Shouts went up as soldiers voiced their agreement.

"No!"

Captain Buras raised his pistol and fired as he yelled. Schumer felt a burning sting in his side as the echo of the shot reverberated in his ears. *No, not an echo*. It had been another shot. The captain, too, was falling, a victim of his own troops. The ground was cold, but it felt better lying there than trying to get up. He felt hands lifting him and carrying him, and then he blacked out.

Schumer opened his eyes and saw nothing but white, not the pure white luminescence that he imagined would fill Heaven, but the pale white of a hospital room. He lay in a bed, an IV tube dripping blood into his arm. A white curtained partition blocked most of his view, but outside, the sky was blue and clear. The sun was shining bright. He could feel its warmth bathing his face. He remembered the cold night and felt as if he had suddenly shifted through time. He remembered being shot and grew woozy. After the dizziness passed, he explored his injured side with his hand, wincing as it encountered a bulky bandage.

"You'll live."

He looked up and saw a smiling Bahati standing at the edge of the partition.

"How long?" he asked.

"Two days," she said, her voice cracking with emotion. "It was touch and go for a while. You lost a lot of blood, but they removed the bullet and you'll be up and around in no time."

"The Captain?"

She frowned. "One of his own men shot him. He's dead. The others all joined us."

"All of them?"

"Yes, all of them."

He fought down the dread that had been building in him since awakening, the fear that he had lost.

"They were too busy concentrating on the troops they could see to look for a surprise. You're a pretty good engineer. They weren't expecting camouflaged ditches. We won."

"No, not yet," he reminded her, "but it's a start." He winced as a wave of pain swept over him. Bahati saw and frowned.

"You're still in pain," she said, "I'll call a nurse."

"No. I'll be fine. Sit. Talk with me."

She took a chair by the window and smiled at him. He noticed hastily wiped smudges in her mascara where she had been crying and felt a moment of joy that she should express such concern for him. She had all but admitted her love for him, and he had hesitantly expressed his feelings for her, but withheld the depth of his passion for fear last night's conflict would go badly. Perhaps it was time he showed her.

"You look beautiful," he said.

Tears welled in her eyes. "You're lying. I haven't slept in two days. I look awful."

"Not to me."

"I was so scared. When that captain shot you ... I almost died."

She saw his facing the captain alone as an act of bravado, of courage. He knew it was one of desperation. He had to focus the captain's attention away from the possibility of a trap. He had been the bait and had almost died springing the trap. He had not expected all the captain's troops to defect. It was a major coup.

"Did they say why?"

Bahati's face revealed a moment of confusion. "What? Oh, you mean the soldiers. Yes, they said because of the fact that civilians were willing to fight and the fact that you didn't simply shoot them down. They were expecting just that."

He nodded. He had won this battle, but not the war. Still, it would take time for the others to mount a larger attack. He could not afford to give them that time. "It's not enough just to sit back and hope. We have to take the battle to them."

Bahati leaned forward in her seat, stunned by what he was saying. "What?"

"We have to attack Phoenix. We have to take the battle to them."

"How?"

"A convoy." He began to speak faster as his vision began to take shape in his head. "We have tanks, artillery, and now we have manpower. We'll fill every jeep, truck, automobile, and school bus with people and head for Phoenix. We have enough helicopters to provide air cover support. Just the fact that we're coming will be enough to scare the bejeezus out of them."

"I don't know …"

Bahati's reluctance didn't surprise him. It was a bold plan fraught with risks, but not as risky as doing nothing. "It will work." He tried to rise to a sitting position. Bahati leaped up from her chair and pushed him back down in bed.

"You're going to stay in bed for at least another week. Doctor's orders."

"There's work to be done," he insisted.

"You tell me what needs to be done and I'll see to it." She smiled at him. "After all, I am your liaison."

He settled back and relaxed. It looked as though it was going to be a rough week.

By the week before Christmas, everything was ready. It had been a long, agonizing six days stuck in bed relying on Bahati to see to his preparations, but she had performed miracles. When she entered the room, he was sitting on the edge of the bed with maps spread out around him.

"You're looking better," she said and plopped down beside him. Her hand slipped into his. He squeezed it gently.

"I'm ready to get out of here. Look, I've been planning the route." He showed her one of the maps, tracing the route he had chosen with his finger. "We'll split into two groups. Half will follow I-15 to St. George, and then take 59 to Fredonia and hit 89A. The rest will take 14 from Cedar City to 89. We'll join up outside of Page, Arizona, follow 89 to Flagstaff, and make a mad dash down I-17 straight into Phoenix." He raced his finger along the route and jabbed Phoenix. "I'll send scouts ahead to check the route. If everything goes well," he looked at her and sighed, "meaning we don't get snowed in or come across a washed out bridge, we should reach Phoenix by Christmas Eve. We might catch them off guard."

She looked at the map, tracing her finger along I-15. "Wouldn't the Interstate be faster?"

"By taking the smaller roads, the column will be more difficult to locate from the air. We'll carry every drop of fuel we have with us. This will be an all or nothing operation. If we lose … well, you know what's going to happen."

"Maybe they won't fight at all," she said. "Maybe they will join us."

"I sent a message stating that the men they sent have joined us, but I doubt they will spread the word. In fact, they probably told everyone we killed them. We'll meet resistance, but I'm hoping it will be light."

"What if they use jets again?"

She had hit upon the one thing Schumer dreaded most. He could spare the fuel for the five helicopters as scouts, but not for multiple flights of the A-10 Thunderbolts. They needed a clear runway to be effective. He didn't have time to stop and clear one, or the facilities to keep them operational. An idea tumbled around in the back of his mind, dangerous but possible.

He smiled at her. "I just might have a solution for that little contingency."

13

Uncompahgre Plateau, Colorado

The long, cold winter days became a blur of tasteless meals and boring tedium, a flurry of complaints and bouts of apathy, the nights an interminable blackness begging for release. Nerves stretched taut, ready to snap, and tempers rode the razor-sharp edge of anger. Jeb began to spend more time with Brother Malachi simply to escape the burning hatred he saw each day in his wife's cold blue eyes. After her blowup, Karen had become taciturn and uncooperative, refusing to help with the chores and taking long walks alone in the forest. Instead of concern for her absences, he almost considered her frequent disappearances a godsend. Her abrasive manner alienated the others and placed him in the untenable position of defending her.

Adding heat to an already touchy situation, Halliwell was once again causing trouble, this time by making unwelcome advances toward one of the New Apostle women. At first, Jeb had let it slide, attributing Halliwell's actions to his youth and his raging hormones, but he had steadfastly ignored both Jeb's advice and Brother Ezekiel's less than friendly warning to leave the woman alone. He had thought speaking with Halliwell alone in the cabin would smooth matters. He was wrong.

Halliwell voiced the same objection he had used earlier. "If she doesn't like me, why does she smile at me every time she sees me?"

"They all smile all the time. It's the way they are."

Halliwell paced the cabin, his hands thrown into the air expressing his exasperation. "What do you expect me to do? It's been months since I've been with a woman. Some of us can't freeze up inside like you do."

Jeb brushed aside Halliwell's pointed barb. He didn't have time for a fight. "I'm not frozen, I'm tired, and I don't have the energy to fight you. We're here on sufferance. We can't afford to antagonize the New Apostles."

"I told you we shouldn't come," Halliwell snapped at him.

"We didn't have much choice then, and we don't have much choice now. It may be months before we can leave. The snow's too deep for travel. We have to make the best of the situation. Just keep it in your pants."

Halliwell spun and yelled, "You can't tell me what to do, you cold bastard! You can't even keep your own wife under control."

It was as if Halliwell's accusation had pressed a button in Jeb's head. Before he realized what he was doing, he grabbed Halliwell by the collar and yanked him forward. "Shut the hell up," he growled. Halliwell's eyes opened wide as he saw the look of madness on Jeb's face. Jeb drew back his fist. Halliwell saw the blow coming but couldn't move quickly enough to avoid it. Jeb's fist landed just below his chin. The force of the blow snapped Halliwell's head sideways. When Jeb released him, he stumbled backwards out the open door of the cabin, landing on his back in the snow. People stopped what they were doing and stared. Jeb stepped out of the cabin and stood over Halliwell, his fist still clenched, his blood boiling. He ached to pick up the downed man and hit him again, take out his rage and frustration on the only target available. He fought to quell his out-of-control anger. He stooped to grab a handful of snow and rub it in his face to cool off. Misunderstanding his gesture, Halliwell curled into a ball and began blubbering like a child. This angered Jeb even more.

"I won't warn you again," he yelled. "No more trouble."

He stared down the curious onlookers and stalked away, leaving Halliwell lying in the snow, allowing the cool, crisp air to drain away his anger. He was now angrier with himself than at Halliwell. He should have been able to defuse the situation without resorting to violence. After all, he was still a psychiatrist, but it seemed each passing day carried him farther from those calm, steady clinical days and deeper into a state of fluid chaos where the rules constantly changed and anarchy ruled. With no rules, how could he expect others to follow them? He realized he was no longer leading them but bullying them into following. Maybe they were better off assimilating into Brother Malachi's New Apostles. At least they would be safe from zombies.

"You can't solve your problem by creating more problems."

Jeb spun on Antonov. "I don't need your advice, Mikal. I know I was wrong, but I can't put it back in the box. Now, maybe Halliwell will be frightened enough to listen. I have enough problems without babysitting everyone here."

"Is that what you think you're doing, babysitting?"

Jeb sighed. "I don't know. It certainly feels like it. 'When are we leaving, Jeb?' 'We need more wood, Jeb'. 'Why won't Karen help us, Jeb?' Just leave me alone."

"We can't. You are our leader, remember."

A harsh laugh escaped Jeb's lips. Antonov's soft-spoken rebuke was like a sharp knife twisting in his heart. He leaned against a pine tree, his eyes closed. The cool, rough bark felt good against his back. He wished he had the strength of the pine tree, but it had cellulose and sap for strength. He had only flesh and blood. "I don't want to lead anyone. I'm tired. We're not going anywhere. You don't need a leader. Take care of yourselves."

"You've taken good care of us so far."

Jeb turned and stared at Antonov. For the first time, he noticed how pale and thin the old Russian looked. His face was gaunt and sallow, and loose skin sagged from his cheeks. The long journey had been rough on him.

"Good care? There are seven us left. We were fourteen when we left Biosphere2. We were three times that number there. Good care? Get real. I'm killing us off one by one. Have you looked in a mirror? You may be next."

Antonov's smile disarmed him. "Yes, I may be dying. My kidneys aren't working very well, and my appetite isn't what it once was, but my heart still beats." He held up his arm. "Blood still flows through my veins. I haven't given up."

"Maybe you should. Maybe we all should grab a white robe and join Brother Malachi. Die with some dignity where it's warm and dry. The only place I can lead you is into hell."

Antonov's soft sigh rebuked Jeb more eloquently than his words could have and wounded him more deeply. He stared at Jeb for a few moments before turning and walking away, leaving Jeb wondering if he had won or lost the exchange. Certainly, he felt no better for unloading on his close friend.

He banged the back of his head against the tree. Remembering Brother Malachi's words, he said, "If there was a neighborhood pharmacy nearby, I would prescribe myself some *Zoloft*."

He walked, aimlessly he thought, trying to sort through his feelings, but it came as no surprise when he found himself standing on the ridge overlooking the Children of God village. He found it difficult to think of them as zombies. They were no longer the vicious, mindless creatures craving only flesh and blood that he had feared and fought against for almost a year. They now appeared almost human, building fires, living in simple daub-and-wattle shelters, hunting with clubs and stones, even communicating in a rudimentary fashion – typical Paleolithic savages.

He brushed the snow off a large flat rock and sat on the edge of the ridge watching the children running and playing, accompanied by frenzied yells of joy and laughter, a very human trait. He thought of his six-year-old son, Josh, now dead over a year, an early victim of the very virus that had produced these creatures. *If FEMA had not burned his body, would he be one of the children down there?* All the emotions that he had suppressed for so long rose to the surface in a flood of anger, joy, and fear that burst from his throat in a harsh guttural sob. Tears burned furrows in his skin as they ran unchecked down his cheeks. He pulled his knees up to his face and cried, releasing the pent up disappointment inside him. For all the mistakes he had made, for all the wrong decisions, he forgave himself. The burden he had carried had been so heavy for so long that he felt that he would float away from the bonds of the Earth from his emotional release.

He didn't know how long he sat there, but when he felt empty, he opened his eyes. The sky was growing dark. Fires dotted the village below. His catharsis, a year in the making, had taken only hours to complete. He was not a new man, nor was he the same old man. He was different in ways that he did not yet fully comprehend. It was as if he could see himself through new eyes, see the nexus of decisions that had subtly changed him, follow the threads as they wove the future that was now his past. He stepped outside his body and saw the tangle of threads that intertwined with his, twisting into other irrevocable futures. Karen, Renda, Mace, Vince, even Erin and Elliot – he had changed their lives as they had changed his. For better or for worse, he had affected them, unintentionally and unknowingly. He could feel the threads leading back to his companions in the New Apostle village. He knew he could pluck them like a violin string and they would dance like marionettes. Was that what he had been doing, playing with them? It was too much responsibility for one man.

A sound, hauntingly sad, arose from the Children village below. It was primitive, simple, but the rhythmic cadence was unmistakable, a mournful song. He wasn't sure if the song even had real words or just guttural repetitions conveying emotion, but it welled from the gathered throats as an offering to a god, to the night sky, or to nature itself. He wasn't sure which, but it was a plaintive cry from those offering it. The Children stood beside the fires, surrounding an object on the ground, swaying like reeds in a soft breeze.

Movement at the edge of the woods caught his attention. He knew immediately it was no animal, for what animal would dare come so close to the Children. It was too small for one of them unless one of their children had wandered away. A trick of the light as the moon passed from behind a cloud revealed the visitor just as it turned its face toward him. His heart fluttered in his chest.

"Karen," he muttered.

Almost as quickly as she had appeared, she vanished back into the woods. Had she come here often to observe the zombies, the creatures she hated more than she did him? He was disturbed by how her attention had been focused so intently on the ring of young children around the fire. Had he seen the flash of a knife just before she vanished into the woods? Of that, he could not be certain, but even the thought frightened him. He retraced the dark path back to the New Apostle village hoping to catch up with her, but saw no sign of her.

He sensed the change in the mood of the village as he entered. New Apostles were standing in quiet groups, the normal evening chores forgotten. His companions huddled around a large fire on their small rise at the edge of the village. A chill raced through him when he saw that they were armed. Brother Ezekiel saw him coming and raced to intercept him.

"One of the children is dead," he said in a rush.

"There are no children here."

"No, one of *their* children."

Jeb went cold. *That explained the mournful song. They were lamenting the dead.* "An accident?"

A look of anger crossed Brother Ezekiel's face. "No. The child was murdered, its heart cut out." He pointed at those gathered around the blazing fire. "One of them did it," he accused.

Jeb noticed the guarded tension in his group and knew that Brother Ezekiel had made his accusation against them earlier. "How do you know?"

Brother Ezekiel drew himself to his full imposing height and replied, "None of us would do such a thing."

He ignored Brother Ezekiel's protest of innocence. "Do you have proof?"

"Proof? No, but who else …?"

Jeb cut him off. "Where's Brother Malachi?"

"He's gone to speak with the Children."

"Alone?"

"He insisted."

"If what you say is true, they'll tear him apart. We need to go find him."

"That will not be necessary," Brother Malachi called from the edge of the village.

Jeb was glad to see the group's spiritual leader was unharmed, but his happiness ended when several of the Children stepped into the light behind him. Each carried a large cudgel.

Brother Malachi spoke loudly so all could hear him. His voice carried across the village. "I'm not sure I understand all they have tried to tell me, but this much I know. Someone murdered one of their children. The Alphas are trying to restore calm, but the Children are crying out for vengeance. They know it was one of us. They followed the murderer's scent here. If we do not produce the killer, they will slaughter us all. I cannot stop them." He turned to Jeb. "They saw you at their village."

"I didn't …"

"They know you did not do this foul thing. Did you see who did?"

He hesitated. "I … I don't know."

Brother Malachi stared at his reluctant response. "If you did, you must tell us, for the sake of us all."

He knew he could not reveal Karen's presence there. They would condemn her without proof. She had angered too many people for anyone to offer to defend her. Even he had his doubts. Was she capable of such a heinous act? Then, he remembered that he had killed scores of zombies without blinking an eye, coldly and without mercy. Why would she, who hated them with such vehemence, consider killing them wrong? A loud grunt from one of the creatures surrounding them startled him. He looked up to see Karen emerging from one of the cabins, her shirt smeared with dried blood, her face twisted into a manic smile. In one hand, she held a knife. In the other reposed a bloody object. She held it in her open palm. A loud moan went up as someone recognized it as a severed heart.

"Karen," he gasped.

"A child for a child," she said, and then laughed as she threw the heart into the blazing fire. Sparks exploded as the flames greedily licked up the bloody object like an offering. The Children of God began wailing and stamping their feet. One repeatedly slammed his club into the bole of a tree.

"The guilty must be punished!" Brother Malachi cried. Several of the New Apostles stepped forward.

Jeb growled, "No!" and raced toward Karen to protect her. To his astonishment, she thrust the knife out toward him.

"Stay away from me," she screamed, stabbing the knife in the air at him. "You're one of them, one of the undead." Her eyes were wild. He didn't think she recognized him. Her tortured mind had finally snapped.

Arms grabbed him from behind. He struggled but could not break free.

"Take her," Brother Ezekiel called to those around him.

Karen, unhinged by her deed, raced in a circle, jabbing the knife at attackers real and imagined. The Biosphere2 survivors backed up to give her room, while New Apostles surrounded her, waiting for a chance to grab her. Jeb knew he could not allow them to harm her. Her deeds were his responsibility, her lack of guilt, his. He sagged in his captor's arms; then stiffened and lunged backward, throwing them from him. Ignoring them, he faced Karen.

"Karen," he called.

She stopped and stared at him. Spittle ran from the corners of her mouth. Her eyes were unfocused, unblinking. He took a step toward her and reached out his left hand. She stared at it. With his right hand, he slowly drew his pistol. Her eyes went from his outstretched hand to his pistol. Instead of running or lunging at him with the knife, she smiled at him. For a brief moment, he saw a glimpse of the old Karen behind her cold green eyes. He raised the pistol and fired one round into the center of her forehead. She embraced the bullet as she had once embraced their son, as she had embraced him. She fell in slow motion, her knees giving away first. She landed kneeling and smiling. A single drop of blood ran down her forehead and marred her cheek. She remained in that position for several seconds as her heart stopped pumping blood. Then she slumped to the ground and lay on her side, dead. The woods erupted into a cacophony of hoots, growls and grunts, as dozens of zombies displayed their approval. Spent, Jeb fell to his knees in front of her, wanting to touch her, but couldn't bring himself to do it.

"It's over," Brother Malachi intoned like a benediction.

Jeb did not see, but could feel the forest emptying as the Children, satisfied by Karen's execution, returned to their village. The New Apostles did the same. The tension left as if blown away by a cleansing wind. He did not know how his mad wife's deeds would affect the Children's relationship with the New Apostles, or the New Apostles' relationship with his group, but he did know that everything had changed suddenly and irrevocably. Another thread had been plucked. He would never be the same again. He could never heal anyone again. He had lost that right when he had pulled the trigger and murdered his wife, the same crime with which his wife had accused him in the death of their son. The circle was now complete.

He remained on his knees for a long while until hands helped him to his feet and marched him to the cabin he had so recently shared with his wife. He looked up to see Craig Tyndale and Mikal Antonov holding him. Tyndale refused to meet his eyes, but a look of profound sorrow crossed Antonov's face as if he knew what Jeb's action had cost him. He collapsed onto the cot, ignoring all attempts to draw him into conversation or to drink some of the foul smelling alcoholic concoction his people had produced from rotten vegetables, a drink they playfully called 'squeeze.'

He had failed. He had failed his son, his wife, and his friends. He had failed in his promise to keep them safe and to guide them to safety. He could no longer lead them. They deserved better. He could no longer remain among them. Each face, each pitying expression would only remind him of the magnitude of his manifest failures. He would have to leave before dawn, while everyone was sleeping. He packed his few belongings, a small bag of food, his weapons and ammunition and donned a pair of snowshoes. In silence, he left the village. He did not look back. If any Children observed his leaving, they did not announce their presence. If his people decided that they needed a new leader, he hoped they chose Tyndale. Antonov was too old and too caring to lead. Such a burden would surely kill him.

He journeyed the ten miles back to the hunting cabin as a condemned man marching to the gallows. He eyed the ATVs but knew he could never maneuver one through the deep snow. He went to the shed and broke off the lock with the butt of his rifle. Inside, he found skis, an old Arctic Cat snowmobile in good condition, and a small tent. A carefully sealed five-gallon can of gas rested on a shelf. Loading his equipment into the snowmobile, he coaxed its frozen engine into life with the electric starter, and shot out the shed into the waist-deep snow. He didn't bother closing the doors. He didn't know how far he could go on a tank of gas, but he wanted to place as much distance between himself and the others as possible. He did not want anyone coming after him out of misplaced loyalty. He chose no particular direction, driving where the terrain looked less steep and the snow packed, but when dawn came, he saw he was facing east toward the rising sun. *How appropriate*, he thought wryly.

"As good a direction as any," he said aloud. A sudden thought hit him as he recalled the date, eliciting a round of dark laughter that caught in his throat. "Merry Frickin' Christmas, Jeb."

14

San Diego, California

Guy Ferguson had been a railroad engineer for thirty-five years, most of that time running Amtrak's *Sunset Limited* between New Orleans and Los Angeles three times per week. At sixty-five, forced into what he considered an early retirement and a boring life of fishing and daydreaming, he had often stood on the side of the tracks watching trains pass by, remembering his glory days of driving two, one-hundred-ton locomotives and twenty passenger cars through the southwestern countryside at seventy miles per hour. Twice, after a few too many shots of Ronrico rum, he had considered stepping onto the tracks in front of an oncoming train and embracing it one last time, but his resolve had abandoned him at the last minute.

If not for the zombie plague, he would still be sitting in his comfortable recliner in his one-bedroom condo in San Diego drinking himself to death. He didn't know why he of all those tens of thousands around him, had not caught the Avian flu, or why he had not died and arisen as a zombie, but it had been the turning point in his pointless life, a catharsis of monumental proportions. When the military had discovered that he was an engineer, he was spared the trip to the army barracks from which no one immune ever left. He knew what went on in those cold, sterile rooms, but forced such images from his mind. The only thing that mattered to him was that he would once more be behind the controls of a locomotive.

He had driven crews from San Diego to various points along the line making repairs and clearing the tracks, but not long trips. Now, the new train they were making up destined for Phoenix would be a big one, two engines and twenty cars. He would once again be carrying passengers, but none of them would be watching the scenery. His customers would be more freight than passengers, four-hundred and eighty-four comatose munies. The thought of so many silent bodies riding behind him gave him the creeps, but he would be an engineer and that was all that counted. He personally oversaw the coupling of the flatcars and the loading and securing of the medical trailers onto each one. Two cars would carry freight and two more guards, as if anyone would want to steal comatose patients.

He was eager to go, but delay after delay postponed the scheduled departure. First, someone filled the diesel engines with the wrong kind of oil and the tanks had to be drained and the crankcase cleaned. Next, an intoxicated crane operator dropped a trailer onto the tracks, forcing hasty repairs to both the trailer and the tracks. Now, word from Phoenix was that a rebel army was on the way there. Ferguson wondered what army in its right mind would take on the US Military, even one so depleted by the plague. Such concerns were not his. His job was to deliver a train and he was eager to get on with it. It was to be his Christmas present to himself.

As he climbed aboard the bright yellow Union Pacific lead diesel engine, he patted its smooth metal sides lovingly. In the 'cow-calf' arrangement, he could control the second engine from the lead engine, utilizing its 3000 horsepower to augment the lead engine and its generator to power the cars. Alone in the cab, he was God Almighty. No one could command him and he brooked no counsel on how to do his job. He longed to push forward the throttle and roll the mighty behemoth in which he sat, down the twin steel rails and away from man and his works. He eyed the battered old railroad lantern hanging from a peg above the controls, a reminder of times when railroading was man and machine, no electronic switchers and no computers.

With the collapse of the country, railroading had almost returned to such a simple system. Along with the soldiers who would accompany him, he would carry two men whose job was to hop off the train and move the switches. He had refused to allow them into his cabin. It was sacrosanct, holy ground. Instead, they had been assigned places in the calf engine. The King did not tolerate peasants.

15

Agua Caliente, Arizona

Believing in something does not make it true. Belief is an opinion, a conviction, a state of mind. A hope. Truth is an accord with reality. Truth supersedes belief. When reality blurs into the realm of dreams and nightmares, truth becomes suspect, and belief becomes as tenuous as a wisp of smoke. Renda clung to that wisp as tightly as she could, as she had done for the last fourteen days. Mace was alive and unharmed. His occasional brief radio messages slowly built up a picture in her mind of a community under siege, of people fearful for their lives, their belief in their security as tenuous as hers.

Mace had described the zombies surrounding the warehouse that the Tucson Survivors Society called home as determined and cunning, much cleverer than any zombies any of them had previously encountered. After being repulsed in the first attack, the zombies had settled into a series of probing raids designed to test the weaknesses of the defenses. Twice, they had managed to gain entrance into the fenced parking lot but died before reaching the warehouse. For now, Mace and the others were safe, but from his short, terse messages, she knew that he believed it was only a matter of time. She feared for his safety.

Agua Caliente felt empty with so many people missing, like summer camp on the last day of summer when all the kids are leaving for home. Life was on hold. They were all still reeling from the death of Seth Brisbane. They ate, they slept and they worried. After Krell's conversion to zombie, those dependent on Blue Juice watched nervously for any telltale sign of zombie infection. It was winter and people caught colds. Each sneeze, every runny nose created panic. Renda alternately cursed Trish Moon and Bob Krell for crashing so near to their new home and cursed Elliot for noticing their presence and rescuing them.

Renda worried for Mace. They had not been apart for more than a few hours in the past year. Now, it was going on two weeks. Alone, he took too many chances. Since splitting up into two groups after Biosphere2, he had taken on the role of sole protector and leader, a responsibility that he had so often accused Jeb of needlessly shouldering. Doubtless, he would assume responsibility for this new group as well. Mace missed Jeb with whom he could share the task of leadership. She did too, but unlike her husband, she knew the real reason Jeb had left with the other group – Karen.

Karen's dementia had been increasing steadily toward the end. Her misplaced hatred of Jeb seemed to be her sole reason for living, to serve as a constant reminder of his failings, at least in her eyes. Jeb, faithful and devoted, didn't have the balls to cut her loose as a lost cause. He thought he could cure her as he had done with so many other patients, but she wasn't a patient and she didn't want his cure. He had left with her so that the others, Erin and her researchers, could find a vaccine. Renda was so thankful for Mace. He was hard when he needed to be, so thoughtful that he often surprised her, and so devoted it frightened her. How could she tell him that she was dying?

Some days she imagined that she could feel the cancer eating its way up her leg like some parasitic worm, writhing and twisting just beneath the skin. It evoked memories of her early days with breast cancer, fearing she would lose her breast. With drugs and a strong determination to live, she had beaten it for several years, sent it into remission. When she discovered that she was pregnant, she decided that the cancer drugs were too strong to expose the growing fetus inside her to them. It was a conscious decision to put the health of her unborn child above her own. Now, it seemed she would pay the price. She only hoped she lived long enough to watch her child take its first steps. She knew she would not live to see it grow up.

She irked at inactivity. She wanted to grab her rifle and her *guan dao* and wade through the zombies keeping her husband trapped, slashing and killing to see her man. Instead, she clenched her fist, opened it, laid it on her belly to feel the new life growing inside her, and sighed.

"We'll wait, little one. Daddy will be home soon."

Erin was ecstatic. A sample of Trish's blood to monitor her health had proved unique. Besides the normal immunity from the airborne virus that many of the others exhibited, Erin had discovered a second immunological property in Trish's blood. Certain B-cell lymphocytes, *plasma* cells, acted as antigens to the airborne virus in those with normal immunity. In Trish's case, the cytokine messenger proteins the plasma cells secreted activated other T-cell lymphocytes that attacked blood-borne Avian flu virus cells, making her immune not only to the airborne virus, but also to infection through zombie bites. Her blood contained a permanent vaccine, but she and her team could do little about it until the new equipment was operational and the Level 4 lab up and running. She drove the workmen and her team ruthlessly and herself even harder.

Any animosity between her and Ang Lee was set aside as they sought the elusive cytokine messenger. Without an active virus to experiment with, they could only hope they were moving in the right direction, but any activity beat the morose feeling of defeat she had been experiencing. She felt alive again. She could kick herself for not saving a sample of Bob Krell's, but his death and conversion had come so suddenly that blood samples had not been possible.

She was certain that they were very close to the answer. Once they had the right cytokine protein, they could synthesize it using their own blood. It would be a slow process, but they should be able to produce enough vaccine for everyone at Agua Caliente. All she needed was more of Trish Moon's. Given her mood when she left, that might prove an insurmountable obstacle.

Tucson, Arizona

Renda was not the only one bored with inactivity. Two hundred miles away, Mace paced the roof of the warehouse that had been his prison for nearly two weeks. He was eager to return to Agua Caliente and Renda, eager to return to the small bit of normalcy he had found there. Zombies milled about seemingly aimlessly out of gun range, but he knew they were watching intently, waiting for any opportunity to get inside the protective fence. He sensed that hunger did not drive them. These were not the flesh-eating animals he knew. These were cunning creatures that cooperated and planned. Given sufficient time, he knew they would breach the fence and the walls of the warehouse.

Of even greater concern than the zombies, was a train that had passed by the previous day on the Union Pacific tracks less than half a mile away. Where there were trains, there would be military. It would only be a matter of time before they were discovered. He knew the military, as methodical as they were, would not fail to inspect a warehouse district. He did not want a repeat of the battle at Biosphere2 where they had simultaneously fought the military and zombies. If trains were moving, it would not be long before the military decided to use Sarin gas to clear the city. They were damned if they stayed and damned if they tried to leave.

Elliot sat on an upturned crate at the edge of the wall watching Mace's agitated pacing. He sensed Mace's frustration. "Sit down, Mace. You're making me nervous."

Mace stopped long enough to glare in Elliot's direction. He noted that nothing seemed to perturb the lanky, slow talking former FEMA liaison. "You should be nervous. These creatures are different."

Elliot nodded. "I can see that. It's not so much that you make me nervous. You're making everyone nervous. They need to see a rock steady hand at the helm."

Elliot's observation surprised him. "Me? Garza runs the show here." He resumed his pacing.

"Garza's out of his depth, and he knows it. That's why he confides in you. He respects you. If we're going to get out of here, you're the one who's got to do it."

Mace stopped at the edge of the roof and looked out. "Any suggestions?"

"Not really, but it's time to do something. Everyone's tired and tired people make mistakes. They're frightened as well. They know what that train means."

Mace realized Elliot was right. They had been standing long watches for two weeks with little sleep and even less chance to relax between constant zombie attempts to break through the fence. All it took was just one inattentive guard and they would all die.

"We have to break out of here," he said. "No one's going to rescue us."

"We have enough vehicles for the people, but not enough supplies to keep so many people fed for any time," Elliot reminded him, "and where do we take them?"

That, he knew, was the bigger question. They could load all the people onto the bus and the Chevy Tahoe and various other vehicles, but the eighteen-wheeler that he wanted to load with supplies would never make it through the maze of abandoned automobiles and trucks outside the fence. With the constant threat of zombies, removing the wrecks would take too much time and would be riskier than vacating the warehouse.

"Maybe we could come back later for supplies when the zombies move on," he suggested, avoiding the hanging destination question.

Elliot looked at him doubtfully. He knew as well as Mace that the chances of their returning were slim. There was no guarantee the zombies would leave the area once the military moved in with Sarin gas, but it would still be too dangerous for a return trip. The risk of capture would be too great. "Maybe."

"So we go soon," he said.

Elliot shrugged. "Today is as good a time as any day."

Mace shook his head. "It'll be dark in a couple of hours. We'll need daylight to see what we're doing. Tomorrow. I'll let Garza know."

Elliot rose from his crate, stretched his arm and rubbed his aching shoulder. "I'll go with you. I'm tired of sitting. I need to stretch my muscles."

Mace suspected Elliot wanted to see if he invited the TSS people back to Agua Caliente. It went against everything he felt, but he could come up with no other viable option. He could simply get them out of the warehouse and onto the road, but his sense of responsibility wouldn't allow him to abandon them to the vagaries of chance. Garza had proven himself a capable leader, but he didn't fully realize the seriousness of the situation. They had never dealt with a threat bigger than some gang bangers. They weren't ready to face a well-armed military.

He found Garza talking to two men about mounting guard shifts. He decided to couch his suggestion to Garza in such a way that would not usurp the man's authority. This was Garza's house and he was the visitor.

"We're not safe here anymore," he said.

Garza scrunched his face into a scowl. "Yeah, I know." He paused and searched Mace's face. "Any suggestions?"

"We can load up the bus and the Tahoe and break out."

Garza looked around the warehouse. "We would have to leave all the supplies behind."

"They're not worth dying for."

"Some of us did die for them, but I guess you're right. Staying here is too much like being in prison. I would like to be able to walk in a straight line for a few miles just to see how it feels."

Mace was glad Garza was so agreeable to his idea. The last thing he wanted was a fight. He respected the Afghan vet. "We should leave in the morning."

"Where do we go?"

Mace saw Elliot smiling and silently cursed him. "Back to Agua Caliente with us. A few more people won't hurt. We can always scrounge up a few more trailers."

Garza frowned. "I thought you were against that."

Elliot answered for Mace, eliciting a scowl from him. "Mace has a heart as big as Arizona. He changed his mind."

Garza looked doubtful but nodded. "I'll tell the others. We'll bring what we can."

"Cots, blankets, and weapons only," Mace suggested. "We can forage for the rest later."

The two men with Garza had been following the conversation without interrupting. The youngest one, barely in his twenties, posed the question everyone had been asking themselves for the past twenty-four hours. "What if the military comes before we leave?"

Garza looked at Mace, leaving the answer to him. "I'm going to fight," Mace replied.

"But they're …"

"Human?" Mace finished for him. "Son, they'll kill you just as quickly as the zoms. If they don't, you'll wind up a human Popsicle dripping away your life's blood. Neither option suits me. You fight or die. It's that simple."

The young man swallowed hard and nodded. "Yeah, I guess so."

Then Elliot smiled as Mace did a decidedly un-Mace-like thing. He reached out and lightly punched the young man in the shoulder. The young man smiled at the small act of encouragement and walked away. Mace noticed Elliot's grin and said, "If you tell anyone …"

Elliot dropped his smile and held up his hands in mock surrender. "I never saw a thing." He glanced toward the dining area and said, "I think I'll eat."

While Elliot went to eat, Mace located Vince and Amanda to inform them of his decision. When he suggested that someone would drive the Tahoe, leaving first to draw away as many zombies as possible, Vince immediately volunteered.

"I'm a better driver and Amanda's a better shot," he challenged.

"That's why you're driving the bus," Mace countered. "It's my plan, so I take the risks. Garza feels the same way."

Vince attempted to stare Mace down but gave up seeing that Mace was determined. He stepped back and nodded. "Okay. I'll drive the bus, but if anything happens to you, Renda will kill me."

"Nothing will happen. I'll lead them away like the Pied Piper and meet up with you later."

Vince looked dubious. "I'd feel better if Amanda and I rode shotgun."

"And I would feel better with you on the bus. I need you there."

Vince relented. "Okay."

"Good."

He left Vince and Amanda and found Elliot sitting at a table with Trish Moon. Since he had told Trish of Erin's discovery a few weeks earlier, she had been strangely quiet. He thought she was probably still angry with him for the long delay in returning her to her friends. He had not pressed the point of her returning to Agua Caliente with them to provide more blood for a vaccine. He knew that she fully understood the significance of Erin's find. A vaccine would provide permanent immunity for everyone, even those bitten or badly injured. It would mean the end of forced blood banking and the military's monopoly on Blue Juice. It was not lost on her that such a vaccine could have saved Bob Krell. She held a mug of coffee in her hands, but did not drink from it as she stared blankly at the tabletop deep in thought.

"We're leaving in the morning for Agua Caliente. Garza and I will lead off with the Tahoe. The rest of you will follow in the bus."

Trish looked up at him but said nothing. He wondered if she thought their destination had anything to do with her.

"Why just you and Garza?" Elliot asked. "You might need more firepower."

"We'll move fast and rely on speed. The bus is slower. That's where I want your gun."

"Okay," Elliot agreed.

"I suppose it was inevitable," Trish shot at him with undisguised anger.

Mace stared at her. "What?"

"That me and my blood end up back at Agua Caliente."

Her insinuation irritated Mace. He snapped at her. "Look. You can go wherever you want. We won't force you to come with us or to give blood if you do. Both are up to you. If we did, we would be no better than Hunters. You could save an awful lot of lives. In fact, you might be the only person who could, but don't let me sway you."

He turned to walk away.

"Wait!" she called.

He turned back to her. Trish set her mug on the table. "I'm sorry. You saved my life, and now you're trying to save all our lives. I didn't mean to … to bark at you like that. It's just that …," she sighed and her shoulders slumped, "I don't feel worthy of this gift you say I have. I don't feel like I'm the one to save the world."

Mace softened his voice. He realized it was a heavy responsibility to bear. "There may be more like you. I don't know. You've got a chance to make a difference. Maybe that's the only reason any of us survived – to make a difference. All of us have this monster hanging over our lives. You might be the one to lop off its ugly head. If you decide to come with us, I'll see that you get there safely and guarantee no one harms you once we're there."

"I believe you."

"Good, I don't lie unless I have to," he replied, smiling. "Now, is there any more coffee? I have a feeling I won't get much sleep tonight."

Few zombies were visible as they rolled open the gate to let the Chevy Tahoe through, but by the time they had gone less than a hundred yards, zombies came from everywhere. Mace gunned the gas and careened the Tahoe through the maze of automobiles, clipping several as he fought the wheel. A zombie leaped from the top of an overturned car and landed on the hood, slamming its fist into the windshield in front of Garza. The windshield cracked but held. Mace slammed on the brakes. As the Tahoe skidded sideways to a stop, the zombie tumbled off the hood onto the road. Garza fired through the open side window and killed it. Mace pressed the accelerator and ran over a second zombie racing at them head on. More zombies attacked from both sides. Garza fired short bursts from his M16 into their midst. The 5.56x45mm rounds were smaller than the AK47 Mace preferred but had a higher muzzle velocity. He fired short, tight bursts of three, killing several and slowing the advance of others, but Mace's evasive driving made it impossible to aim.

Zombies poured from buildings and from behind parked automobiles and gave chase. He fought the urge to outrun them, but the purpose of their excursion was to distract them. He slowed the Tahoe until it kept just ahead of them. Garza glanced at him as the truck slowed but said nothing, turning his attention to zombies in front of them. When they neared the end of the street, Mace picked up the walkie-talkie in the seat beside him.

"It's time," he said to Garza, and then keyed the mic and spoke into it. "Time to go, kids. Drive slowly. Most of the bastards are chasing us. See you later."

Vince's reply was terse. "Leaving now."

Mace glanced through the rearview mirror and saw the bus coming out the gate. It stopped for thirty seconds as one of the men closed the gate behind them, as if expecting to return. The bus then sped off in the opposite direction. Very few zombies noticed its departure; their attention was focused on the Tahoe.

"Looks like it's working," he told Garza as he fishtailed the truck onto Contractors Way heading south toward Irvington Road. From there he intended to take Alvernon Way south to Interstate10, the quickest route out of town.

He had barely uttered the words when a large Alpha male ran up to the side of the road and flung a car tire at them. It all happened far too quickly for Mace to avoid it. The heavy tire and rim smashed through the already damaged windshield. Mace threw his hands up to shield his face from a shotgun scattering of shattered glass. The tire caught Garza full in the face, pinning him to the seat. He barked out a quick *humph*, and then went silent. The out-of-control Tahoe rammed the right rear fender of a Honda Accord parked in the opposite lane, sending it spinning. The airbags deployed, smothering and blinding Mace. He fought the steering wheel in a fruitless attempt to straighten the truck. The airbag deflated. He hung on helplessly as the Tahoe careened out of control up the side of a pile of sand deposited by the summer monsoons, plowed through a chain link fence, hit a shallow ditch sideways, and rolled twice, ending up on its side across the railroad tracks with the engine running and the rear wheels spinning uselessly.

Mace was shaken up and disoriented, but not seriously injured. He quickly checked Garza, but he had no pulse. The impact of the tire had snapped his neck. The former sergeant was beyond pain. Mace struggled with the release of his safety harness, finally falling on top of Garza's dead body. He grabbed his rifle, the walkie-talkie, and crawled out the driver's side window. His head spun and his knees ached from colliding with the dash. He had to brace himself against the chassis of the truck to keep from falling. The Alpha male zombie that had thrown the tire still stood beside the road fifty yards away howling in triumph. Mace fired at it but missed, his aim spoiled by his dizziness. More zombies gathered on the far side of the road. He glanced around but found no cover other than a small building a hundred yards up the tracks. The wrecked truck offered no protection. The engine chugged and sputtered a couple of times as the engine flooded; then died. He took off at a quick clip toward the building, hoping his legs held out long enough to get him there. He tried the radio.

"This is Mace. I'm down. Garza's dead. Don't come back for me. I'll make my way home."

He waited for a reply but heard nothing, not even static. He quickly checked the walkie-talkie and saw that the battery cover plate had jarred loose during the crash and the batteries were gone. He glanced longingly back toward the truck where the batteries probably were, but zombies were already closing in around it. He had no choice but to go on. He ignored the pain in his knees and increased his pace.

He thought he was hallucinating when the warning lights at the railroad crossing on Irvington Road began to flash and the railroad barricade cross arms slowly lowered across the road.

"Zombie crossing," he muttered, grinning at his black humor.

It suddenly became even more surreal when a train whistle began to blow in the distance.

Dingane Soweta swung the ten-pound sledgehammer as easily as a slugger swings a baseball bat. He struck the seven-and-a-half-inch-long railroad spike squarely on its head, driving it into the hard wood of the crosstie. The metal sang out as he hammered it home. In three blows, it snagged the flare of the metal rail, securing it to the crosstie. Finished, he leaned on the handle of the sledgehammer and surveyed his work.

He and his crew of snipes had just tightened down a couple of loose rails noticed by the engineer of the last train using the rail on its way to Texas. So far, the line ended outside El Paso, but soon the line would be open all the way to the railroad hub of Ft. Worth. Soweta smiled as he thought of Ft. Worth. He had visited the city once when he first came to America. Even wearing a cowboy hat and boots, the six-feet-seven-inch African had stood out in a state noted for its tall citizens. He turned to his crew. Most sat on the edge of the Hi-Rail crane watching him work while three others stood around with rifles ready for zombies.

"Show's over," he said. "I hope you learned something."

One of the men laughed. "Yeah. I learned not to fuck with you when you're mad. You swing that hammer like you're in love with it."

"Yeah, boss," another chimed in. "You're poetry in motion. We didn't want to get in your way."

Soweta picked up the sledge, threw it over his shoulder, and began walking back to the crane. "If any of you did an honest day's work, you might love your tools also."

Ira Phillips, one of the youngest snipes, grabbed his crotch. "I love my tool. I just don't get much chance to use it."

"Your sticky sheets say that ain't true," one of the guards replied.

Phillips offered an obscene gesture toward his detractor.

Soweta tossed the sledgehammer onto the short flatcar attached to the crane. "It's time to return to camp." He looked around him. "It is too quiet here."

"We haven't seen any zombies since we got here."

Soweta nodded. "That is so," he agreed, "but the noise we were making should have made them curious."

"Maybe they're gone," the guard said. "The ones in Phoenix left."

"Yeah, the ones that didn't die from the gas," Phillips reminded him as he looked around nervously. "They sure tore up the captain's boys last week. I'll feel better when they gas this burg."

Soweta frowned. "People will die."

"Lots of people died," Phillips replied. "If they kill off the freaking zombies, I'll personally help repopulate the world."

One of the guards laughed. "That's what the world needs, more little Phillips running around. As if zombies aren't bad enough."

"Load up," Soweta said.

They all found a spot on the flatcar or inside the crane. From his vantage point inside the crane, Soweta looked out the tail fins of mothballed jets rising in the distance at Davis-Monthan Air Force Base. The military wanted the base. Now, thanks to his hard work and that of his snipes, they could bring men and material to the base from Phoenix by rail. Soon, he and his crew would be moving farther east. He looked forward to seeing Ft. Worth again.

He cranked the engine and began pushing the flatcar west towards their camp. After crossing Valencia Highway, the tracks turned north through the heart of Tucson and the marshalling yard near 22nd Street, the section Soweta hated the most because it passed through subdivisions, business districts, and neighborhoods, easy places for a zombie ambush.

"Keep an eye open," he yelled to his crew, even though he knew they were as wary of the area as he was.

They heard the first shots as the tracks turned north.

"Someone's in trouble," Phillips said from the seat next to him as he picked up his M16 and flicked of the safety. He smiled at Soweta. "Maybe it's a woman."

Soweta knew someone was in trouble ahead of them. He pressed the accelerator and the Hi-Rail sped up. A few minutes later, he spotted the truck across the tracks and a man running along them. A horde of zombies on the road kept pace with the man but kept their distance. Soweta hit the horn on the crane. He had no choice but to hit the truck head on and hope the weight of the heavy crane could shove it off the tracks without derailing.

"Hold on," he yelled.

He braced himself as best he could but still the impact almost threw him from his seat. Tossed about and shaken up, his men managed to stay aboard. The heavy truck screeched as crumpled metal scoured the rails ahead of the crane. Soweta used the crane's boom to shove it off the tracks. Zombies came at them from their right side, but Soweta spotted more in the distance to their left. His crew recovered quickly and began firing at the leading edge of zombies. They were railroad men and brawlers, but necessity had made them expert shots with their weapons. M16s, shotguns, hunting rifles, and pistols laid down a withering volley of fire that kept the zombies at bay. Those foolish enough to stand on the tracks went down crushed beneath twenty-five tons of speeding metal.

To his credit, the man from the truck did not stop running to wait for them. He angled closer toward the tracks, firing as he went. Soweta was pleased to see him drop two zombies with as many shots. As the flatcar drew nearer to him, Soweta slowed just enough for one of his men to reach out, grab the runner's hand, and swing him aboard. He then sped up. The zombies became enraged at losing their quarry and rushed the crane and flatcar, but none lived long enough to pose a serious threat. At forty miles per hour, the zombies soon lagged behind.

The man they had rescued lay on his back trying to recover his breath. After a few minutes, he gave Soweta a big thumbs' up. Soweta chuckled inwardly at the man's aplomb. It showed courage, though he supposed most cowards had died early on in the plague. It was a world filled with brave men full of testosterone. He turned to Phillips.

"I guess we set one more plate for dinner."

16

Agua Caliente, Arizona

Renda rushed outside when she heard the bus returning, but her heart sank when she saw the load of passengers it carried. She knew immediately that something had gone terribly wrong. With mounting trepidation and an ache in her heart, she watched them climb down from the bus, searching their troubled faces for some idea of what had happened. When she failed to see Mace, she confronted Vince.

"Where's Mace?" she demanded. Her breath came in ragged gasps as she forced the words from her throat. "What happened?"

Vince glanced away uneasily. Amanda walked up behind him and laid her hand on his shoulder for support. "We don't know," he said.

Her legs felt wobbly, not from her cancer or any pain in her legs, but from the realization that Mace might be lost to her. Her voice cracked as she repeated, "What happened?"

"He and Garza, the leader of this group," he waved his hand in the direction of the TSS people standing around looking lost, "took an SUV and left first to draw away the zombies. We left a few minutes later with the bus. His plan worked perfectly. The zombies left us alone. We waited at the rendezvous point for an hour." He paused for a few seconds. "He didn't show up."

When Renda stared at him in mute silence, he quickly added, "I'm heading out right now in the jeep to search for him."

Renda closed her eyes and turned away to hide the tears streaming down her cheeks. "I'm coming, too," she said as she started walking toward the trailer for her gun.

"No you're not," Vince said, stopping her in her tracks. When she whirled on him, he quickly added, "You need to stay here. These people need someone to help sort things out, a place to bed down."

"Erin and Elliot can do that," she insisted. "My place is with Mace."

"Do you think the seatbelt will fit?" Vince said looking down at her swollen belly. "Do you think you can hang on if I have to go off road? You're eight months pregnant for Christ's sake! Do you want to have your child on the side of the road?"

She knew he was right but she felt as if she was abandoning Mace. Her chest ached from the empty cavity growing there. Then her baby kicked, reminding why she doubly needed him back safe. "You've got to find him," she begged as she grabbed his hand.

"I will. I promise."

She did not doubt Vince's ability to find her husband, but resented his logical reasons why she shouldn't go with him. He was right and she hated him for it. He spoke a few words with Elliot before he raced into the kitchen to grab some food for the journey. She didn't notice Cy until he nudged her elbow, startling her.

"I heard about Mace," he said. "I'm going with them."

She nodded to him, unable to speak. She appreciated his volunteering. Because of his quietness and solitary behavior, some people thought him slow-witted and unfriendly, but she knew him to be intelligent and strangely loyal to her, one of the few people he trusted. He walked away to retrieve his weapon.

Vince was inside for only a few minutes. He rushed out of the trailer and headed for the shed where the jeep was stored. Amanda held open the door to the shed, and then jumped in beside him. He cranked the jeep and began to back out of the shed. Cy walked up and stood behind the jeep, stopping him. Renda could not overhear the animated conversation between him and Vince, but could tell by Vince's expression that he was not pleased. However, Cy was insistent and finally climbed into the rear of the jeep. Vince shrugged and continued backing out of the shed. Renda watched until the jeep disappeared over the ridge, her heart traveling with it.

"I'm sure he's okay," Elliot said as he walked up with Erin clinging tightly to him. For a brief second, she envied Erin for having her man so close.

Renda was not in a conciliatory mood. She wanted answers. "How did you separate? Who is this Garza he was with?"

Acutely aware of Renda's anger and unwilling to become the target of her wrath, Elliot did not hold back. "We were trapped. We knew we didn't have much time before the zombies found a way in. Mace decided that a decoy might draw them off while the bus escaped. You know Mace. It was his idea so he insisted on driving. Vince was against it, I might add. He thought he should be the one to drive the truck." Renda felt a momentary twinge of guilt for attacking Vince but set it aside as Elliot continued. "Garza was the leader of the Tucson group. He's an Afghan vet, so he and Mace hit it off from the start. He seemed quite capable, but he deferred to Mace's judgment. They got away safely allowing the bus to break out and head off in another direction. We heard shots in the distance, but we expected that. We tried the radio several times but heard nothing. We just figured he was too busy for conversation. We waited for him near the intersection of I-8 and I-10. He didn't show." Elliot paused. "We had to get these people back here first, Renda. We'll find him."

Renda refused to give in to the flood of emotions threatening to overwhelm her. She knew Elliot had done exactly as Mace would have wanted. She knew as well that Vince would not return until he had found her husband, dead or alive. She would not trust her voice to reply. She simply nodded her head and walked away.

Erin was elated to see Elliot return safely, but the news of Mace's disappearance tempered her joy with a bittersweet taste. She knew Renda was in no emotional state to deal with the possibility of Mace's death, not on top of her cancer and her pregnancy. She wished there was more she could do. She did not have long to celebrate Elliot's return. She had to help settle the newcomers into the now overcrowded quarters. They would all have to be checked for disease and immunity to the zombie virus. A dining schedule had to be decided upon since the kitchen could not accommodate so many people at one time. Until they could locate more trailers, things were going to become very cozy.

She noticed Trish Moon staring at her from across the room. At first, she thought Trish might harbor ill feelings for the death of Bob Krell, but then she noticed that the woman looked frightened. She approached her.

"I see that you're back," she said.

To her surprise, Trish smiled. "So it seems. Mace wasted no words telling me how selfish I was. He said you needed my blood."

Erin suppressed a grin. "Mace has never been one to mince words. Your blood is unique. If my tests were correct, you may very well hold the answer to a vaccine."

"So there's a cure."

"Cure?" Erin questioned, and then shook her head. "No, no cure. It won't affect zombies. Their condition is genetic. However, it does mean that Blue Juice will no longer be necessary to keep us safe."

Trish rolled up her sleeve and offered her arm. "Take all the blood you need. Let's get started. I don't want anyone else winding up like poor Bob. How long will it take?"

"I'm afraid you're laboring under a misconception. Even if we replace all our damaged equipment, with only your blood to work with, creating sufficient serum for even a few of us will take weeks, maybe months."

Erin watched in sympathy as Trish seemed to deflate, her disappointment obvious. She had expected Erin to make gallons of vaccine overnight. She tried to offer Trish some hope.

"Once we discover the particular cytokine that triggers your immunity, we can synthesize it using other blood."

"So Mace was right?"

"Yes, we really need you. I'll try to be as easy on you as possible."

Trish shrugged her shoulders. "Like I told Mace, I owe him my life. I'll do what I can."

Erin winced as she thought of Mace missing. "Thank you?"

"You could show me where I'm going to bed down."

Erin pursed her lips and said, "Hmm? That could be a problem. For now, we'll sleep in shifts. You can take my bunk."

"I don't want to put you out."

"No problem. I don't think I could sleep until Mace comes back safely."

"Everyone around here seems to hold him in high regard."

Erin had never considered it from an outsider's viewpoint. "Yes, I guess I do. He, Renda, Vince and Jeb Stone came to San Diego to free us from the military. I guess we all owe him our lives."

Trish nodded. "I see. I hope he makes it back."

Once she had shown Trish and the TSS refuges into which trailers they were to bed down, she sought Elliot, needing his presence to reassure her things would be all right. She found him directing the workers rebuilding the Level 4 lab, jumping it to help replace the heavy, two-inch thick acrylic window. He glanced in her direction but quickly turned his attention back to the installation of the window. She waited patiently until he was satisfied that it was seated properly.

"Do you think he's still alive?" she asked.

"Mace can handle himself. There are a number of reasons he's been delayed."

She nodded. She could see that despite his faith in Mace's abilities, Elliot was concerned. "Renda is at her wit's end. I'm worried for her."

Elliot walked over to her and gently touched her cheek with the palm of his hand. She leaned into it as he caressed her cheek. "She's a strong woman. She'll be okay."

She recoiled at Elliot's words. She wanted to tell Elliot just how wrong he was, that she was dying of cancer, but she had promised not to reveal Renda's secret. "I guess you're right."

He focused his attention on the work going on around them. "You'll be up and running in another day or two."

"Good. Ang had a great idea about how to pinpoint the exact cytokine messenger proteins we found in Trish's blood." She paused, removed her glasses and looked into his eyes. "If we're right, this may be the vaccine we've been hoping for."

Elliot drew her to him and kissed her. To Erin, it felt like a small slice of heaven, but before she could respond fully, he pulled away.

"Now quit distracting me so we can get on with our work."

When she frowned at him, he spun her around, smacked her on her bottom, and said, "Go."

She smiled and sashayed to the door, knowing his eyes followed her every move.

17

Tucson, Arizona

Mace carefully studied the men who had saved his ass. He was glad for the timely rescue but wondered what he had gotten himself into. By their looks, the men weren't military, but they had to have some connection with the military. Their leader, the biggest black man he had ever seen off a basketball court, continued to stare intently at him through the window of the crane. From the snatches of conversation he overheard over the singing of the steel wheels on the rails, the group ran the gamut from Latino to white redneck to Northern Yankee. The oldest might be pushing sixty, the youngest barely out of his twenties. The one thing they all had in common, other than the weapons they carried, was the look of men at ease in their natural environment – big, burly, roughhouse railroad men. He turned to the man nearest him, the one who had helped him aboard the moving flatcar.

"The name's Mace Ridell. Thanks for the lift."

Around him, the others continued taking pot shots at zombies, but the crane was quickly leaving them behind.

"I'm Jake," the man replied. He jerked his thumb over his shoulder at the crumpled Tahoe. "That your ride blocking our nice clean tracks?"

Mace looked at the smashed Tahoe containing Garza's body and grimaced. He felt an overwhelming guilt at leaving Garza's body behind. Garza deserved better than that. "It was. I left a friend with it."

"Too bad. Friends are hard to come by these days. You can't have too many. You from around here?"

Mace didn't want to reveal too much to protect the others. He quickly thought of a likely cover story. "No. We were exploring. Poked our noses in the wrong neighborhood."

"We'll take care of the buggers soon. Looks like you're along for the ride."

"Where are you headed?" He was afraid they might be returning to Phoenix.

"We've got a place north of here at the edge of town – Marana, I think."

"Just you railroad boys?" he probed.

"Nah, the army's keeping us company." Jake looked at him and raised an eyebrow. "You got a problem with that?"

Mace shrugged. "No. No problem."

Jake's grin surprised him. "Yeah, I don't like those smarmy army bastards either, but we have to keep them safe."

Mace looked back at the big black man driving the crane, who was still staring at him. "Who's the big man?"

"Dingane Soweta. He's one of them Zulu tribesmen, but he knows railroads like he knows the pimples on his ass. He's a good boss. Looks after his crew."

Coming from a railroad man, Mace took the latter as high praise. The crane and flatcar entered the marshalling yard just south of downtown. Dozens of locomotives and boxcars sat idle and rusting on the dozens of side rails, trains frozen in place by the plague. Mace was surprised there was no activity. He mentioned this to Jake.

"Our yard's in Phoenix, but we'll crank this one up soon enough."

"Once you gas the city, you mean. You know a lot of people will die."

Jake frowned. "Not me. It's them army jerks. If you ask me, they're too scared to face them zombies man-to-man. Besides, they'll probably warn everyone to clear out."

"They didn't warn Phoenix."

Jake stared at him with suspicion. "How do you know about Phoenix?"

Mace realized he had let too much slip. He tried to cover his mistake by shrugging his shoulders. "A friend told me. He got out just in time."

"You've got a lot of friends."

"Like you said, a man can't have too many friends."

Jake continued to stare at him for a moment, and then broke into a wide grin. "Yeah, right."

The silent buildings of downtown Tucson presented a haunting sight. The shattered glass and blackened facade of the sixteen-story Bank of America building reminded him that he still had a few hundred dollars inside somewhere rotting away, not that it would do him any good now. The twin towers of the Diamond Rock Plaza had suffered severe damage from fire. The smaller West Tower was now eight stories shorter after the top floors collapsed. Window curtains moved behind broken windows like wandering ghosts of the people who once worked there. The sprawling Tucson Convention Center, where he had once watched a Ringling Brothers Circus, had collapsed in the center. Mace noticed everyone had fallen silent as the small procession passed the downtown area, either out of respect for the dead or in contemplation of what they had lost.

As the crane reached Speedway Boulevard and began to parallel the Interstate, they came under another zombie attack. Mace joined the work gang as they fended off zombies. He noted that for railroad men, the workers were handy with their weapons. He killed two zombies that rushed the crane. After their initial charge in which six died, the zombies retreated out of rifle range and howled their anger and frustration. Soweta favored him with a toothy grin.

"Ugly brutes," Jake said, shaking in disgust. He carefully reloaded his rifle before setting it aside.

Mace nodded in agreement, but his mind was elsewhere. The zombies' casual attitude both puzzled and disturbed him. This group seemed more intent on showing their displeasure than in killing intruders. By contrast, the zombies surrounding the warehouse had seemed more interested in killing than in consuming. Zombies were no longer a homogenous group of flesh-craving creatures. Different bands had staked out individual territories, which they vigorously defended. Their use of utility poles to breach the fence spoke of a remarkable degree of organizational skills earlier zombies hadn't shown. They were becoming smarter, better organized, and more dangerous. If they had declared war on the human survivors of the plague that had spawned them, he wanted to win.

"You had many dealings with them?"

He knew Jake was referring to zombies. "Enough," he answered carefully. "Too much."

"Yeah, you handle your rifle like you've used it a bit."

Jake settled back and watched the countryside. Mace knew his best bet was to slip away from his rescuers before they reached their camp. He had no desire to fall into the hands of the military. He waited for an opportunity but the area was too open. If they wanted to kill him, they would have ample opportunity before he reached the safety of cover. He didn't think they would shoot, but he wasn't ready to take that chance. All it took was one overeager shooter. The spot he had chosen for a rendezvous with the bus was just south of the junction of I-8 and I-10. He would need a vehicle to reach it in any reasonable amount of time, and running vehicles were hard to find after a year of idleness. His only choice was to remain with the train and hope for the best. He trusted Vince to make sure the bus reached Agua Caliente. He expected that someone would come searching for him. He had to be well away from his present rescuers before then.

The little train pulled into a sidetrack in the middle of nowhere. He spotted movement at a farmhouse in the distance. He noted its strategic location in an open field. The group trudged across the field talking and joking. He moved next to their leader, Dingane Soweta.

"Thanks for the lift."

In spite of his own height, he had to crane his neck to look up at the giant South African.

"We could not let you become zom food," Soweta replied.

"I wouldn't like that myself."

"Do you have friends who will miss you?"

"They won't come around the military, if that's what you're asking."

Soweta broke into a deep *basso profundo* laugh. "We do not like them so much either, but they are necessary. Without them, there would be no railroad."

"Am I your prisoner?"

"If you were, you would not have your rifle."

"What about your military buddies?"

"I do not know." A big grin spread across Soweta's face. "Perhaps if you tell them you are a railroad worker, they will let me keep you, like a lost puppy."

"All I know about trains is that they run on tracks."

Soweta thought for a moment. "Tell them you were a grease monkey for the Union Pacific, an oiler. If you can use a grease gun, they will believe you." He looked pointedly at Mace's rough hands. "You have the look of a man who is good with his hands."

"Why do you want to help me?"

Soweta stopped abruptly. "I saw you shoot. I need men who can shoot well. Besides, if it just happens that you're a munie, they would send you to one of the hospitals. I would not want that."

"So I take my Blue Juice and work for you."

Soweta slapped Mace across the back hard enough to make him stumble. "Good man."

After Soweta's glowing recommendation, Hugh O'Malley, the work crew boss, was glad to add Mace to his crew. O'Malley kept his suspicions to himself and made a great show of welcoming him in front of the military leader, Captain Lacey.

"We can always use an experienced oiler," Lacey said. "I guess you worked at the marshalling yard."

"Yeah, not much there now but rusting hulks," Mace replied quickly. "It's a shame."

Lacey was not easily fooled. "How have you managed to survive for so long on your own?"

Mace shrugged. "I was a hunter so I'm good with a rifle, and I wasn't on my own. My friend died today in a wreck. Soweta saved my ass."

Lacey rubbed his chin. "Very convenient for you."

"I've always been lucky. Maybe that's how I survived the plague."

"Are you immune?"

"Immune? No. I bought two doses of Blue Juice from a group of Hunters about five months ago up around Phoenix. Cost me a case of scotch and a box of cigars." He stared at Lacey meaningfully. "I'm probably due for a dose right about now."

"A big yellow school bus passed this way a short while ago heading north. I don't suppose you know anything about it."

Mace's heart lifted to hear the others had made it to safety. He managed a deadpan expression. "Bus? No, I don't know anything about a bus. I was driving a Chevy Tahoe. Ask Soweta."

Lacey returned his stare for a long minute before nodding to O'Malley. "Give him a dose of Juice if you need him, but I want him watched."

When Lacey turned to walk away, Mace slowly released his pent up breath and relaxed. He was inside. Now, he had just to figure out a way to leave.

Vince was certain Mace could take care of himself under normal circumstances, but using himself as bait to draw away the zombies from the warehouse so that the others could escape was pushing luck and experience to its limits. Two men, even two men with military training, could do only so much against a horde of zombies. He recalled with bitterness Dan Mateo's sacrifice. Trapped in a garage surrounded by zombies in Winkleman, Arizona, Mateo, bitten by a zombie and slowly changing, had deliberately offered himself to the zombies to allow Vince to escape. He could not bear the thought of Mace ending up the same way.

Road conditions forced them to travel slowly. Numerous wrecks and drifts of sand from washes slowed their progress. Night fell before they were halfway to Tucson. Driving without lights to avoid attracting attention only made travel more challenging. A gibbous moon outlined the rusting hulks of wrecked autos and semis that littered the highway but did little to highlight numerous potholes, sand dunes, and plants making a toehold in the cracked asphalt. In a few more years, the road would be impassable, almost invisible from a distance.

Beside him, Amanda clung to her safety harness, as he dodged and swerved, occasionally casting encouraging smiles in his direction. That she had accompanied him seemed only natural. Since escaping the New Apostle compound in Phoenix, they had become inseparable. However, Cy's insistence on coming along surprised him. He welcomed the young quiet man's shooting ability but worried that he would have to watch after him. Cy dispelled that concern when he had shot a zombie crouching atop an automobile waiting for the open jeep to pass by. The deafening discharge of the Remington 870 12-gauge shotgun from so close behind him took Vince by surprise. The zombie, a young male, toppled from the auto and landed on the pavement, his chest a bloody mess. Vince swerved to avoid it, and then searched for more zombies. He was relieved to see none. The young male might have been scouting or simply a loner in search of females to start his own harem. Like other predatory animals, zombie males sometimes left their packs and struck out on their own.

"Thanks," Vince said as he reamed his ear with his forefinger.

"It's why I came," Cy answered deadpanned.

"No offense, but you and Mace aren't exactly bosom buddies. Why did you come?"

"For Renda. I could tell she was worried."

"You like Renda?" Amanda asked.

"She's my friend. I wanted to help her." He frowned. "We'll find him, right?"

Vince heard the concern in Cy's voice. "I'm sure he's fine. Maybe something happened to the truck. He might be waiting for us at the rendezvous point, drinking a beer."

Cy was unconvinced. He grabbed the roll bar as the jeep swerved to avoid a fallen utility pole. "If anything happens to him, Renda's going to be upset."

"She'll kill me," Vince said only half-jesting. "If anyone can take care of themselves, it's Mace. He lives for this shit."

As they approached the intersection of I-8 and I-10, he slowed the jeep and flashed the headlights several times. There was no answering flash.

"He might not have his flashlight," he said, but he had a strange feeling that wasn't the answer.

He continued onto the bridge over I-10 and stopped on the other side. He had brought along his night vision goggles, or NVGs, a set of PN-15s he had found in a ransacked police station in Yuma, probably part of their S.W.A.T. gear. He smiled as he thought of the 10,000 dollar-price tag, almost three months pay as an Air Force Technical Sergeant. He swept the glasses across the horizon and along the highways. His heart raced when he spotted a small red blob in the green background of the Infrared spectrum, but slowly it resolved into a series of smaller targets. He dismissed them as a herd of javelinas, or native peccaries.

"Nothing," he announced with disgust lowering the NVGs.

"What now?" Amanda asked. "Do we wait?"

"No, we continue on. I'll leave the headlights on so Mace can see them."

He knew that might invite trouble, but the thought of Mace on foot disturbed him.

"What if he's injured and can't get to us?" Cy asked.

"We'll drive slowly and listen for his rifle. He'll try to signal us if he can." He dropped back down in the driver's seat and started the jeep. "We'll go back to the warehouse area and follow the route he was going to take. We should meet him along the way."

However, things did not go as straightforward as Vince had hoped. Spotting a flashing light a few blocks from the Santa Cruz River somewhere near Starr Pass Boulevard, he left the Interstate to investigate. A tiny, nagging voice somewhere in the back of his mind questioned why Mace would venture so far off his path, but in his eagerness to be thorough, he ignored it. Furtive movement in the shadows surrounding houses in a neighborhood adjacent to the road made him question the rashness of his decision.

"Stay alert," he warned the others. He drew his .45 automatic and kept it in one hand as he drove.

Bitter disappointment accompanied his heartbreaking discovery of the source of the flashing light, a solar powered road hazard sign warning of long abandoned road construction on Mission Road. He slammed on the brakes.

"Damn," he muttered.

He spun the jeep in a U-turn and headed back to the Interstate. As they crossed the bridge over the Santa Cruz River, dry this time of year, shadows scampered up the riverbanks – zombies. As he sped up, the headlights caught the unmistakable shape of a tree across the road. It had not been there earlier.

"It's a trap," he yelled.

Amanda began firing at zombies, shattering the previously quiet night. The sound of Cy's Remington 12-gauge almost, but not quite, drowned out the deafening howls of the zombies as they descended on the hapless jeep. Vince was torn between trying to plow through them with the jeep and grabbing his R-25 to join the others. He quickly decided going farther west toward Starr Pass Resort would be counterproductive. It would be too easy to become trapped. No matter where they went, he would eventually have to work his way back to I-10. He grabbed his rifle.

It was easy shooting zombies caught in the headlights, but most stayed low using the darkness as cover. To solve this problem, he pulled two road flares from beneath the driver's seat and struck them against the door, igniting them. He tossed them to each side of the jeep toward the rear, illuminating a wide swath around the vehicle. Startled by the sudden light, a few zombies froze in their tracks, presenting easy targets. Others, driven by their rage, ignored the flares and continued attacking.

Cy's 8-shot Remington filled with handmade shells containing more powder and four ball bearings each, mowed down multiple targets. His R-25, with its 4-round magazine, kept him busy slamming in fresh clips. Amanda's AK47 barked in short controlled burst to conserve ammo. They made good use of their formidable firepower and marksmanship, alternating their reloading so that at least two were firing at all times, but there were too many zombies. When Vince's last clip emptied after killing a zombie that had climbed up on the hood, he ignored his .45, grabbed the machete slung over the back of his seat and leaped from the jeep. He waded into the mass of zombies, hacking and slicing at heads and arms – whatever target presented itself. Zombie faces, some contorted into masks of rage, some seemingly frightened, fell before him. Zombie fists pummeled him, legs kicked him, but he avoided their teeth and concentrated on not falling. To fall would be to die.

Beside him, Amanda continued firing, amassing her own respectable tally of corpses. Cy's shotgun fell strangely silent, but Vince didn't have time to check on him as he advanced mindlessly into the zombie midst. He slashed and hacked until his arms ached, ripping into zombie flesh in a mad fury, a berserker's rage, seeing nothing but splattering blood, hearing nothing but his own pulse as it pounded in his ears. He continued slinging his machete even after there were no more targets. Finally, exhausted, he fell to his knees. Amanda helped him to his feet. He studied her bloodied face as she stared at him in concern. Other arms steadied him, Cy.

"Breathe, Vince," Amanda urged, "they're gone."

He gulped in lungfuls of fresh air, shuddering as his body heat evaporated, exposing him to the night's chill. His pulse slowed and his rage subsided. Cy and Amanda helped him into the back of the jeep. Amanda drove. He looked at the pile of zombie corpses in the dying light of the road flares and felt nothing. They might be evolving into sentient creatures, but he wanted them all dead, gone from his life.

"Did we kill them all?" he asked.

She looked at him with a puzzled expression. "No. They just gave up."

"What do you mean?"

"I'm not sure. It was almost as if they attacked because we were in their way. They simply left, a whole line of them climbing out of the riverbed and heading north."

With his head throbbing from the adrenalin rush and his arms weak from killing, he didn't have time to ponder the reason they were still alive.

"Let's go," he said.

Amanda steered the jeep around the utility pole blocking the road and headed for the interstate.

"We're low on ammo," Amanda told him, searching Vince's face for some sign of comprehension.

Vince nodded to show that he understood. "We have to go back. It's too dangerous searching for Mace with no ammunition." He had failed to keep his promise to Renda. He prayed that Mace could hold out for one more day.

Cy refused to leave. "We have to keep searching."

Vince pulled out his pistol. "I have half a clip left. Nothing for the Remington. Amanda is out. What about you?"

"I have three or four shells left."

Vince shook his head. "It's not enough."

"Would Mace leave you out here alone?"

Cy's words wounded him because he knew Cy was right. Mace wouldn't stop looking for a friend. He looked at Amanda. She nodded her head. "Okay," he said, "we keep going, but if we run into more zombies, we're outta here."

Cy sat back, satisfied with Vince's decision. Vince just wished he felt as good about it as Cy did.

18

Agua Caliente, Arizona

Nothing could console Renda. The full impact of Mace's disappearance struck her hard. She knew Vince would do all he could do, but she needed to do something, anything rather than sitting and waiting. Luckily, there was plenty to do. Adding over twenty new people to their small community made their tight living conditions even more crowded. Each solution created a series of more problems. Renda didn't know how many of the crises Erin brought to her were real and how many she contrived simply to occupy Renda's mind, but she was grateful for the distraction. If Mace was alive, he could take care of himself. She was sure of that. If he was dead, they could do nothing for him. She preferred to think of him as alive. In her gut, she knew he was. His death would have left a hole too big to fill with make work and arranging sleeping schedules.

When Vince had not returned by dawn, she asked Elliot to make the journey to a RV sales center outside Yuma to obtain a few campers for the overflow crowd. Trailers would provide a more permanent solution, but the long trek to Tucson or Marana would be too dangerous. RVs could provide their own heat and help alleviate the congestion in the dining hall with their small, but well-equipped kitchens. Elliot and a half dozen others he selected to accompany him loaded the bus with car batteries, extra fuel and anything else they felt they might need to bring life to the year-long-idled RVs and set out on the journey. Now, the newcomers far outnumbered the original residents. Throughout the long day, she soothed ruffled feathers and consoled people uprooted from their homes, one ear listening for the return of either Vince or Elliot. She was overjoyed when Elliot and his group returned safely before nightfall with two forty-foot-long Winnebago RVs and a Holiday Rambler longer than the school bus. Each could comfortably sleep five or six people, greatly reducing the overcrowding.

"This should help," Elliot announced after jumping down out of one of the Winnebagos.

She nodded her agreement, unable to trust her voice. She was too worried about Vince and her husband.

Seeing her disheartened expression, he asked, "Vince hasn't returned yet? I'll head out as soon as we set up the RVs."

"No," she replied. "Tomorrow."

He searched her face for signs of doubt. "Are you sure?"

"Yes. If … if Mace is alive, he'll try to reach us. He might cut across the desert. You'd never find him."

Elliot nodded. "Tomorrow then. I'll send someone in the bus and I'll take the ATV into the desert. Don't worry, we'll find him."

As she was thinking about the possibility of Mace alone in the desert trying to reach her, a sudden convulsion shot through her abdomen. She screamed in pain, grabbing onto the side of the bus to keep from falling.

"The baby," she gasped.

To his credit, Elliot did not hesitate. He picked her up and rushed her to the lab, yelling for Erin. He kicked open the door and laid her on one of the cots the researchers sometimes used when someone slept over during long tests. Her insides felt as if someone were pummeling her with karate kicks. She gritted her teeth and clenched her fists until her nails drew blood. The uncertainty of the length of her pregnancy concerned her. If she was eight months along as she had thought, problems might arise. If she was nine months pregnant, as Erin now believed, then she was simply experiencing the first pangs of childbirth. She tried to smile at the thought, but another spasm swept through her abdomen, almost bending her double in agony. She felt liquid run from between her legs. *Oh, God. My water broke.*

Erin rushed in, took one look at Renda, and yelled to Elliot, "Get Suzanne. Tell her the baby's coming." She came and took Renda's hand in hers, patting it gently. "It's alright. It's just amniotic fluid. There's no blood."

Renda wanted to feel reassured, but fear was clasping her with its icy grip. "It hurts," she hissed between clenched lips.

"I can administer a local anesthetic," Erin said.

Renda quickly rejected the idea. "I can handle it." Then she groaned as another contraction hit her. It lasted over a minute.

"Six minutes apart," Erin noted aloud. She smiled down at Renda. "You're going to be a mother."

A mother, she thought. *If only she knew where the father was.*

Tucson, Arizona

If Mace had been aware of Renda's imminent childbirth, no power on earth could have stopped him from being by her side. However, Captain Lacey's distrust of him made him a virtual prisoner. His incarceration was subtle. Lacey was intelligent enough not to wish to aggravate the already uneasy truce between his soldiers and the railroad snipes, but Mace noticed the two armed guards who, although they kept a respectable distance, did not allow him out of their sight. He was sure that Lacey intended for him to be aware of the guards to judge his reaction, so he paid them no heed.

He joined the railroad men for a meal in the farmhouse. Though abandoned by its previous owners, they had locked up tight when they left keeping the contents and décor in pristine condition. Except for a good dusting, the railroad workers had done very little when they moved in. The buff and red flowered rattan sofa and chairs and the heavy gold linen curtains were a bit whimsical and Floridian for his taste.

The cook, a grizzled old man named Sinclair, ladled a large portion of beef stew onto Mace's plate, along with two piping hot dinner rolls. He tasted the stew and smiled. He had expected stew from a can, but a lot of love had gone into the meal and it showed in the flavor.

Sinclair noticed his smile and grinned back with yellow-stained teeth. His speech, somewhat nasal and high-pitched, placed him from somewhere in the Northeast, Vermont or Connecticut. "The meat's canned, but the vegetables are fresh grown in a greenhouse in Phoenix. If you're wondering about the peculiar taste, it's bourbon. The army won't let us drink, so I add a little culinary pick-me-up for the boys." He shivered. "Keeps the chill out. I baked the rolls this morning. Nothing like fresh bread to make any meal a feast."

One of the men laughed. "Sinclair here couldn't hit a spike with a sauce pan, but he can cook like the Devil himself."

Sinclair growled at the man. "I was a better snipe at ten than you are now. My best days might be behind me, but I once…"

"Built a railroad through the Amazon," the man finished for him, "we know."

"Well, I did, and with poison darts stinging my backside from irate natives."

"They must have tasted your cooking."

"I like it," Mace interjected to stop the good-natured bickering.

"You're a gentleman and a man of obvious good taste," Sinclair said. He noticed Mace's nearly empty plate and smiled broadly. "I'll fetch seconds."

"You've made new friend," Soweta told him. The big Zulu was sitting beside Mace working on his second helping as well.

"I don't think Captain Lacey wants to be friends."

Soweta frowned. "Captain Lacey is … *stopien najwyzszy* – most cautious. He seeks advancement in rank and fears to make a mistake."

"Does he trust you?"

Soweta considered the question for a moment. "He knows we will do our job, but we are not military, therefore we are outsiders. No, I do not think he trusts us." He stared at Mace, leaned closer and said softly, "The bus of which he spoke – you know those people?"

Mace wondered if he could trust Soweta; then decided he would have to. He nodded. "Some are my friends. I must get to them."

"That might be difficult. The captain will watch you closely, at least for a while. You must show him you can be trusted. Then, I will help you leave."

"Why would you help me?"

"I am a stranger in this land. These men are all the family I have. A man must have family."

Mace thought of Renda. "It's all we have."

"Yes." He regarded Mace for a moment, and then as he chewed his bread, whispered, "In two days a train will leave San Diego for Phoenix. On it will be over four-hundred munies. I know this because it will be necessary for us to reroute the train near Maricopa."

"Why do you tell me this?"

"You strike me as a man who cares about such things. Besides, it would be a good time for you to disappear."

Mace took a sip of his iced tea. "This train, I don't know what I could do about it."

Soweta shrugged. "Perhaps nothing. Still, it would be good if these people did not reach Phoenix."

"Why don't you do something?"

"I am a railroad man. This country, my adopted homeland, will need railroads to rebuild. I will not destroy them."

"You think I will?"

"I think you are a man of conviction who gets things done." He shrugged again. "Perhaps I was wrong." He stood to leave. "I must inspect the supplies for tomorrow," he said loudly.

Mace watched him leave, wondering if Soweta's information was correct. If so, the lives of four hundred people had just been placed in his hands, but what could he do about it. He leaned back in his seat to think.

Sinclair came up to him. "More?"

Mace waved his hand in the air. "Enough. I'm bursting."

"I'll take more," Phillips called from across the table.

Sinclair sneered at him, said, "Get it yourself," and stalked off.

Now he had two reasons to make it back to Agua Caliente safely – Renda and to plan a way to free four hundred munies. If only he knew how.

"That's Mace's truck alright," Vince said. His heart had grown heavy when he spotted the smashed Tahoe beside the tracks where the train had dragged it. He stopped the jeep and walked slowly to the wreckage afraid of what he might find inside. From the strong odor of decay, he knew someone had not survived the crash. He fanned the flashlight over the crushed Tahoe and breathed a sigh of relief when he saw only one body inside. The crushed body was too mangled to identify the face, but he did recognize the plaid shirt – Garza's. Whatever had happened, Mace had escaped the wreck.

"He's not here," he called to Amanda.

"Zombies," Cy said, pointing to several bodies beside the track.

Vince followed footprints running alongside the tracks until they vanished. "If these are Mace's, he must have hopped the train. But if it was moving slow enough for him, why didn't the zombies follow him?"

Amanda held up a shell casing and inspected it. "Here's why. These are from an M16."

Vince knew an M16 might mean military, especially on a train. They had lost him. "He could be anywhere."

"He's not dead," Cy said.

"No, probably not, but I don't know where to start looking."

Cy's eyes strayed along the tracks. "We could follow the tracks," he suggested, "maybe we'll find him."

"He could be in Phoenix."

Cy stared at him. "So we go back and tell Renda he's gone?" he challenged.

"Hell no! I'd rather face an army as face Renda. We need more ammunition. We can find that at Davis-Monthan. We also might pick up something heavier than your shotgun."

Cy laid the Remington 870 across his arms. "I like my shotgun."

"It's good enough for zombies, but we're going up against men. We'll need more firepower." He looked at the night sky. "It'll be daylight in a couple of hours. We need to move fast. Last time I was at the base, it was overrun with zombies. Let's hope they moved on."

The absence of zombies perplexed Vince. According to the Tucson survivors, they had surrounded the warehouse for months. Now, they were gone, the area deserted. Why had they suddenly vanished? Had they completed the task they had set out to do and left, or were they hiding and watching? The thought of so many unseen eyes watching him sent a shiver through Vince.

"Come on," he said and walked back to the jeep.

On his first visit to Davis-Monthan at the beginning of the zombie plague, while he still wore the Air Force uniform he had been so proud of, Vince had fought his way off the base through a horde of the bloodthirsty creatures. Now, as he sat at the security gate looking in, he could detect no sign of movement. The night was eerily quiet. He welcomed the far off call of a coyote seeking its companions.

"The armory is on this side of the field. We go in fast and quiet. Pick up any weapons you see lying around. We might need them."

He pressed the accelerator and the jeep leaped as it took off. He ignored the skeletons still clothed in the tattered rags of military uniforms littering the street and the sidewalks and concentrated on any movement in the shadows. Although, they now roamed all hours of the day, the pre-dawn hours still belonged to the zombies, their hunting time. The armory looked deserted but he took no chances. One of the loading bay doors stood open. He drove straight through the wide door and slammed on the brakes, skidding to a halt on the concrete. They swept the interior with their flashlights but saw only stacks of crates. He wrenched an Air Force M4-A1 from the hands of a skeleton wearing the blue beret of the security forces, checked it for ammo, and slung it over his shoulder.

"Look for crates marked M4-A1 carbines and boxes of 5.56x45mm ammo."

Amanda and Cy raced down aisles searching the labels on crates with their flashlights. Vince went to a storage area separated from the warehouse by a chain link fence. The gate was locked. Picking up a length of two-inch pipe, he jammed it between the gate and the fence post and levered it back and forth until the lock broke. Inside, he used the pipe to pry of the lid from a wooden crate marked 'M-249, machinegun, light.' There, nestled in a cradle, sat an M-249 light machine gun, a high velocity, rapid-fire weapon that also used 5.56-caliber ammunition. He removed it from its cradle and placed it in the back of the jeep beside the crate of M4-A1's and two cases of ammunition Amanda and Cy had located. He saw that Amanda also carried a box of M67 hand grenades and a second box containing G60 flash-bang stun grenades.

"Trying to start a war?" he asked as she tossed them in beside the other weapons.

She smiled. "No, end one."

He leaned over and kissed her on the tip of her nose, ignoring Cy's look of disgust.

"So where do we go now," Cy asked.

"We take your suggestion and follow the tracks."

Cy looked stunned, and then smiled at him. "All right!"

They returned to the wrecked Tahoe and followed the tracks as closely as they could. When the tracks reached I-10, he paralleled them using the frontage roads so that they had a better view around them. They stopped once just long enough to inspect a train sitting idle on a siding near a warehouse but quickly decided it had not moved in months. Vince knew the odds of finding Mace were not in their favor. If the military had him, he could be a prisoner unable to signal them even if he saw them.

Amanda was the first one to spot the Hi-Rail crane and small flatcar near a well-lit farmhouse on the edge of the city. He killed the engine and turned off the lights.

"Do you think it's them?" Cy asked.

"Maybe."

"Do we go in after him?"

After a few seconds, Vince replied, "No. it's too dangerous. We don't know where he is. We watch and wait. When we spot him, then we can move in."

They left the jeep beside the road amid several other rusting vehicles and took up a position near the Hi-Rail crane overlooking the farmhouse. The open ground between the farmhouse and the tracks offered a perfect killing ground if it came down to a fight. He set up the machinegun at the edge of an irrigation ditch.

Amanda and Cy took positions about fifty yards to each side, Amanda behind an overturned Ford Bronco and Cy in another ditch. In the near freezing darkness, they waited for dawn.

19

Northern Arizona

On the third day after leaving Salt Lake City, the two separate columns met south of Page, Arizona on the Navajo Indian Reservation. The reunion was a grand affair but short-lived. So far, no one had spotted them except for a few curious onlookers, but Colonel Schumer suspected that would not last long. General Hershimer in Phoenix knew they were coming even if he was not aware of exactly when. They would not catch him unawares. After getting the convoy moving again, he ordered his five helicopters to fly only in short hops to avoid radar, investigating the column's path and searching for ambushes against the slow moving convoy of trucks, jeeps, cars and armored vehicles.

They had stopped only once on that first night outside St. George to sleep. Since then, rotating drivers, they had kept the convoy rolling with only short stops for refueling that also allowed the passengers to stretch weary muscles. Lack of sleep and boredom was taking its toll on them, but Schumer pushed his volunteers hard, but no harder than he pushed himself. He was not eager to confront General Hershimer's army, but he was impatient to reach his destination – Phoenix.

Twenty-five tanks, four howitzers, sixteen armored Humvees, and thirty-five trucks filled with over fifteen hundred men and women passed through the outskirts of Flagstaff in the early morning hours. The thunder of vehicles was enormous, but no zombies appeared to investigate the furor. Snowflakes fluttered around the vehicles, the leading edge of a storm moving south out of Utah. Schumer hoped they reached Phoenix before the storm hit, but prayed the inclement weather and low-lying cloud cover would keep search craft to a minimum. He rolled down the window and pulled his coat tighter in the unheated cab of the truck in which he was riding, the second vehicle. Leading the convoy was a five-ton truck on whose front end was mounted a heavy grader blade pushing cars and trucks from the column's path.

Bahati rode in one of the vehicles in the middle of the convoy. She had insisted on riding with him, but he knew that her nearness might affect his decisions. He wanted to keep her safe if possible knowing that no place was safe from an air attack. She had nursed him back to health and for that, he owed her much, but what he felt for her was not simple gratitude. He had been alone for most of his life, too busy for love or for a life outside the army. She had shown him that it was never too late for love. Now, once again facing possible death, he knew he must have her, not as a lover but as his wife. She loved him and he loved her. In a world gone to hell, a small slice of heaven was worth the risk. If they survived Phoenix.

He didn't know if it was a sixth sense or if he actually heard the jets off in the distance through the low-lying cloud cover, but he called the convoy to a halt just south of Camp Verde.

"Kill the engine," he said to the driver. A cold wind blowing down off the Mogollon Rim made him shiver. *Or is it fear?* he asked himself.

A sign beside the road announced the Montezuma's Castle National Monument, not truly Aztec but a misnamed, well-preserved Sinagua ruin built into the white limestone cliffs seventy feet above the valley floor of Beaver Creek. From the valley floor in which they had stopped, I-17 slowly climbed into a series of mountains, an excellent place for an ambush. He had purposely kept his helicopters off to the east to avoid detection. Now, they would be no help to him. He hoped his decision to keep them safe didn't doom them.

He spoke into his walkie-talkie. "Have everyone disperse. Bring up the special trucks and place them across the road."

He waited and watched as fifteen hundred people disembarked from the trucks and scattered into the desert seeking shelter from the attack he only felt in his bones. He could almost sense their fear from where he sat, men and women who had never fired a weapon in anger now engaged in conflict with their brothers and sisters. He had faith in them and hoped he did not betray their faith in him. If his senses had steered him wrong, he was wasting precious time they could not afford to lose.

The six special trucks took their positions just as the first F-16 appeared. Altogether, he spotted four, fewer than he had thought they would face but a formidable array of firepower nevertheless. On its first pass, the lead F-16 flew low to the ground parallel to their position, scoping them out. He knew that on its second pass it would rain destruction down upon the convoy. He hoped his plan worked. If his men got antsy and revealed themselves too soon, all would be lost.

The first jet returned to its comrades, circled their location once, and then all four began to drop toward them. It was a good sign, but he held his breath. If the jets had carried JDAMs, or Joint Direct Attack Munitions, they could release hundreds of tiny, lethal guided bomblets over the entire roadway from fifteen miles away. The F-16s also carried M61A1 Vulcan cannons capable of firing 6,000 20mm rounds per minute. A single one could chew up his entire convoy.

Suddenly two missiles, air-to-ground AGM-65 Mavericks, lanced from beneath the wings of the F-16 into one of the fuel trucks. It erupted into a giant ball of flame, spewing burning fuel onto several other nearby vehicles. He could not afford to lose more fuel.

"Fire!" he yelled into the walkie-talkie.

Six 30mm GAU-8/A Avenger Gatling guns stripped from A-10 Thunderbolts and mounted into the back of six five-ton trucks released their deadly fire at the approaching F-16s. The first two immediately burst into flames riddled with 30mm bullets fired at 4,200 rounds per minute. Pieces of their fuselages fell away as they careened overhead, finally crashing into the desert. Twin geysers of flame and smoke rose from their impact sites. The two remaining jets peeled away in tight, high G turns, but a salvo from the row of

Abrams tanks caught one mid-turn. A 105mm shell ripped away the tail section, sending the F-16 tumbling end-over-end until it too crashed. The surviving jet gained altitude and headed south. Cheers rose around him at their victory. He didn't bother stopping them. Realization that they had been discovered would hit them soon enough.

He checked on the destroyed trucks. Six men had died during that first brief attack. Burning fuel from the tanker still spilled from it, running in a blazing stream down a dry arroyo, setting fire to creosote, tumbleweeds and brittlegrass plants. His heart lifted when he saw Bahati running towards him. He opened his arms wide and she raced into them. He folded his arms around her, savoring with delight the feel of her soft body against his.

"I was so frightened," she muttered into his chest.

"It's alright. They've gone."

"Will they be back?"

"I don't think so, at least not for a while." He stared south. "I'm sure he radioed our location though."

She pulled away and looked into his eyes. "Then we should go."

He nodded and smiled, delighted with her rapid uptake of the situation. "Yes, we should."

"I'm riding with you," she said.

By the tone of her voice, he knew he could not dissuade her. "Okay. I would like that."

Back in the truck, he ordered the convoy forward. He sent two of the Gatling gun trucks ahead to lead the convoy. The remainder he interspersed along the length of the convoy both for added protection and for concealment. By his estimation, it would take at least an hour for the base in Phoenix to mount an offensive force to meet them. If they travelled at the speed of his convoy, 30 mph, that meant that they should meet beyond the outskirts of Phoenix, around Black Canyon City or New River. He didn't want to be caught in open ground where jets and helicopters could attack from all direction. He would need to take a dangerous risk.

Into his walkie-talkie, he announced, "Send all tanks and howitzers forward at full speed. I'll send the choppers to cover you." He glanced at Bahati and off the radio said, "I have to risk them. If the enemy takes the high ground on each side of the

Interstate, they could pick us off as we approach and stop us cold. We have to reach Phoenix before they can mount a major defense. The tanks and artillery can break through."

"I trust you," she said.

If his tanks met the enemy head on before they had a chance to deploy, he had them. If not, he had lost. He was an engineer, not a battle-tested professional. He prayed his judgment was sound.

Phoenix, Arizona

General Hershimer accepted news of the destruction of three F-16's with quiet aplomb. He had gravely underestimated Colonel Schumer's determination and brazenness. Instead of fortifying Salt Lake City against attack, Schumer had brought the battle to him.

"Cagey bastard," he muttered. He turned to his aid, Sergeant Ralph Reid, a tall, lanky Kentuckian with a penchant for slow talk and witticisms that greatly annoyed him. "Sergeant, I want every vehicle and man we have on the road in thirty minutes to intercept Colonel Schumer."

"Heck, Sir, it looks like he's in an all-fired hurry to reach us. Why not just blow up the highway?"

"Because we might need the highway, Sergeant. I want to teach this upstart ditch digger a lesson. Now, move your ass before I bust you to private."

Reid snapped a sloppy salute. "Yes, sir."

Hershimer had ten more F-16s and a dozen helicopters at his disposal, but Schumer's trick with the Gatling guns warranted caution before mounting a second air attack. He just might have other tricks up his sleeve. With no heavy artillery and only a dozen tanks, his heavy weapons arsenal was smaller than Schumer's. His dependence on airpower might prove to be a mistake. He had to force Schumer to spread out where his airpower would be more effective.

Schumer's attack could not have come at a more inopportune time. In two days' time, a trainload of munies would arrive from San Diego, establishing Phoenix, under his command, as the center of military operations in the west, fount of the priceless Blue Juice. He had waited all his life for an opportunity like this. Passed over for promotion twice during the post-Afghan war years, he had expected to go into retirement as a lowly colonel. The zombie plague had saved his ass and pulled him from forced retirement. All he had had to do was survive it. He was now the third highest-ranking military man in the U.S. Even the President listened to what he had to say, and he had plenty to say about their European allies.

Europe had suffered worse than the U.S. Crowded and divided by cultural and religious strife, Europe's countries had fallen to the plague like dominoes. The European Union had first unraveled; then disintegrated, often followed by small local skirmishes. NATO had picked up the pieces and soldered them into a loose-knit collection of camps and compounds under military rule, their version of the *Judgment Day Protocol*. As a member of NATO, the U.S. technically fell under their jurisdiction, but already divisions had occurred between the two former allies. For his part, Europe could go to hell. The U.S. didn't need them as much as they needed the U.S., just as it had always been since WWI. Major Corzine had been NATO's boy in the U.S., wielding his power like a sledgehammer. Now that he was gone, NATO had become as irrelevant as the daily newspaper.

He had recently deployed two squads to Captain Lacey in Tucson to help secure the railroads. If by some miracle Schumer broke through his defenses and into the city, he would need every man and every weapon. He picked up his phone.

"Order Captain Lacey and his men back to Phoenix, ASAP."

He slammed down the phone and smiled. That drunken Irishman O'Malley and his band of misfit railroaders could look after themselves for a few days, at least until his train of munies arrived.

20

Tucson, Arizona

"We've been ordered back to Phoenix. You and your men will proceed to Wellton near Yuma, where you will meet a special train inbound from San Diego. You will transfer it to the Phoenix line through Maricopa. I have a map here."

O'Malley waved the map away with disgust. "I don't need your map, Sonny boy. I know the Mcilheney Cattle Company line like the back of my hand. Who do you think cleared the tracks from San Diego?"

Lacey paced the floor of the living room as the snipes, Hugh O'Malley, and Mace sat around and stared at him. With his hands clasped behind his back, Mace snickered quietly at his conjured image of a slightly taller Napoleon Bonaparte. Lacey's serious face betrayed his self-importance.

"Suppose zombies make a nuisance of themselves during your absence," O'Malley asked. "Do we fight to the last man?"

Lacey stopped pacing and stared down at the Irishman. "You will see that the train arrives in Phoenix without delay at all costs."

O'Malley raised an eyebrow. "At all costs? And what will you be doing, having a parade?"

Lacey glanced around the room with a barely suppressed smirk on his face. Mace knew that Lacey could never resist the opportunity to boast. O'Malley's goading had been all that was necessary.

"Forces, rebellious forces, are mounting an attack on Phoenix. We will repel these misguided miscreants and teach them a lesson they will not soon forget."

"Tsk. Tsk. Dissention in the ranks? That's hard to believe."

Lacey's face rankled at the few muffled chortles O'Malley's remark elicited. "Traitors!" he spat aloud. "We will deal with them quickly and then get on with rebuilding America."

O'Malley stood. "Well, we would see you off but we have work to do."

Lacey stared at him a moment, turned, and left the room. Several men burst out laughing.

"Pompous ass," O'Malley said.

"It must be more than a small force attacking Phoenix if they need Lacey's men," Mace suggested.

O'Malley looked at him and cocked an eyebrow, "What are you saying?"

Mace shrugged his shoulders. "Maybe someone is getting tired of the way the military is running things."

O'Malley dismissed him. "It's none of our concern."

"Isn't it?"

O'Malley walked over to where Mace sat and looked down at him with an interested expression. "What do you mean?"

"He means that perhaps we are on the wrong side," Soweta answered for him.

O'Malley snorted. "They're the side with the Blue Juice. I don't know about you, but I don't want to wind up as one of them olive green creatures running naked with my genitals dragging in the dirt."

"My people may have found a vaccine," Mace blurted. He knew he had to sway them to his side quickly. The 'special train' could only be the one Soweta had mentioned transferring munies to Phoenix. He had to stop them from reaching the city and he was running out of time.

"Your people, you say." O'Malley pointed a beefy finger at Mace. "Just who the hell are you?"

"I'm with a group of CDC researchers trying to find a vaccine. They might have just made a breakthrough. If so, there's no need to keep munies locked up like cattle, milking them for blood until they're dead."

O'Malley winced. "I don't like it either, but it's the way it is."

"I'm sure the men, women and children giving their lives to keep you alive appreciate that sentiment."

O'Malley turned away and growled, "It's not my fault. I can't change it." He turned back to face Mace. "Besides, if you've got a cure, the military will distribute it. They won't need munies."

"Vaccines take time. They'll distribute it to their own people first. A lot of people could die by then." He let that thought sink in before adding, "They're using your trains to transport these people. That makes you responsible."

"My trains …," O'Malley mulled that for a few seconds. "What can I do?"

"By yourself – nothing." Mace's gazed fell across everyone in the room. "Together, we might do something."

Soweta's deep voice broke the silence that followed. "In South Africa, before Mandela, my people were treated badly, but not as badly as the munies. I am ashamed of what I have become."

"Why don't we hijack the train?" Phillips asked.

"Hijack … But where do we take them?" O'Malley asked. He spread his arms wide to encompass the room. "Here?"

Mace grinned. They were slowly coming around to his side, no longer discussing why but how. The railroaders' innate distrust of the military placed them on the side of the munies. Before they became bogged down in the minutiae of details, he needed to focus them on a task they could perform better than anyone else could, a job for which they were particularly suited.

"First, we stop the train from reaching Phoenix; then we figure out what to do with them. I have an idea."

O'Malley cocked an eyebrow at him. "And what might that be."

"My people are near Wellton. They can help."

"There's a crate of M16s and ammo in one of the sheds," Jake volunteered.

"Maybe they'll be too busy with Lacey's 'rebellious forces' to bother with us," Phillips suggested.

"Don't count on it," Mace said, "if the rebels lose, the military will send an army after us."

"We could block the highway at Picacho Peak," Phillips noted. "We have dynamite. It's a narrow valley. We could slow them down."

"No, they have jets and helicopters. They would just bomb us or start dropping Sarin gas."

"Then what do we do?" O'Malley asked.

Mace grinned. "What they least expect – we deliver the train to Phoenix."

O'Malley was aghast. "What? I thought the whole idea was to prevent that."

"There won't be any munies on it, just us."

Soweta grinned. "They would not expect opposition, especially if they are concentrating on these rebels Captain Lacey spoke of."

Phillips shook his head. "No, it sounds too dangerous to me."

Mace looked at him. "It was your idea to hijack the train."

"Hijack, not commandeer. Hell, if anything goes wrong, we'll be stuck there."

Mace shrugged. "You either accept the risk or do nothing." He looked around the room at all of the railroaders. "I have to try. I saw what the military does with munies in San Diego."

O'Malley stared at Mace. "Were you one of the ones who busted in and made off with a helicopter load of munies?"

"I was."

O'Malley smiled broadly. "I heard about that little feat. You're notorious." He turned to his men. "This here's a bona fide hero, boys. He spit in the eye of these military boys once before. What say we help him do it again? What the hell? Do you want to live forever?"

The silence following O'Malley's remark seemed to fill the room with static electricity. Mace could feel a charge building to an explosion. Finally, it sparked into life.

"Hell, no!" they shouted. "It's our railroad."

O'Malley turned to Mace. "Looks like you have an army of misfits and miscreants, God help us all. What now?"

Vince watched the soldiers load into five trucks and leave the farmhouse. He was relieved that he did not see Mace among them, but afraid that Mace was not at the farm, perhaps already in Phoenix. Trying to move closer to the farmhouse across the open ground in daylight was too risky, but they could not sit and wait all day. Just as he had arrived at the conclusion that they needed more help, he spotted group of men leaving the farmhouse headed toward the crane. To his relief, he saw Mace among them.

He cautioned Amanda and Cy to hold their fire. When the men drew nearer, he noticed the apparent camaraderie between Mace and the railroad men and shook his head smiling. "Only Mace could step in shit and come away smelling like roses." When the men reached the crane and flatcar, he stood casually, pointing the M-249 machine gun at them. They stopped, startled but unafraid. Mace stepped forward grinning.

"Hold on," he said to the railroad men, "these are my friends. Good to see you, Vince."

Vince casually looked over the men surrounding Mace. "Renda was worried about you."

"I bet she gave you hell."

"Damn right she did. If she could have buckled a seat belt around her big belly, she would have come with us."

"Garza didn't make it."

"I know. We saw his body. Let's go home."

Amanda and Cy rose from their positions and casually walked toward the group. Phillips whistled appreciatively at Amanda. Soweta shot a scowl in his direction and he quieted.

"Change of plans," Mace said. "We have to hijack a train."

Vince stared at him to see if Mace was joking but saw no humor in his eyes. "I see. Anything special or will just any old train do?"

"This one is full of munies headed for Phoenix."

Vince's eyes narrowed as he furrowed his brow. "Where?"

"Wellton, not far from Yuma. We intend to stop the train, free the munies, and fill the train with armed men."

"Isn't attacking the military a little dangerous?"

"Someone's doing the job for us. Phoenix is under attack by rebels, according to Captain Lacey. They won't expect us. I think it's time for a little retribution."

"Are they helping?" Vince asked, nodding to the railroaders.

"Yes."

Vince nodded. He was ready for a little retribution himself. "Okay. I'm in, but first you have to see Renda or she'll come looking for us."

Mace turned to Soweta. "You and your men go on to Wellton. We'll meet you there later today."

"According to Lacey, the train is due in Phoenix in ten hours," O'Malley reminded him. "That would put it in Wellton in about six hours. Don't be late. If you're not there, we'll take the train on in to Phoenix. I'll not be responsible for these men's deaths for no reason."

"We'll be there," Mace assured him.

O'Malley stared at Mace for a long moment. "Okay, I trust you. We'll leave now."

Vince watched as the railroad crew boarded the crane and proceeded north along the track. "I'm sure there's a story there. You can fill me in on the way back."

Mace slapped Vince on the back. "Good to see you." He looked at Cy and smiled. "Thanks for coming."

Cy grinned. "Renda was worried about you."

All four loaded into the jeep. "I have a short stop to make before we return," Vince said. "We could use a little more firepower."

Agua Caliente, Arizona

Renda felt as if her insides were trying to crawl out, and in a way, they were. Her contractions were less than a minute apart and lasting longer. With each spasm, Erin urged her to push harder. The baby badly wanted out and she wanted nothing more than to help it into the world. She regretted not accepting Erin's offer of a local painkiller, but it was too late now.

"I'm pushing as hard as I can," she hissed through clenched teeth, and then took in a lungful of air to prepare for another push.

"I know. I'm sorry. I'm nervous. This is my first baby," Erin admitted.

"It's not like I've had a house full," Renda reminded her. She bit down on her lip as another wave of pain seized her. "Oh God!" she moaned.

Of all the people now swelling the camp, only Dale Cuthbert seemed to know anything about childbirth. The technician hovered over her like protective nurse, wiping her perspiring forehead and squeezing her had during the contractions. Susan McNeil, whom Erin had chosen to help her, had almost fainted early on, forcing Erin to send her outside for air.

"You're doing fine," Cuthbert said gently, "it's almost here."

"He's right," Erin said. "You're at 10 centimeters, fully dilated. One more good push."

Renda pushed, dragging Cuthbert closer as she grabbed his arm. Pain swept through her. She dug her heels into the makeshift stirrups Elliot had cobbled together using a photo of a delivery table as a guide.

"I can see the head," Erin shouted.

Renda saw stars. Her vision was blurred and her pulse pounded in her ear. She fought to keep from passing out.

"It's coming! One more push."

Just as she thought the pain could get no worse, it did. Then, she felt the baby leave her cervix.

"It's a girl," Erin shouted, "a beautiful girl."

She heard a slap and a baby's cry. Tears rolled down Renda's cheeks but not from the pain. She fell back on the table exhausted. She had done it. She had delivered Mace's baby. Now, she could die contented. But she didn't die and the pain didn't go away. Every muscle in her body ached. She listened to the crying and smiled.

"Thank you, God," she whispered.

21

Outside Phoenix, Arizona

When Colonel Schumer received word that his tanks had broken through the hastily positioned Phoenix tanks south of Black Canyon City, he refrained from shouting with joy knowing that the worst was yet to come. There was no time for jubilation. His helicopters keeping pace and flanking the convoy had reported air traffic on their radars – F-16s. He could not afford to stop or disperse his convoy in spite of the imminent threat of air attack. Schumer could only thank his good luck that controlling the air space around Phoenix from attack had not been uppermost in General Hershimer's mind. He had access to all the jets mothballed at Davis-Monthan in Tucson, even though he might not have enough trained pilots to fly them. Had he concentrated on increasing his air power, Schumer's more vulnerable rolling column would be at a serious disadvantage.

After the earlier attack, Schumer had radioed Salt Lake City to launch his own small fleet of A-10 Thunderbolts, also known as Warthogs by the pilots that flew them. Even though he had stripped them of their GAU Gatling guns, they were still formidable weapons platforms with their impressive array of air-to-air missiles. At the first sign of trouble, he would order them in, but he could not keep them in the air much longer and hope for them to reach Salt Lake City with enough fuel to land safely.

The attack came with little warning from two separate directions – west and south. From the south, five F-16s swept down from the clouds firing AGM-65 anti-tank missiles, destroying two tanks and damaging two more. Gatling gun fire from the trucks brought down only a single attacker. Four more F-16s attacked from the west hugging the ground to avoid return fire. They raked the column with machine guns scattering defenders. Two trucks went up in flames. Schumer saw a few survivors race from the trucks before the fuel tanks exploded. This time, all four jets got away. He knew he could not stand many such attacks.

"Bring in the Thunderbolts," he told the radio operator. He hated to commit them to battle this early, but saving them might cost him his entire convoy.

They were more prepared for the second attack. A barrage of tank shells and Gatling gun fire brought down on jet and damaged a second. It turned and flew away, black smoke trailing from its engine. Even this did not stop the attackers. Two more tanks and several more trucks exploded as more air-to-ground missiles and accurate machinegun fire made deadly contact. As the remaining F-16s began their third attack run, his own A-10 Thunderbolts joined the fray. Armed with AIM-9 air-to-air Sidewinder missiles, the Warthogs plowed into the attacking formation with a vengeance. The F-16s broke off the attack on his convoy and scattered. It became an aerial dogfight at speeds difficult to follow because of the low-lying clouds. Flashes of light, followed by loud booms indicated hits or near misses by one side or the other. He could only hope that it was not his side suffering the losses. One F-16, intent on avoiding the Stinger missile fired by an A-10 Warthog, flew directly into a barrage of GAU Gatling gun fire and exploded. Two more became victims of accurate Sidewinders.

His A-10s did not escape the battle unscathed. One took an Aim 120 AMRAAM (Advanced Medium Range Air-to-Air Missile) missile in the rear and exploded in a blazing fireball. He watched the flaming wreckage crash into the desert. He had known the A-10's pilot, a young woman with long red hair that loved reading poetry. He had lost many people today that he knew personally, but he could not let that stop him. He was their commander and had committed them to battle. Now he could only see that their deaths were not in vain.

The AH-64 Apache helicopters, using the contours of the canyons as cover, sneaked into the fray and quickly turned the tide of the battle. The choppers provided a stable firing platform for their 30mm M230E1 chain guns and AIM-92 Stinger missiles. Three more F-16s fell to this withering assault. Finally, the F-16s had had enough. They regrouped and headed south in defeat.

Cheers erupted from the men and women around him. He did not try to stop their spontaneous exuberating but did not join in. As the numbers of casualties came in, he wept openly – forty-five dead and twenty-one wounded. The number could have been far worse. He ordered the A-10s back to Salt Lake City for refueling. He suspected he would need them again before the battle was over. He refueled the helicopters two at a time from fuel trucks, keeping three in the air to protect the convoy.

They did not have time to lick their wounds, nor could he give General Hershimer time to lick his. Grabbing the radio, he said, "Move the tanks forward." He gave the map coordinates of the intersection of Piestewa Freeway, named after the first Native American killed in Iraq, Lori Ann Piestewa, and I-10, also known as Papago Freeway, the old name for the Tohono O'Odham tribe. The position was less than three miles from the Phoenix airport and downtown, the two strategic locations of the local military. Both would be well within range of his tanks and artillery. It would also place them in a no-retreat situation. If he failed to secure a foothold quickly, they could lose the battle.

He turned to Bahati. "Coptic Christians have the same God as regular Christians don't they?" he asked.

She looked perplexed by his question but answered, "Yes, the same God."

"Good. Will you pray with me?"

Phoenix, Arizona

General Hershimer was so livid when he received the news of the ill-fated attack by his F-16s that he threw his crystal paperweight across the room. It passed within inches of his aide,

Sergeant Reid, and shattered against the wall. Reid grinned, but quickly dropped it when he saw the look of anger on the general's face.

"That upstart ditch digger just blew away my air force. He has dedicated soldiers and I have a base filled with pencil pushers and medical personnel."

Reid could not resist cracking a corny pun. "Maybe he'll dig in."

Hershimer scowled at Reid; then smiled. "Perhaps you would like to go to the front lines, Sergeant."

Reid gulped and stuttered, "N-n-no, sir. I'm a pencil pusher, sir."

Hershimer pushed away from his desk and walked to the window. The sky was gray with the threat of snow – perfect weather for a sneak attack. His forces were divided between downtown where the medical facilities were located and the Phoenix Sky Harbor Airport. Defending both could prove difficult. He could not abandon the airport. He might need it to ferry in reinforcements. However, the reason for moving the munies to Phoenix was to make it the center for vaccine production and distribution. He could not afford to let it fall into enemy hands.

He knew that the reason for the attack was to release the munies. Colonel Schumer and General Perry had made their feelings on the forced detention of munies abundantly clear. The President and his advisors did not agree. Perry had been dealt with. It was up to him to eliminate the colonel.

"Sergeant, order the F-16s to Luke."

Luke Air Base, west of the city, served as an auxiliary field. Sending the F-16s to Luke would remove them from danger and keep them nearby for emergencies.

"And bring my car around."

Sergeant Reid, in an attempt to put himself back into Hershimer's good graces, snapped a crisp, military salute. "Yes, sir."

In the backseat of his personal Humvee, General Hershimer surveyed his domain. Phoenix airport was operational. Downtown was clear. The trains were beginning to run. The future had been looking bright for him. Now, it could all tumble around his ears. If he failed to repel the rebels or showed any sign of incompetence, the Brass would remove him just as they had General Perry. He would not let that happen. He had delayed the special train from San Diego once. He could not afford to delay it again. The train must roll, attack or no attack. If the President suspected that he could not insure its safety, he might as well slip into civilian clothes and find a deep hole to hide.

He had his driver stop the car beside a harried-looking second lieutenant. The lieutenant saw the markings on the vehicle, stood at attention and saluted. The general rolled down the window and read the man's name patch – H. Simpson.

"Lieutenant Simpson, I want you to take twenty men to the marshalling yard and guard it."

The lieutenant's salute wavered slightly as he leaned forward to ask, "The marshalling yard, sir?"

"Damn it, Lieutenant! Yes, I said the marshalling yard. A train is due to arrive in a few hours. I want it secured as soon as it arrives."

"Yes, sir."

Simpson stood there staring at the general's car as it sped away wondering why he was guarding a train when an army was advancing on the city. He didn't wonder long. He yelled at the first men he saw.

"Find Sergeant Weiderman. Tell him to grab twenty men and get his ass to the motor pool ASAP." He thought a second, and then added, "Tell him to bring a couple of 30mm's."

If the general expected trouble, he should at least go in prepared.

22

Agua Caliente, Arizona to Wellton, Arizona

When they arrived in Agua Caliente and Mace discovered that he was now a father, he rushed to Renda's side giddy with excitement. When he saw her lying in bed so pale and weak, he stopped and stared. He had never seen her look so helpless. He realized that the birth must have been a hard one. She was groggy from her ordeal and the sedative she had finally relented to allow Erin to administer, but she was awake. Even in her drugged state, she wasted no time in admonishing him for his prolonged absence.

"Leave it to you to be gone when your baby's due."

He fought back his concern and smiled. He sat down beside her bed and clasped her hand. It felt soft and delicate, but cold. "I didn't know," he said as he leaned over and kissed her knuckles gently.

"Well at least you made it back in one piece. I was beginning to worry."

He laid her hand on the bed but continued to grasp it. "Vince found me. He was afraid to come back without me."

"He damned well should have been." She reached over with her other hand, pulled back the blanket to reveal his new daughter asleep by her side. "It's a girl, six pounds and eleven ounces. She has blonde hair and green eyes. I want to name her Tia."

Mace smiled as he gazed down at his child. *My child.* She was so tiny and delicate, so beautiful. Overcome with emotion, he choked as he said, "Tia sounds nice. She'll be strong and beautiful like her mother." He reached out to touch her but hesitated seeing his grimy hands.

"Tia, meet your father. Mace, meet Tia. I hope you two get along."

"We'll be BFF, all three of us."

Renda chuckled. "BFF? Since when did you learn text lingo."

He shrugged. "Looking to the future." He didn't understand why Renda suddenly frowned and teared up, but suspected that it had something to do with what he had to tell her. She always seemed to know when he was hiding something. He took a deep breath and blurted, "I'm afraid I've got bad news."

"What is it this time?" she asked, sniffed and wiped her eyes with her hand.

He understood Renda's disappointment in him. He should have been with her at a time she needed him most. Instead, he had abandoned her for what he felt was a more compelling duty. Now, he was telling her of another such duty. "There's a train load of munies headed for Phoenix. We have to stop it."

Renda rolled her eyes and looked away. Her voice was flat and even but filled with frustration. "Just like that?"

"Well, I made a few friends, railroad men. They're going to help."

She lifted herself from the bed on her hands and stared at him. "There's more you're not telling me."

He tried not to flinch under her reproachful gaze. She had every right to be angry. He was a new father and he was already deserting her. "There's a rebel army attacking Phoenix. If we take the place of the munies, they won't be expecting us. We could make a difference."

Renda sighed and collapsed back onto the bed. Tia stirred beside her but fell back to sleep. "Are you trying to die? I understand freeing the munies. I really do, but attacking Phoenix … are you mad?"

"If we hijack the train, the military will just come after us. If we help the rebels, we might just end this constant threat that we live under. We can start over." He glanced at Tia. "What kind of life can she expect if we don't take this chance? I would like to see her grow up, go to school, get married."

Renda turned away and whispered, "So would I."

Mace did not detect the sorrow in her voice. "Then we have to go, all of us."

"Go on, fight your fight. You would never be happy if you didn't."

"Babe, I … I have to tell everyone."

"Go on," she said more firmly.

He leaned over to kiss her, saw the tears staining her cheeks, and felt sorry for her. She deserved a better man than he was. A good husband would be more concerned about his wife and new daughter, not a trainload of strangers. How could he explain that he saw a chance to end the military tyranny and return power to the hands of survivors? Defeat Phoenix and the other city bases would fall. They still needed the military, but as an ally, not a threat.

"I'll be back soon," he said.

She didn't answer. He walked to the door fighting the urge to look back, knowing that if he did, his will would fail and he would remain by her side.

Outside, he saw Vince speaking with a small crowd, outlining the plan he had developed on the trip back to Agua Caliente. All eyes turned to him expectantly as he stepped through the door. He knew that he was not good at making speeches. He could not sway them with poetic phrases or lofty ideals. He decided to keep it short and to the point.

"A few miles from here, hundreds of people just like you are being used like cattle, the same fate most of us would face if the military captured us. Some of you have suffered this fate. We have the opportunity to end this threat. A rebel army is attacking Phoenix." He waited for the excited murmurs to die down. "They won't be expecting us. I think we have a good chance of getting in undetected. If you're willing to fight for your freedom, for your future, then come with me."

A few heads nodded. People whispered to their neighbors. Mace couldn't get a good sense of their attitude. Had he swayed them?

Vince stepped forward with Amanda close on his heels. "I'm in."

A few others joined him. Elliot moved to stand beside Vince. "Count me in."

One by one, they made their decision. To his surprise, only a handful decided against joining him, mostly the old and the young. When Trish Moon stepped forward, he stopped her.

"No, Erin needs you more."

"I can fight," she said.

"You might be the key to saving us all. We can't risk you."

She glanced away and said, "Okay, I'll stay."

Altogether, twenty-six would accompany him to the Phoenix. Even combined with O'Malley's snipes, they made a very small army. He hoped the extra firepower Vince had insisted on bringing from the Davis-Monthan arsenal would be enough.

"We can't bring them here. We don't have the facilities. Instead, we'll uncouple several of the cars, leave them at the junction, and transfer the other people to them. I need Erin's people and a few more to remain with them to help them recover. The rest of us will take the munies' places on the remaining cars. When we arrive, we break out and do some damage."

"What if we run into real trouble?" someone asked.

He had considered that point. "Once we arrive in Phoenix, our options are limited. If we have to retreat, we board the train and come back. If for some reason we can't, split up and head south. When you reach the Salt River, head west. We'll rendezvous a few miles away from the city and take it from there. Our goal is not to openly attack the rear of the Phoenix defenders, but to hit and run, make such a nuisance of ourselves that it draws soldiers away from the attacking rebels. If it gets too hot, we cut and run. I don't want any heroes," he cautioned.

He hadn't expected a rousing cheer, but the silence when he finished surprised him. Had he asked too much of them? Was he biting off more than he could chew? Vince broke the silence.

"Can I toot the whistle?"

"And wear the conductor's hat if you want."

"The military will be well armed," someone said. Several heads nodded in agreement. "All I have is a hunting rifle."

"Vince took care of that. In the back of the jeep are cases of automatic rifles, ammo, grenades, and some heavier stuff, enough to arm a small army." He scanned the crowd for more questions but no one spoke up. "Well, I guess the moment's come. Let's load up and get started."

The small convoy of buses, RVs, jeeps and ATVs kicked up a plume of dust easily detectable by any passing patrol plane, but Mace wasn't concerned. Phoenix was probably too busy defending itself to look for more trouble. They covered the short distance to Wellton with no mishaps following old highway US 8. It ran parallel to the tracks for most of the way before crossing over the northern leg of tracks after the split.

O'Malley and his crew were waiting for them when they arrived. Mace was surprised to see a smaller version of a locomotive instead of the Hi-Rail crane. O'Malley walked over with a broad grin on his face, his ubiquitous cigar dangling from the corner of his mouth. He waved an arm at the locomotive.

"How do you like it?"

"What is it," Mace asked.

"It's a mule, a shunting engine."

Mace did not understand the terminology. "What's it for?"

O'Malley frowned. "To move the flatcars. Did you intend to move them by hand?"

Mace tried not to show his chagrin. "I thought the crane ..."

O'Malley threw back his head and laughed. "Civilians, ha! The crane doesn't have the power. This baby can do it with ease."

"Where did you get it?"

"At the Tucson marshalling yard. All it needed was fuel and oil."

Mace realized he would have to leave the details to O'Malley and his crew. "So what's first?"

O'Malley checked his watch. "The train should be due in about an hour. We'll pull onto the eastbound track as we were going to shunt the train north, and then stop it. We secure the train, uncouple the cars we want and board the train. We move the uncoupled cars onto the eastbound line to wherever you want them."

It sounded easy as O'Malley spoke, but things seldom went as smoothly as planned. He eyed the terrain with a frown. The plan he had formulated in his head was quickly falling apart. The tracks split in an open area between old highway 8 and Interstate 8. Other than a canal that crossed under the tracks, the nearest buildings were an RV park half a mile away. They had no cover. There was no place to conceal the vehicles.

"It's too open," he said.

O'Malley scratched his head and removed his cigar. He jabbed it at Mace. "I noticed that, but I thought maybe you had a plan."

"You'll have to flag down the train further up the tracks, say near those silos." He pointed to a pair of grain silos half a mile away. "There are buildings nearby we can use for cover." He looked at O'Malley. "Is that a problem?"

"No, we can stop her anywhere. I don't think the driver will miss seeing this mule on the tracks."

Mace nodded. "Good. I'll scatter everyone. We brought some real firepower if we need it."

"Don't damage the engine," O'Malley cautioned.

"Right."

The railroad crew wasted no time getting started. They went directly to the switch section and began oiling the moving parts and digging loose sand from between the rails. It seemed everyone was as impressed by Soweta's size as Mace had been. They watched in awe as his broad shoulders swung the heavy hammer he carried to loosen rust from the gears. When he noticed them watching him, Soweta's laughter filled the air, putting them at ease. Phillips was delighted to see women among the crowd, moving from one to the other in an orgy of pleasure.

It took almost an hour to hide the vehicles and get everyone in position. Vince deployed .30 caliber machine guns on each side of the train. Mace was glad they had cut the timing so close. It meant less time for everyone to get nervous. O'Malley's men were in the greatest danger. They rode on the outside of the mule, easy targets for the military. He hoped he had made all the right decisions.

His heart began pounding when he heard the train's whistle a few miles away. They had noticed the mule on the tracks. There was no more time for second guesses. O'Malley's answering blast pierced the still air. The train slowed to a crawl and stopped just a dozen yards short of the mule. O'Malley waved at the engineer and smiled. Everything looked normal, until one of the car doors and fifteen soldiers leaped out and took up positions alongside the train. Hijacking the train was not going to be as easy as he had hoped.

Guy Ferguson had pushed the heavy train up the steep grade on the west flank of the Gila Mountains outside Yuma, Arizona, past Sheep Peak and down into the flat floor of the Dome Valley basin. Once on the flat, the train picked up speed. He checked his watch. He was on time and running smoothly. Once or twice, he had blown the whistle to hurry deer or stray cattle across the tracks, but he had seen no people or zombies.

Months earlier, the entire area along the Colorado River had been in the path of hordes of zombies migrating north out of Mexico. They had left few survivors in their path of destruction. Yuma was deserted, a ghost town. Once fertile fields gone idle now sprouted with weeds and a resurgence of desert flora. He remembered his earlier trips through the area on the *Sunset Limited* when children waved from trackside and urged him to blow the horn. Now, it was like driving through a graveyard.

He spotted the small locomotive on the tracks as he entered the outskirts of Wellborn and slowed, wondering if there was trouble ahead. He sounded the horn to let them know that he saw them. He saw the railroaders standing around the mule and waved. O'Malley waved back. He stopped almost nose to nose with the mule engine and was not surprised when soldiers exited one of the cars alert for any sign of trouble.

"Dumb ass soldiers," he said aloud. "Who in their right mind's going to attack a train?"

He stepped out of the cab into the chilly air and leaned on the rail as the soldiers fanned out alongside the tracks. He waved once more to O'Malley, somewhat surprised that the usually talkative and cheerful Irishman looked so somber. He wondered why he had not yet exited the cab of the mule. He noticed that O'Malley's men were armed but gave it no second thought. Everyone carried a weapon in zombie country.

"What's the matter, O'Malley?" he yelled. "Too good to come out into the cold?"

He noticed movement out of the corner of his eye just as O'Malley's men dropped to the ground and aimed their weapons at the soldiers.

"What the fu...?" he mumbled.

The soldiers noticed as well and raised their weapons.

"Don't shoot!" he yelled, but it was already too late.

The soldiers opened fire on O'Malley's men. Ferguson didn't know what was going on, but he knew which side he was on. They were attacking *his* train. He dropped to the deck and crawled back into the cab for his pistol. He felt a sudden surge of adrenalin course through his veins and smiled.

"I guess I ain't too old after all."

When Soweta and the other railroaders dropped to the ground, Mace waved to the men on each side of the tracks. Gunfire erupted as the soldiers fired on Soweta. He had hoped to confront the soldiers with superior firepower and force their surrender. Now, it looked as though they would have to do it the hard way.

The two .30 calibers opened up, followed by automatic and semi-automatic weapons fire. The soldiers, though better trained, were taken by surprise. They scrambled for safety beneath the train and between the cars. Supporting fire also erupted from the open doors of a second boxcar.

"Don't fire at the medical trailers," he yelled, but wasn't certain if anyone heard him over the cacophony of gunfire. The trailers were clearly marked with white crosses on their sides, but he was afraid stray bullets might kill or injure some of the patients.

One of the grenades Vince had brought exploded beside a boxcar, killing two and showering the remaining soldiers with gravel and dirt. This forced them deeper beneath the cars. He watched as Eliot and two others made a mad dash for the rear of the train. They reached it safely and entered one of the medical trailers. After a few moments, he emerged and waved to Mace. At least one trailer of munies was free.

One of Soweta's men lay dead on the ground but Mace could not see who it was. They had to secure the train quickly before more people died. Too long a delay in Phoenix might attract unwanted attention. He signaled Vince. Suddenly, a LAWS rocket shot toward one of the boxcar's open door. Those that saw it coming dove out the door. It exploded, splintering one metal wall and catching the wooden flooring on fire. With the car burning, Mace knew he had to take a chance. He motioned for his people to stop firing. When the gunfire died away, he stood and walked slowly toward the train.

"There's no need for more bloodshed," he called. "As you can see, we have more firepower than you. We don't want to kill you. We only want to free the munies."

"I have my orders," a voice called out from beneath the train.

"This train isn't going anywhere. Your mission is over. Now you have to decide if you want to live or die."

"They're expecting us. If we don't show up soon, they'll send more men."

"I'm afraid Phoenix has enough problems to deal with. They're under attack. They won't send help. Surrender and you won't be harmed."

He waited while the soldiers digested his information. He didn't know if they were aware of the attack or if they believed him. He felt exposed standing in the open. All it would take was one trigger-happy shooter to start the war anew with him in the middle of the action. To his relief, the soldier's leader, a young lieutenant, crawled from beneath the car and stood. The lieutenant eyed the men and women behind the guns facing him casually, showing no fear. He took a few steps toward Mace and stopped.

"Who are you?"

"We're just survivors, son. We're tired of the way the military is treating munies, and we decided to do something about it. Will you surrender?"

He stared at Mace for several seconds before answering. "Is Phoenix really under attack?"

"It is."

Mace tensed as the lieutenant reached for his pistol, then relaxed as he slowly removed it with two fingers and dropped it to the ground. "Will you allow the doctors to treat my wounded?"

"Certainly."

The Agua Caliente and the TSS people emerged from hiding and walked toward the train. Curious medical personnel exited the trailers and stared apprehensively as they approached. Feeling it was now safe to bring in Erin and her people, he motioned to the bus, safely out of range of gunfire. Soweta walked over to him. Mace noticed the sad expression on Soweta's face.

"Who was shot?"

"Phillips. He's dead."

"I'm sorry."

Soweta shrugged. "Men die. At least he finally saw some women."

"Let's move the train and start uncoupling the cars. We don't have much time."

Soweta nodded and walked away. Erin and her medical crew went directly to the cars.

"Be careful," Mace warned.

He had no wish to see more comatose munies. He had seen enough to last his lifetime. While O'Malley and his crew moved the train's first few cars past the switch and began to uncouple the flatcars with medical trailers, he inspected the boxcars carrying troops. He found three dead in the car struck by the LAWS rocket. Several more had serious injuries. He directed them to the medical cars. As Vince and the others disarmed the soldiers, he was struck by an idea.

"Lieutenant, have your men disrobe."

The lieutenant glared at him. "Take off our clothes. In this weather?"

"In one of the trailers. We need your uniforms."

The lieutenant didn't move. "I don't know what you intend, but it won't work."

Mace shoved the lieutenant in the stomach with the barrel of his rifle, not enough to hurt him but enough to make his point. "We'll see. In the meantime, disrobe."

Erin quickly scanned the first medical trailer trying to keep her emotions under control. The pitiful sight of so many men, women and children treated like medical lab animals stacked along one side of the trailer in two-tiered bunks made her blood boil. Her anger surprised her. She wanted to hurt someone. Instead, she vented her rage on one of the beeping monitors, smashing it to the floor. She began shutting down the sedative drips and blood pumps. Two medical personnel cowered in the corner watching her. Finally, one of them spoke up.

"What are you going to do with us?"

She glared at him. "If you help us, nothing. If you try to stop me," She raised her pistol and pointed it at him, wanting badly to shoot him, "I'll kill you."

"Who are you?"

"Survivors." She nodded at the comatose munies. "Like them. I was with the CDC. In case you're interested, I think we've discovered a vaccine."

The man's fear gave way to interest. "Vaccine? How?"

"How isn't important. What is important is that you help me."

He turned to look questioningly at his companion, and then the two began to shut down IVs.

Of the over four-hundred munies aboard the train, fifty began to come around quickly. Most had been sedated for so long and were so weak that they would require extensive medical care to recover. She felt the jarring as her car took its place among those uncoupled from the train. It took less than twenty-five minutes for O'Malley and his men to transfer the trailers to the other track. By moving as many patients as they could fit into other cars, they freed up eight medical trailers. They also removed the two boxcars of supplies, including medical supplies. The new train's makeup consisted of the twin engines, two boxcars and the remaining medical trailers. She hoped it was enough to fool anyone waiting in Phoenix.

Almost thirty medical personnel had accompanied the train. Among them was one of the doctors she had met in San Diego, Charles Lucas. He did not recognize her until a bearded young man dressed in white rushed up to her, wrapped his arms around her and called by name.

"Doctor Kostner!" he yelled.

She broke free and looked at the young man, finally recognizing him as Mike Jensen, one of her Atlanta CDC members that had gone missing during their escape from San Diego eight months earlier.

"Mike! It's good to see you. We didn't know what had happened to you."

"After the excitement you caused died down, they let me keep working. I often wondered what happened to you." He looked around at the men with guns. "Looks like you haven't changed much, still fighting. Can I help?"

She kissed his cheek and smiled, pleased to see him again. In her worst nightmares, she saw him killed in retaliation for their defection. "Yes, Mike. We need you."

"Good. I hated this. The vaccine research has gone nowhere. I don't think they really wanted it to."

"We found a vaccine," she said and watched his face go through contortions as he fought back tears of joy.

"Thank God," he said quietly.

"Is that true?" Dr. Lucas asked. "Do you have a vaccine?"

"Yes. We found the key."

"Then I wish to help as well."

"Come," she said, taking him by the arm. "We need to get these people ready to move, at least the ones who can."

As she hurried to the next car, she could not help smiling. It seemed finally that things were going their way.

23

Phoenix, Arizona

After six hours of tank and artillery bombardment, General Hershimer still refused to surrender. Colonel Schumer could not understand why he was not willing to discuss terms. His position must have been obvious. His men were deserting in droves. No help would arrive in time. He looked toward downtown through his binoculars from his position on the overpass at I-10 and Piestewa Freeway. Flames lit up the night and smoke curled up from damaged buildings downtown and around the airport. They had destroyed several planes on the ground, but most of the jets were missing. He worried about those missing jets. The F-16s could cause a lot of damage. They had fought off two foolhardy and badly bungled attempts to rush their position and had received some fire from enemy tanks, but most of them moved constantly and only took ineffective potshots that did little damage. They seemed more afraid of drawing fire from his artillery than in inflicting damage.

He had hoped Hershimer would realize the hopelessness of his situation and surrender quickly, but the general's intense opposition quickly dampened his optimism. Schumer detested unnecessary damage to the buildings and the airport. He also grieved at the loss of life on both sides. Casualties on his side had so far been light, but each death disturbed him. He could only stiffen his resolve and push on with the assault.

He turned to his second in command, Major Terry Richards, and jabbed his finger at a point on the map lying across the bridge railing. "Order the helicopters to sweep in from the east to take out any further resistance from the airport. Captain Wells and his men will move toward downtown under the cover of darkness. Once they set up a forward base of operations, we'll send in tanks to support them."

Richards followed Schumer's finger as it traced the route the tanks would take with the narrow beam of his penlight. It was a bold move but one that could end the conflict. He nodded his agreement.

"It might work. They seem to be losing interest in fighting."

"We can't stop until they surrender completely." Schumer pointed to another point on the map. "Luke Air Base. This must be where the general moved his F-16s. It's the only field close enough that can handle them. If he sends them against us, we'll lose more good people. I don't want that to happen. Contact Salt Lake City. Order our Thunderbolts to attack Luke tonight." He turned and looked at Richards. "If I'm wrong, we'll pay dearly, but I can't take the chance of waiting until morning to be certain. Pray I'm right."

"Yes, sir."

"When the A-10s signal their attack, we move in with everything we've got. We'll overwhelm them. I can't let this battle degenerate into a house-to-house melee. Urban warfare is messy enough as it is. We need this city intact."

As Richards left for the radio, Schumer glanced at the sporadic bursts of flame as the tank and artillery shells found targets.

"God, I hate war," he muttered.

General Hershimer well understood the hopelessness of his situation but did not let that sway his confidence. He had underestimated Colonel Schumer's tactical abilities and was paying the price. At dawn, he would unleash the F-16s he had held in reserve and make short work of Schumer's tanks. Without armor, it would be an easy job to mop up Schumer's civilian army. He also had one last hold card left to play if all else failed.

Captain Lacey's foray to *Red Rock* nuclear first strike base in Marana had produced several low-yield tactical nuclear warheads. Before he allowed the city fall into enemy hands, he would destroy it; obliterate it from the map completely. The new United States government could afford to lose one more city but it could not afford to lose control.

He ducked as another artillery round whistled overhead. It landed in the Salt River a hundred yards away, but the explosion shook the earth, splashing whiskey from the glass he held in his hand. He quickly downed the remainder, his third shot of the night, and slammed the empty tumbler on the table beside him.

"I'll show that black bastard what I'm made of."

Bahati was afraid. If she had known that war meant killing and destruction, she would never have suggested that they fight. It had been an impulse, a desire keep the freedom she enjoyed. She had not realized then what a coward she was. Each time a tank fired she almost jumped out of her skin. She wanted to dig a hole and hide or run until the noise stopped. She was no good with a weapon, so she had chosen to help in the first aide station, but the battered and bleeding bodies pouring in had been too much for her. Overwhelmed by their pain, she had eventually fled into the night. Now, ashamed to return, she stood alone, staring into the city, wondering how many more would die.

On the journey from Salt Lake City, she had tried to get closer to Martin Schumer, but ensconced in his persona of Colonel Schumer, he had held her off, intent on what he had to do. She had not known him during the zombie attack and the digging of the Big Ditch except as a figure of authority. Now, she knew he was a warm, caring man, but he had set such feelings aside as he contemplated the attack on Phoenix. She worried for him more than for herself. She knew that when the fighting stopped, she would return to normal, haunted by her experiences but still the same. She wasn't as sure about Colonel Martin Schumer. He seemed to take each death personally. He seemed determined to inflict as little damage as possible on his enemy. The little she knew about war, which admittedly came mostly from books or movies, such an attitude could lead to defeat, especially if your enemy held no such convictions.

Voices to her right startled her until she saw that it was just two people sneaking away from their duties to smoke cigarettes. She watched them, noted the calmness in their voices as they spoke, and felt ashamed at her own fears. She could not help Martin if she fell to pieces. He needed her, now more than ever. She took a deep breath and went to find him.

24

Wellton, Arizona to Phoenix

It mattered very little to Guy Ferguson that his train was shorter and now under the command of strangers. His friend Hugh O'Malley had told him that they were doing the right thing and he believed him. All that mattered was that his train was moving once more and he was the engineer. It rushed through the night like a serpent threading its way toward prey, dark and silent. He held no opinion on the munies that had been freed. That was beyond his expertise. He knew trains.

O'Malley stood beside him in the cab of the locomotive engine, bracing himself against the wall as he swayed like a drunken sailor. Without constant repair, sunken ties created almost imperceptible dips in the rails, difficult to see with the naked eye, but easily felt by the rushing locomotive.

He turned to O'Malley. "What do your friends have planned once we reach Phoenix?"

O'Malley smiled and rubbed his hands together as if he were on his way to a tavern brawl. "Oh, a wee bit of ruckus to liven things up."

"They won't hurt my train, will they?" He had felt the damage to the boxcar as if it had been an extension of his body, a dull ache in his side.

"No, Guy. Just a bit of mischief with the locals."

Ferguson nodded, and then cocked one eye wide open and glared at O'Malley. "Okay, but no more of them rockets." He stared out the window into the darkness a few moments before adding wistfully, "You know, I haven't pulled a train into Phoenix since the *Sunset Limited* stopped running there in '96."

Amtrak had discontinued direct service to Phoenix in 1996. Passengers had to ride a bus from Phoenix to Maricopa to meet the *Sunset Limited*.

"You've been running this train for a long time. You weren't at Big Bayou, were you?"

Ferguson frowned at mention of Big Bayou, the worst rail disaster in years, when in 1993, a barge damaged a bridge outside of Mobile, Alabama, and the *Limited* derailed and went into the water, killing forty-seven passengers.

"No, I was off duty. If I had been, I might have kept her upright on the tracks." He reached out and patted the control panel. "In 2011, we carried 100,000 passengers from New Orleans to L.A. without so much as a scratch, but the only thing anyone remembers is Big Bayou."

"Don't get riled, Guy. No one thinks it was your fault. You're the best railroader of us all."

This brought a smile to Ferguson's face. "Damned straight."

"When we reach Maricopa, I'll hop off and set the switches. Then we'll be on our way."

"It'll be good to see Phoenix again," Ferguson mused. "Unless they've blown it up by the time we get there."

Two cars back from Ferguson and O'Malley, Mace was checking his weapon. Around him, Soweta's men joked and spoke casually, as if forgetting that one of their own, Phillips, was dead. He did not know the TSS people very well, but they appeared nervous and frightened, even more frightened than the Agua Caliente people who had been through fights before. He and twelve others wore the uniforms of the original escort. When the train reached the marshalling yard, he hoped they would pass any casual inspection. He wanted to subdue any guards quickly and quietly with as little bloodshed as possible. His desire was not from any loyalty to the military. Their deaths would not bother him that much, but a prolonged fight would put his people at risk. The entire operation was riskier than he cared to admit, but if they fanned out, destroyed a few buildings, and made some noise, the city's defenders might think the rebels had surrounded them, breaking their will to fight.

Vince, in the car behind his, had brought with him several LAWS rockets, a case of C-4 plastic explosives, and a case each of hand grenades and flash grenades. He was like a kid in a toy store. Only the limited space in the jeep had prevented him from emptying the Davis-Monthan arsenal.

He had forced each one of his people to view the munies as Erin's people moved them from the train. It was almost a scene from a Holocaust movie – thin, emaciated bodies; empty, staring eyes; sunken cheeks, pale from loss of blood. Many of the munies would not make it. They were too far gone in their illness, their bodies used up, kept alive only by the medical devices connected to them. He wanted each of his fighters to carry that picture and that thought in their mind as they fought.

He felt the train slow and looked questioningly at Soweta.

"O'Malley's throwing the switch at Maricopa."

Sure enough, the train had barely slowed before it once more began to pick up speed. Ferguson, the recalcitrant engineer, seemed determined to push the train to its limits, even if he rattled and jolted his passengers to the point of seasickness. Mace opened the door just a crack and looked out as Maricopa passed from view. Next stop – Phoenix.

Lieutenant Simpson watched the train slow as it entered the Phoenix marshalling yard. As it stopped, ten soldiers jumped down from two of the cars.

"You're late," he said.

One of the men replied, "Trouble on the tracks."

The man glanced to the north as an explosion lit up the night sky. "There's trouble here too," Simpson said. "We'll watch the train until morning. Trucks will come then to transport the munies to the hospital."

"What's happening there?" The man pointed to the sound of gunfire.

"Nothing we can't handle."

As he spoke, the soldiers from the train began casually to move away from the train and ease along the tracks, stretching their muscles as if exhausted from the long ride. Simpson didn't notice anything awry until the tall man with whom he had spoken pointed his weapon at him. At the same time, the boxcar doors slid open, revealing two .30 caliber machine guns and many armed civilians.

"Can you handle this, Lieutenant? Order your men to stand down. There are no munies aboard, so there's no reason to die for an empty train."

Simpson tensed. His men nervously pointed their weapons toward the train. He had machine guns as well and almost as many men, but his orders had been to protect the train, not attack it. In the last few hours, his faith in his commanding officer had slipped and his desire to die with it. What they had assumed to be a small band of rebels, was in fact an entire army, well equipped and determined. Now, he confronted more rebels coming from the south. He lowered his weapon.

"We surrender."

His men dropped their weapons and walked toward the train, hands in the air. The tall man turned to one of his companions. "Vince, lock them in one of the medical trailers. Have two men keep an eye on them but don't harm them."

The man nodded. "Follow me, please," he said.

Simpson shook his head. In his first and only fight, he had meekly surrendered without firing a shot. He fell in line with the others.

Mace observed the artillery fire falling into downtown Phoenix and the airport and realized that the rebel army was very substantial. For the first time in two days, he felt things were going their way. The lieutenant's surrender without a fight probably spoke of most of the city's defenders. It was easy to don a uniform, take orders, and chase down and capture unarmed munies, but fighting an army as well equipped as your own was another matter entirely.

He recalled his days in Afghanistan cowering in a foxhole or any available cover during an enemy mortar bombardment, frightening under the best of circumstances, even more so when you did not know when the attack that the barrage usually presaged would come or how many men would come with it. Each explosion, each whistling round had sent shivers up his spine. Even the reality that you didn't hear the one that got you didn't help. Those he did not fear. It was the one that maimed and mutilated that he dreaded most. Too many of his friends had gone home missing an arm or a leg. Too many had gone home in body bags.

He spoke to those gathered around him. They had already discussed their plans. This was more of a friendly reminder to be careful. "Okay, spread out in groups of five. Don't engage if you don't have to. Set C-4 charges in buildings, fuel tanks, anything to attract attention just as Vince showed you. Set the timers for one hour, and then get back here."

Vince and Elliot led two groups. Men from the TSS led two others. Mace watched them disappear into the darkness, hoping they all returned safely. Soweta and his men remained at the yards to watch the train and the prisoners. Taking his own four men, he headed east along the tracks past the repair sheds to Jackson Street. In the distance, explosions wracked the airport. His destination was not that far. Half a mile from the marshalling yard, in a formerly quiet residential neighborhood, he and his companions placed their allotted six C-4 explosive devices beneath propane tanks, inside houses, and parked vehicles. The resulting explosions would make the defenders think an opposing force was near the city's southern edge and send troops to investigate.

A series of loud blasts from the west rocked the night. At first, he wondered what was happening. Then he saw the telltale streaks of air-to-ground missiles. Someone was getting plastered by an air strike. He hoped it was the good guys doing the plastering.

Once they had placed and armed the devices, they began the return trek to the train. The lack of small arms fire nearby led him to believe that his ruse was working. No one had spotted them yet. Sporadic firing from the direction of the train ended that hope.

As they got nearer to the train, they saw that Soweta's men were under attack, not from soldiers, but from zombies. Almost fifty of the creatures raced around the train where Soweta and his men had taken cover. Some had leaped onto the top of the cars, pounding uselessly on the metal roofs. Men fired from open doors and windows, killing several zombies, but the remainder disappeared into the darkness only to emerge from another direction.

Mace checked his watch. Twenty minutes remained until the C-4 went off. He had planned on being long gone by then. The zombies were going to make their escape more difficult. Attacking with only his four men would be suicidal. *Time for a change of plans.*

"Come on. We'll swing north and meet the others."

He hoped Soweta did nothing foolish until he returned with the remaining men. Together, they could kill of chase off the zombies. Their presence had been a surprise. Most of the zombies in the area had left or died during the Sarin gas attack months ago. He remembered Soweta's observation that he had seen many zombies moving north as others had before. They had been unlucky enough to run into a pack of migrating zombies. If other zombies were moving through the city, perhaps it would throw a little scare into the defenders; help break their resolve.

Vince was the first to show up. He smiled as he said, "We found a gas station with fuel in the tanks. It should put on quite a show."

"We have other problems – zombies."

Vince looked toward the train. "How many?"

"Enough," Mace replied. "We'll wait on the others."

Mace was eager to help Soweta, but could not leave the remaining teams to straggle back to the train unaware of the danger. The chance for an accidental crossfire was too great. Elliot showed up next with his group. The others followed closely on his heels.

"Zombies," Mace cautioned them. "Be careful firing at the train. Don't hit any of our people."

The sound of more small arms fire in the distance made him wonder if more zombies had wandered into the city. The unexpected zombie incursion would cause more confusion than his small group could. Separating the volunteers into two groups, they approached the train from the side and from the rear, avoiding the train's headlights and the flares Soweta had tossed out the door of the boxcar. Mace shot one zombie beating uselessly at the roof of the boxcar. He fell to the ground. Several others fell as bullets found their mark. Thirty nearly simultaneous C-4 explosions rent the air, sending geysers of flame high into the night sky. The zombies stopped attacking and looked at the fires; then slinked away into the darkness. Mace had the distinct impression that fear had not been the reason for their retreat. Whatever the reason, the battle was finished, at least for his people. In the distance, the sound of tanks firing indicated a more intense attack was beginning. It was time to retreat.

"Let's load up and leave," Mace ordered. "Inform the lieutenant that he and his men can come with us or stay here. Their choice."

Vince smiled. "I think maybe he'll come with us. They seem a bit disillusioned with their leader."

Mace looked back upon at the destruction they had caused. Flames billowed into the air from five different areas. "I hope this takes the pressure off whoever is attacking the city."

Ferguson leaned out of the cab of the engine. "All aboard!" he yelled. "Get on or get left behind. This train's headed for Yuma."

Mace took one last look around counting heads before climbing aboard. He had lost no men or women in the raid, but he knew luck had played as big a part as his planning had. He also knew that his luck was not likely to hold.

"Let's go," he yelled as the train began to move.

General Hershimer leaned against the window and looked out over his city. The airport was in flames. Buildings downtown burned. His F-16's had been destroyed on the ground at Luke. Even his train of munies was lost. Explosions in the area told him that the enemy had infiltrated his perimeter. He had lost.

He grinned at his reflection. "I may have lost, but I won't let Schumer win."

Beside him, one of the .5 kiloton tactical nukes reminded him of the power at his disposal. Unlike the nuclear weapons depicted in thriller movies, this one did not have a shiny glass exterior or a digital readout ticking down the minutes. Designed for a missile, it exploded at a preset height and distance, but he had attached a simple timing device. He rested his tumbler of whiskey on top of the nuke, smiling at the juxtaposition.

He checked his watch. "Four am. In two hours, Boom!" He spread his hands apart mimicking an explosion. The resulting blast would destroy everything within a three-mile radius, him included. He had no intention of leaving. He knew that losing Phoenix ended his career. It would be better to die in the heart of a nuclear fireball than face President Hastings.

He groaned and turned to Sergeant Reid, sitting as far from the nuke as he could. "That dumb shit's probably never even fired a weapon."

"Yes, sir," Reid answered nervously, afraid to say anything else that might cause the general to detonate the nuke sooner.

Hershimer stared at his aide, saw the sweat streaming down his face and knew he was a coward. The thought of dying did not bother him. Perhaps it was the three-quarters of a fifth of Cutty Sark he had consumed, or perhaps it was his acceptance of the inevitability of defeat. He would not face his end sober. That would be asking too much of his resolve. Many of his troops had defected to the enemy when word spread like wildfire that the rebels had destroyed his small fleet of jets. The artillery barrage from Schumer's tanks had slowly broken their spirit. Soon, Schumer would move his troops into the city and he couldn't stop him.

"I'd give anything to see that bastard's face as the city turns into a mushroom cloud." His laughter burned his throat, so he downed the rest of the whiskey. He eyed the bottle. "No, I have to make it last until morning."

"Yes, sir," Reid answered carefully. "I can go find another bottle, sir."

Hershimer patted the pistol on his hip. "Oh no, sergeant. I want you right here beside me. I won't let you desert."

"There's still time to escape, sir," Reid suggested hopefully. "We could just disappear, the two of us. No one would know or look for us."

His sergeant's desperation was not lost on him. "Coward!" he spat. "It's our duty to remain, Sergeant. It's our ... duty." He let the last word roll off his tongue. He had done his duty for twenty years and one mistake was going to end it. He would not live out his life with the taste of failure in his mouth. "Duty."

He turned to stare out the window again and heard footsteps as Reid scrambled for the door. When he turned back, Reid was gone. He smiled. He preferred to die alone rather than in the company of cowards.

25

Phoenix, Arizona

Colonel Schumer was beginning to relax. His A-10 Thunderbolts had caught General Hershimer's F-16s on the ground and had destroyed them all without a single loss. Resistance was weakening along the perimeter and some unknown ally was attacking south of the downtown area. Scores of Hershimer's troops had surrendered. It looked as if victory was just a matter of time. Therefore, the startling news that Major Richards brought shook him badly.

"That crazy bastard, Hershimer, has a nuke!"

Schumer stared at his second-in-command to see if he was joking. He saw nothing but fear in the major's eyes.

"How do you know?"

"We just picked up his aide, a Sergeant Reid, trying to get through the lines. He said it's set to detonate at 6 a.m."

Schumer glanced at his watch. "That leaves us just over an hour to evacuate. How big?"

"Half a kiloton."

"We have to pull back well beyond the blast radius, say five or six miles."

"Impossible!"

Schumer knew that Richards was right. They would barely have time to move their own people, much less the people in Phoenix, but they had to try.

"Order everyone north. Tell them to keep moving. Load every vehicle that runs. Bring in the choppers and find anything that will fly at Sky Harbor. Just get them in the air for now. We'll decide where to send them later. Announce to Hershimer's men what's he's done. The war's over. Nobody won. Now, it's just a matter of survival."

Richards nodded and raced off.

Schumer could not understand Hershimer's reasoning. To kill everyone to prevent him from taking the city took a special kind of madness. As he looked out over the city, he thought word had already spread of the nuke, but then he realized that what he had thought to be wholesale desertion was in reality sporadic fighting between cornered troops and zombies. In such chaos, he could do little for Hershimer's men. To delay his army would only invite disaster.

He now questioned his decision to attack Phoenix. His desire to free the munies and to protect his own charges had driven him, but the result was poor payment for his good intentions. Men and women on both sides had died and more would die in the next hour and a half. They had no time to transport the munies from the city. They had no time to accept the enemy's surrender. At the very moment of his victory, he now had to retreat.

Through his binoculars, he saw his tanks returning, sometimes driving through pockets of the enemy. Some clambered aboard the tanks. Half an hour earlier, the tank crews would have repelled them with withering machine gun fire. Now, to the credit of his men, they allowed this, often encouraging it. Vehicles began to head out of the city in all directions, but not enough to hold the thousands trapped within the city.

With their weapons turned to face the threat from the north, the defenders of Phoenix were not prepared for the zombie attack. The creatures swept out of the darkness and through them in a bloody fury, pausing only long enough to rend flesh and break bones. They would reach his position in less than half an hour. He lowered his binoculars from the sickening blood bath.

"It's time to go," he called to those waiting around him.

Captain Lacey realized the battle was lost long before the chaos began. General Hershimer had been big on talk but poor on delivery. The airport was gone and Colonel Schumer's helicopters controlled the airspace. The haphazardly thrown together defenses were falling quickly, and without leadership, the men were in a blind panic. No word had come from Hershimer in hours. Word had come of an attack near the marshalling yard about the time the train from San Diego was due to arrive. He immediately suspected O'Malley had something to do with it. He had never trusted those snipes. They were too damned cocky. He had been on the point of withdrawing his men when the rumor that Hershimer had a nuke began to spread. He knew this was no mere rumor. He had delivered the six *Red Rock* nuclear warheads to the general personally. While he had always wanted to witness a nuclear detonation, he had no desire to be standing on ground zero when it went off. It was definitely time to fend for himself.

"Men," he announced, "this war is lost and Hershimer's gone ape shit on us. It's time to get the hell out of Dodge."

No one argued the validity of his statement. He could read the fear in their eyes. If he looked into a mirror, he would probably see the same fear in his. He knew that if O'Malley was responsible for the attacks near the marshalling yard, he had an escape plan, probably by train. Maybe it was time for a lift.

He gathered as many lost and confused men as he could along the way. They encountered zombies twice but fought their way through. Luckily, the zombies seemed more intent on moving north than in killing humans. Avoiding them seemed to work. He didn't question their motives. Let them have the city for as long as it lasted. They could fry with the general.

The train was just beginning to pull out of the yard when he arrived with his ragtag collection of refugees. He stood on the tracks in the train's path, his hands raised in the glare of the train's three headlights. He was not surprised when O'Malley stuck his head out of the cab and yelled for him to move.

Lacey stood his ground as the locomotive inched toward him; then stopped. "I thought I might find you here," he said,

"Don't start anything you can't finish," O'Malley warned. He held a rifle in his hands. "There are over fifty armed men aboard."

Lacey laughed and threw down his rifle. "I'm through playing soldier, O'Malley. The general has a half-kiloton nuke to play with. He intends to blow up the city rather than lose it. We're just looking for a ride out of here."

O'Malley's face went pale. He stepped back into the cab to confer with Ferguson. In the meantime, another figure that Lacey recognized jumped down from of one of the boxcars.

"The oiler. Why am I not surprised to see you here?"

Mace shrugged. "It seemed too good an opportunity to waste. We freed the munies. They're safe."

"Well we're not. Very soon, a big old nuclear bomb is going to wipe Phoenix off the map, courtesy of General Hershimer."

"What?"

"The general's gone off the deep end. I brought him the nukes from *Red Rock,* a nuclear base near Tucson."

"I know the place. One of my friends was stationed there."

That somehow didn't surprise Lacey. Mace had not struck him as a simple oiler looking for a job. "My, my, you are informed. Did he tell you how big of a mess a half-kiloton nuke makes?"

"No, but I can guess. I don't suppose you know when."

"No idea. I don't expect him to wait too long."

"Are you looking for a ride?"

Lacey bowed. "Humbly."

O'Malley walked out and looked over the crowd of over a hundred men and women waiting nervously. "I can't leave them," he told Mace. To Lacey, he said, "We'll have to couple more cars to the engine." He started to climb down from the engine. "I'll get Soweta."

"No," Mace yelled.

O'Malley stopped halfway down the ladder and looked at him. "For God's sake, man! These people need to come with us."

"You take this train out of here now," Mace answered. He pointed to a second locomotive coupled to a string of boxcars. "What's wrong with that one? Show me how to get it started. I'll worry about stopping it later."

O'Malley scowled at him. "You ain't in the union. I'll drive."

Mace waved Ferguson and the train they had arrived on out of the yard. Lacey was a little apprehensive as he watched it pick up speed. A few of his men, worried that the next train might not leave in time, hopped aboard wherever they could find space to stand or sit. He too was worried, but he didn't really believe that any of them would have enough time to escape the blast anyway. At least he would have a ringside seat for the biggest explosion he had ever seen.

It took O'Malley fifteen minutes to get the engine cranked and ready to go. Men and women clambered aboard the boxcars. With each minute they waited, more people poured in as if word had spread that escape might be possible, but each minute they waited also kept them in the danger zone. Finally, the train was ready. Lacey crawled up onto the engine with Mace.

"You're taking a big chance," he said.

"The war's over," Mace told him, "for now anyway. Once we're clear of here, you can help us rebuild Tucson or go your own way. We need good men."

"They won't give up, you know. The military doesn't like rebels or traitors."

"We have a vaccine. If they want some, they'll return to protecting the citizens, not exploiting them. If not, well, we've got guns."

"A vaccine." Lacey nodded. "That makes a difference. Maybe I'll stick around for awhile."

"You two hang on," O'Malley warned as he pushed the throttle forward. The train began to move. O'Malley pointed up ahead of the train. "One of you boys jump down and throw that switch to put us on the right track."

"I'll get it," Mace replied.

"I know how to throw a switch," Lacey said. "I'll do it. I'll ride in back. I should have a good view from there."

He hopped off the train, threw the switch, waited until the last boxcar passed, and then swung aboard. Stragglers hurried to catch the last train out of Phoenix. No one knew when the bomb was set to detonate, but Lacey suspected that they would be cutting it very close. It was with great relief that the train finally slipped behind the shelter of the North Maricopa Mountains. He stood at the open door and stared out. The flash caught him off guard. He closed his eyes, but the light was so intense he could still see it through his eyelids. It was as if the sun had risen directly over Phoenix. If not for the intervening mountains, the flash would have blinded him. As it was, he had to turn away and wipe the tears from his eyes. When he looked back, ribbons of red and orange etched the predawn sky racing away from the blast.

The blast was less powerful than he had expected, but more frightening. He watched the shock wave approaching the train across the desert floor like a ripple, preceded by a blast of air hotter than any summer haboob. Grains of sand dug into his flesh and peppered the side of the car. Behind them, the rails lifted and rolled like a plucked guitar string, racing toward the train at breakneck speed. The boxcar bucked, bounced and swayed as the wave passed beneath them. The entire train became a Coney Island roller coaster but continued down the tracks. A dirty mushroom cloud rose over the city. Downtown, Sky Harbor airport, and everything north of the Salt River and south of Piestewa Peak was now dust in that cloud. He would learn later that buildings collapsed up to a distance of six miles from the epicenter of the blast. Windows shattered in buildings fifteen miles away.

Even with warning, he knew most of the several thousand people in the city could not have escaped the blast zone. The irradiated dust containing their ashes would follow the prevailing winds and fall slowly on cities and communities to the east. In normal times, tens of thousands would have died of radiation sickness. Now, it would be a mere handful; people who had managed to survive the plague and zombies only to succumb to another of man's follies. Some of the dust would reach the east coast, eventually Europe, no Chernobyl-style disaster, but a parting gift from General Hershimer. He imagined NATO would not be pleased with its American ally.

He counted himself among the lucky.

Bahati leaned against Martin Schumer's shoulder and wept. They were returning to Salt Lake City, not in defeat, but certainly not in victory. They had lost over two hundred people during the battles along I-17 and in Phoenix. They had escaped only minutes ahead of the bomb. She had watched it through the rear view mirror, a sight that would forever haunt her dreams. They had rescued less than four hundred of Phoenix's defenders. Others might have escaped in other directions, but thousands, including the very people they had sought to rescue, had perished. It seemed only fitting that snow was falling, blanketing the landscape in a cold, white shroud. It was as if the planet wept for them.

There was no sense of celebration in the convoy, only the realization that some factions of the military would go to any lengths to keep the status quo as it was. They would have to wrest the country from their grip by force.

"Will it ever end?" she asked.

Schumer tightened his arm around her. "I think more and more people will come over to our side. The tide has turned in our favor. Once word spreads about what General Hershimer did, they will begin to have doubts. People who doubt the rightness of their cause will waver. In the end, we'll win."

"How many more deaths?" She had seen too many deaths to contemplate a prolonged fight. So many had died during the plague, it seemed such a waste to continue.

"Too many," he answered. "I'll try to persuade people to our side, but any threat has to be met with force or we will all become slaves."

She nestled in his arms. All she wanted now was to return to Salt Lake City, leave the war behind her. In her new adopted country, she must forget her past and look forward to the future. She would not share Martin Schumer the man, with anyone else, but she knew that she must share Colonel Martin Schumer with everyone. At least for the next few days, she had him all to herself. That would have to do.

26

Agua Caliente, Arizona

Renda held her little girl, Tia, in her arms as she watched Mace and the others position another trailer along the road leading to Agua Caliente. He worked bare-chested in the warm spring sunshine. She marveled that at forty-six, in spite of the few gray hairs on his chest, he still had the lean, well-muscled body of a much younger man. He was a doting father and a natural leader. The small community around the solar farm had grown to over eight hundred people. Lines had been run to the sewer and the nearby waste treatment plant was brought back into operation. Newly drilled wells provided sufficient water. At first, there had been a discussion of reclaiming houses in Tucson or Yuma, but Mace's wisdom prevailed. Agua Caliente was self-sufficient and well protected. Everyone participated in the local militia exercises and armed patrols scoured the area. The threat from the military had not vanished, but they were now better prepared.

Mace had made radio contact with Colonel Martin Schumer in Salt Lake City, the man who had led the assault on Phoenix. Envoys would arrive soon by helicopter to coordinate the distribution of the new vaccine. Erin's medical staff now numbered thirty-five people, augmented by many of the San Diego medical team. Of the over four-hundred munies rescued from the train, fifteen had died and forty remained under medical care. An additional fifteen had arrived with radiation poisoning from

Phoenix. She was treating them with *Neupogen,* a granulocytic stimulating factor that promoted white cell growth. She held high hopes for a complete recovery. Her labs had taken over all of the original trailers and a large metal building recently constructed for vaccine production.

Renda had revealed her cancer resurgence to Mace, who after the usual bout of anger and fear, had taken it in stride, claiming that she was too tough to die. Together, they tried to wring as much from each day as possible. She knew she would not live long enough to see Tia grow up, but each day with her and with Mace was a blessing she had never thought to know.

"Wave to daddy, Tia," she said as Mace looked toward them. She lifted the three-months-old's arm and waved it. Mace smiled and returned the wave.

Later, they would all meet in the second metal building, larger than Erin's lab, which had become a community center and dining hall. Six couples would be married, wanting a new start on life, including Erin and Elliot. A warm feeling of satisfaction swept over Renda. In spite of all that had happened, in spite of her cancer, she would not have wanted it any other way. She had sought and found her own redemption and now her retribution would be in refusing to give up, to allow the world to snuff her out. Her daughter would grow up in a new world. Reports had come in that most of the zombies had disappeared, gone into remote areas and now avoided man. At some point, conflict would arise anew, but in the meantime, the world was a big place and both species had room to develop.

Mankind had almost been wiped from the face of the Earth, either through an act of nature or by the folly of man. He had survived through tenacity and the ability to cooperate when necessary, just as early man had done. If the lessons learned took, the future might become something in which both species could coexist.

"Let's go see if daddy's almost finished," she said.

The sun felt warm on her after the long, cold winter months. She now walked with a slight limp but refused to use a cane, at least for now. It was difficult to exercise with the *guan dao,* but she still occasionally found time to work off her frustrations. A roadrunner broke from the cover of a brittlebush plant and raced across the road in front of her. Tia giggled.

"Look, Tia. New life."

The world was not perfect. It never had been, at least not since Adam and Eve had been chased out of Eden. They now had the chance to create a refuge in their own small corner of Eden.

Tia giggled again and leaned forward as if she wanted to chase the roadrunner. To Renda, it was the happiest sound in the world.

Red Rock Park, Colorado

Jeb Stone stood atop a hill overlooking the city of Denver. With his hair grown long and a full beard, he barely resembled the psychiatrist he had once been. He was now a man of the wilderness, a wanderer. It was not yet night, but a few lights shone in windows from candles or lanterns. There was no electricity in the city of only a few hundred. Since the Children of God had abandoned the cities for more remote areas, people had slowly trickled back into them. It would be many years, perhaps many lifetimes, before they once again became metropolises.

Jeb turned at the sound of a tree branch moving. Behind him stood an Alpha male that he had named Blondie because of his long, white hair. Blondie grunted a string of guttural sounds at him, of which Jeb understood only two – 'bad' and 'leave.' Like most of the Children, he did not like cities or the smell of man. The extended family that Jeb travelled with was moving into the high country for the summer and had chaffed at his side trip to view Denver.

Jeb nodded and said, "We go now."

He wondered if Brother Malachi had ever imagined that he would someday walk with zombies. It had certainly never crossed his mind until Blondie's family had adopted him. Jeb walked into the forest, forever turning his back on Denver and the works of man. Whatever future he had left he would spend with the Children, easing them forward in their rapid evolution. What place they would hold in the future was beyond his ability to predict, but he suspected they would not surrender to mankind easily. He had once doubted mankind's ability to coexist with another species.

Man's record had not been one to inspire confidence. Somewhere, a happy medium existed where the two species could, if not cooperate, at least tolerate the other's existence.

It was hard to imagine that just a little over a year had passed since the outbreak of the zombie virus. It seemed more like a lifetime. Around him, the Children of God snorted their pleasure at leaving Denver's environs. He understood their eagerness. A whole world awaited them and a new future for him. He could forget his past, his failures, his nightmares, and face whatever challenges each new day brought.

The shadows of the forest deepened as night fell, but the Children did not need the sun to guide them. Their footsteps were measured and certain as they marched into their future, Jeb beside them.

THE END

NIGHTMARE OF THE DEAD
VINCENZO BILOF

In a world of war and mayhem, a twisted nightmare of undead cannibals begins.

The outlaw Neasa Bannan uncovers a horrifying conspiracy engineered by the psychopathic mastermind behind the Confederacy's deadly flesh-hungry weapons. A homicidal gunslinger and a brotherhood of killers emerge out of Neasa's tragic, blood-soaked past while the living dead ravage the land.

With the fate of the country in the balance, Neasa must decide: save the Union from the undead menace, or surrender to Saul's vision of ultra-violence.

www.severedpress.com

ICE STATION ZOMBIE
JE GURLEY

For most of the long, cold winter, Antarctica is a frozen wasteland. Now, the ice is melting and the zombies are thawing. Arctic explorers Val Marino and Elliot Anson race against time and death to reach Australia, but the Demise has preceded them and zombies stalk the streets of Adelaide and Coober Pedy.

www.severedpress.com

The Coalition

When the dead rose to destroy the living, Ron Cutter learned to survive. While so many others died, he thrived. His life is a constant battle against the living dead. As he casts his own bullets and packs his shotgun shells, his humanity slowly melts away.

Then he encounters a lost boy and a woman searching for a place of refuge. Can they help him recover the emotions he set aside to live? And if he does recover them, will those feelings be an asset in his struggles, or a danger to him?

THE STATE OF EXTINCTION: the first installment in the **COALITON OF THE LIVING** trilogy of Mankind's battle against the plague of the Living Dead. As recounted by author **Robert Mathis Kurtz.**

www.severedpress.com

MACHINES OF THE DEAD

The dead are rising. The island of Manhattan is quarantined. Helicopters guard the airways while gunships patrol the waters. Bridges and tunnels are closed off. Anyone trying to leave is shot on sight.

For Jack Warren, survival is out of his hands when a group of armed military men kidnap him and his infected wife from their apartment and bring them to a bunker five stories below the city.

There, Jack learns a terrible truth and the reason why the dead have risen. With the help of a few others, he must find a way to escape the bunker and make it out of the city alive.

www.severedpress.com

JUDGMENT DAY

Dr. Jebediah Stone never believed in zombies until he had to shoot one. Now they're mutating into a new species, capable of reproducing, and the only defence is 'Blue Juice', a vaccine distilled from the blood of rare individuals immune to the zombie plague. Dr. Stone's missing wife is one of these unwilling 'munies', snatched by the military under the Judgment Day Protocol.It's a new, dangerous world filled with zombies, street gangs, and merciless Hunters desperate for a shot of blue juice. Has the world turned on mankind? Is Mortuus Venator the new ruler of earth?

www.severedpress.com

TIMOTHY
MARK TOFO

Timothy was not a good man in life and being
undead did little to improve his disposition.
Find out what a man trapped in his own mind
will do to survive when he wakes up to find
himself a zombie controlled by a self-aware
virus.

www.severedpress.com

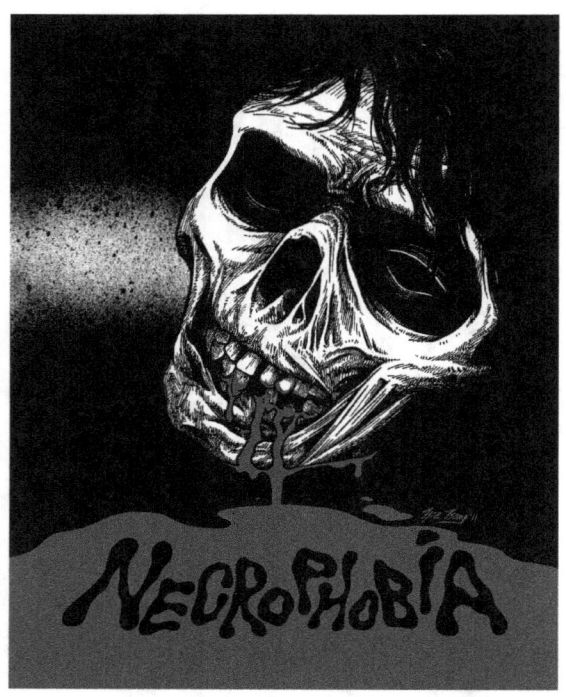

NECROPHOBIA

An ordinary summer's day.
The grass is green, the flowers are blooming. All is right with the
world. Then the dead start rising. From cemetery and mortuary,
funeral home and morgue, they flood into the streets until every
town and city is infested with walking corpses, blank-eyed
eating machines that exist to take down the living.
The world is a graveyard.
And when you have a family to protect, it's more than survival.
It's war.

Zombie Fallout
Mark Tufo
CURRENTLY IN DEVELOPMENT WITH
Illuminandi Media
ShaedStudios.com

www.ingramcontent.com/pod-product-compliance
Lightning Source LLC
Chambersburg PA
CBHW060155180626
46813CB00007B/2757